"Landon Beach's debut novel *The Wreck* is a modern-day *Treasure Island* that keeps the reader turning pages."

     - Steve Alten, *NY Times* & international best-selling author of *The MEG* and *The Loch*

"*The Wreck* has tons of fun stuff, like the log of a long-dead lighthouse keeper and flooded caves. Great underwater scenes, with a real sense of place and an action-packed climax that will make you jump out of your reading chair."

     - Paul Kemprecos, *New York Times* Best-Selling Author

"For a fun, exciting twist on the greatest mystery in Great Lakes maritime history, *The Wreck* by Landon Beach is an excellent summer read! Beach has crafted a story full of colorful characters; the bad guys are really bad and the good guys are really great. The Michigan summer cottage experience is perfectly captured, and then enhanced by a gripping adventure aboard boats, on shore, and best of all, underwater. Because the tension builds unbearably, the reader will not be able to turn away from the book and should take care when reading on the beach because of the danger of forgetting to re-apply sunscreen! We're looking forward to more terrific Landon Beach Great Lakes novels!"

     - Cris Kohl and Joan Forsberg, Hall of Fame scuba divers, maritime historians, founders of Seawolf Communications, Inc., and co-authors of *The Wreck of the Griffon: The Greatest Mystery of the Great Lakes*

THE WRECK

Landon Beach

Cover designed by Design for Writers

This book is a work of fiction. Names, characters, places, and incidents either are products of the author's imagination or are used fictitiously. Any resemblance to actual persons, living or dead, events, or locales is entirely coincidental.

Landon Beach
Visit my website at landonbeachbooks.com

Printed in the United States of America

First Printing: April 2018
Landon Beach Books

ISBN-13 978-1-7322578-0-1

For Meri. You have made all of this possible and have done it with love, generosity, and a sense of humor. The book's flaws are mine; your contributions are flawless.

THE WRECK

PROLOGUE

LAKE HURON, MICHIGAN
SUMMER 2007

The Hunter 49's motor cut, and the luxury yacht glided with no running lights on. Cloud cover hid the moon and stars; the water looked black. A man in a full wetsuit moved forward in the cockpit and after verifying the latitude and longitude, pushed the GPS monitor's "off" button. The LCD color display vanished.

Waves beat against the hull, heavier seas than had been predicted. He would have to be efficient or he'd need to reposition the boat over the scuttle site again. The chronometer above the navigation station read 0030. This should have been finished 30 minutes ago. Not only had the boat been in the wrong slip, forcing him to search the marina in the dark, the owner—details apparently escaped that arrogant prick—had not filled the fuel tank.

He headed below and opened the aft stateroom door. The woman's naked corpse lay strapped to the berth, the nipples of her large breasts pointing at the overhead. A careful lift of the port-side bench revealed black wiring connecting a series of three explosive charges. After similar checks of the wiring and charges in the gutted-out galley and v-berth, he smiled to himself and went topside with a pair of night vision goggles.

A scan of the horizon. Nothing.

He closed and locked the aft hatch cover. Moving swiftly—but never rushing—he donned a mask and fins, then pulled a remote detonation device from the pocket of his wetsuit. Two of the four buttons were for the explosives he had attached to the outside of the hull underwater, which would sink the boat. The bottom two were for the explosives he had just checked on the interior.

He looked back at the cockpit and for a moment rubbed his left hand on the smooth fiberglass hull. What a waste of a beautiful boat. How much had the owner paid for it? Three...Four-hundred thousand? Some people did live differently. With the night vision goggles hanging on his neck and the remote for the explosives in his right hand, he slipped into the water and began to kick.

Fifty yards away he began to tread water and looked back at the yacht. It listed to starboard, then to port, as whitecaps pushed against the hull. He pressed the top two buttons on the remote. The yacht lifted and then began to lower into the water; the heaving sea had less and less effect as more of the boat submerged. In under a minute, the yacht was gone. He held his fingers on the bottom two buttons but did not push them. The water was deep, and it would take three to four minutes for the boat to reach the lake bed.

At four minutes, he pushed the bottom two buttons, shut the remote, and zipped it back into his wetsuit pocket. He treaded water for half an hour. Nothing surfaced.

He swam for five minutes, stopped, scanned the area with his night vision goggles, and swam again.

After an hour of this, he pulled the goggles over his head and let them sink to the bottom. He continued his long swim to shore.

1

HAMPSTEAD, MICHIGAN
SUMMER 2008

The sand felt cool under Nate Martin's feet as he walked hand-in-hand with his wife down to the water. A bonfire crackled away on their beach behind them—the sun had set 30 minutes ago and an orange glow still hung on the horizon. The Martins' boat, *Speculation*, bobbed gently in her mooring about twenty yards offshore.

They parted hands and Nate stopped to pick up a piece of driftwood and toss it back toward the fire. Brooke Martin continued on and dipped her right foot into the water, the wind brushing her auburn hair against her cheek.

"Too cold for me," she said.

Nate took a gulp of beer before walking ankle deep into the water beside her.

"Not bad, but colder than when I put the boat in," Nate said.

"Glad I didn't have to help," Brooke said and then took a sip from her plastic cup of wine.

"Not up for a swim?" Nate joked.

"No way," Brooke said.

They started to walk parallel to the water, with Nate's feet still in and Brooke's squishing into the wet sand just out of reach of the lapping waves.

Four zigzagging jet skis sliced through the water off the Martins' beach. Two were driven by women in bikinis and the other two by men. They weren't wearing life jackets, which usually meant these were summer folk who spent June, July, and August in one of the beach castles smoking weed in mass quantities. These four were probably already baked.

One girl cut a turn too close and flew off.

"Crazies," Nate said.

She resurfaced and climbed back aboard. Her bikini bottom was really a thong and her butt cheeks slapped against the rubber seat as the jet ski started and took off.

"Should they be riding those things this late?" Brooke asked.

"No," said Nate, "but who is going to stop them?"

They continued to walk as the sound of the jet skis faded. A quarter mile later, they reached the stretch where the larger homes began. The floodlights on the estates' back decks illuminated the beach like a stage. The Martins turned around.

When they arrived at their beach, Nate placed a new log on the fire and sat down in his lawn chair. Brooke sat down but then rose, moving her chair a few feet further away from the heat.

"What are your plans for tomorrow?" Nate said.

"I think I'll lay out. I looked at the weather report and we're in for a few good days until rain arrives," Brooke said, "then I'll probably go to the bookstore." Her voice trailed off. She gathered her thoughts for a moment. "We need to make love the next four nights."

"Okay," Nate said.

"You could work up a little enthusiasm," Brooke said.

4

He had sounded matter-of-fact. "Sorry. It's just that scheduled sex sometimes takes the excitement out of it. We're on vacation. We should just let it happen."

"So, you get to have your strict workout regime every day, but when I mention a specific time that we need to make love in order to give us the best chance at conceiving, it's suddenly 'We're on vacation'?"

She had a point. He thought about trying to angle in with a comment about her obsessive need to clean the house the moment they had arrived earlier today, but as he thought of it the vision of his freshly cut and edged grass entered his mind. If they really were on vacation, as he had put it, then the lawn being manicured wouldn't be so important to him. Damn.

"What is your plan for tomorrow?" she said.

A switch of topics, but he knew she was circling. "I'm going to get up, take my run, and then hit the hardware store for a new lock for the boat."

"What happened to the lock you keep in the garage?"

"It broke today," Nate shrugged.

"How does a lock break?"

"I put the key in, and when I turned it, it broke off in the lock."

"You mean our boat is moored out there right now without a lock?" Brooke asked, while shifting her gaze to the white hull reflecting the growing moonlight.

"Yep."

"Do you think someone would steal it?"

"Nah. The keys are in the house. If someone wanted to steal a boat worth anything, they'd go down to Shelby's Marina and try and take Shaw's *Triumph*." Leonard Shaw was a Baltimore businessman who had grown up in Michigan and now summered in the largest beach mansion in Hampstead. Once his two-hundred-foot custom-built yacht was completed, he'd hired a dredging crew to carve out a separate berth in the marina to dock the boat. With the dredging crew working mostly at night, locals and vacationers complained of the noise and threatened to pull their boats out of Shelby's. Nate was glad he had avoided the hassle by keeping *Speculation* moored off of his beach.

Brooke swiveled her eyes between Nate and the boat. "Why didn't you get a new lock today?"

He moved behind her and started to kiss the back of her neck. *We're on vacation, relax, baby.* "Is that a hint? Do you want me to swim out and sleep on board tonight?"

"Of course not," Brooke whispered back, enjoying the foreplay. "Are you trying to get a head start on tomorrow night?"

"No. Just trying to enjoy *tonight*," Nate said. "Can we concentrate on that?"

She leaned her head back and he kissed her lips.

Ten minutes later, the fire started to die with two empty lawn chairs sitting in front of it.

2

Sun rays peeked around the edges of the horizontal blinds in the Martins' bedroom window. Nate opened his eyes and looked at his watch, eight o'clock. He was normally up by six. Brooke was snoring, and he eased out of bed and lifted one strip of the blinds. *Speculation* was in her mooring. He smiled and dropped the blind back into place.

After putting on a pair of shorts and a tank top, he grabbed a pair of socks and his running shoes and exited the bedroom. The hallway was dark as he made his way to the kitchen. He pressed "start" on the coffee pot, and the coffee he had prepared the night before began to brew as he put on his shoes.

The past year had been a revolving door of pain, uncertainty, and disappointment. They had been trying to conceive for six months when his father died. Only last month had it felt right to try again. He hadn't been himself in the classroom either. His ninth-grade physical science lessons at W. M. Breech High School had wandered aimlessly, his tests were rote memorization, and the usual passion he brought to each day had been missing; his students let him know they knew it.

His mother had lasted in the beach house until Christmas. The original plan had been for Nate and his older sister, Marie, to share ownership when their parents were unable to handle the upkeep, but Nate had bought Marie's half and the house was now his and Brooke's. His mother had left in January to move in with his sister in St. Petersburg.

He pushed the brass button on the doorknob and closed the door behind him. After wiggling the knob to make sure it was locked, he hopped off the small porch onto the stone walkway, went past the garage, and followed the dirt driveway until he was parallel with their mailbox. After stretching, he looked at his watch and started to jog down Sandyhook Road.

Each lakeside house had some sort of identifying marker next to its mailbox. A red and white striped lighthouse carved out of wood. A miniature of the house painted on a three-foot by three-foot board. A post. A bench. Something with the owner's name and the year the house had been built on the marker. This five miles of beach, once sparsely populated with neighbors in similarly sized residences, was now dominated by beach mansions that looked more like hotels than houses. The lots were owned by lawyers, congressmen, real-estate tycoons, government contractors, Detroit businessmen (of the few businesses that remained), and a few others who had money. Some were migrants from the already overcrowded western shore of Michigan. White collar Chicago money had run north and was moving around the Great Lakes shoreline like a child connecting the dots to make a picture of a left-handed mitten.

The sun flickered in and out of Nate's face as he ran under the oak trees spanning the road. He thought of the advice his father had given him when he was searching for his first teaching job: "Make sure that you buy a house east of the school so that when you go into work you'll be driving west, and when you come home from work you'll be driving east. That way, you'll never be driving into the sun. Just a simple stress reliever that most people don't take into consideration—that is, until they rear-end someone for the first time." As with all of Nate's father's advice, it had sounded too simple but ended up being right.

Last June his father had been diagnosed with stomach cancer. Three months later, on an overcast September day, Nate had buried him.

Brooke heard the back door close and rose from bed. She turned off their box fan and opened the bedroom blinds. The entire beach was motionless, and their boat was still moored, surrounded by flat water. The aroma of coffee drifted into the bedroom as she put on her robe.

By the time she reached the kitchen, Nate had already filled his mug and was headed down to the water. She poured herself a cup and started a bacon and eggs breakfast.

The sand parted with each step as Nate walked toward the water. Bordering both sides of the Martins' property was a wooden fence; the spindles were flat, painted red, and held together by wire with a metal rod driven into the ground every fifteen feet or so. The fence was not only a "beachy" way to mark property lines but served its primary purpose of trapping sand. Nate took off his shoes and set his mug down by the end of the northern fence line. He began to walk south.

The water ran over his ankles and then receded. It was cool and felt good on his tired feet. The beach looked abandoned. No more than twenty yards from where he started, Nate stepped down with his right foot and felt something sharp. He stood, balancing on his left leg as he inspected the bottom of his right foot. No apparent cut. No bleeding. He rubbed in circles and the pain went away. As he stepped back down onto the wet sand, he saw something sparkle in the place he had stepped before. Glass? A toy left behind by some toddler? As Nate picked the object up, he saw that it was neither. He submerged the object, wiping the wet sand off it, and then dried it with the bottom of his tank top. He held the object a foot in front of his face and studied it. In his hand was a gold coin.

* * *

Brooke saw Nate returning from the water. Assuming that he was coming in to complete his morning routine of running three miles, taking a walk to the water with his coffee, and now eating breakfast and reading the newspaper, she rose to unlock the sliding glass door from the deck. However, he walked right by the deck and headed for the garage. She unlocked the door anyway and refilled her cup. She took a seat at the worn kitchen table, which she wanted to replace but didn't as it had been in the family since Nate was a child. She had plans to redo many parts of the house, but Nate was adamant that the table remained and that the bedroom he stayed in as a boy not be changed. When his father was alive, Nate would have coffee with him in the morning and read the paper at this table. Brooke would still be sleeping and his mother would be cooking breakfast. He had remarked to her that at times he still felt like a visitor, expecting his father to pull up a chair and start a conversation with him about the old days and family stories he'd heard over and over again.

Brooke finished the paper, breakfast, and her cup of coffee and Nate had not come in yet. What was he doing? His bacon, eggs, and toast were cold. She grabbed the coffee pot and headed to the garage.

Nate heard the garage door open as he stared at the coin through a magnifying glass, mesmerized by it.

His wooden writing desk sat in the middle of black carpeting that covered one-quarter of the garage's concrete floor. Two bookcases that he had constructed from odds-and-ends left over from the addition that his parents had done a few years ago rested against the wall behind the desk. Favorite authors had taken up permanent residence on the top two shelves of the first bookcase, and the remaining three shelves were full of paperbacks, read according to his mood at the time he had purchased them. On the top shelf of the second bookcase rested a pair of fins and a mask that he used when cleaning off the bottom of his boat. His father's dive knife was next to the mask.

The shelf below the diving gear contained books that Nate had almost worn the covers off: a Marine Biology desk reference set, half-a-dozen books by Dr. Robert D. Ballard from the Woods Hole Oceanographic Institute, a few by Jacques Cousteau, and five years' worth of magazines from his National Geographic subscription.

The bottom shelves contained books about Great Lakes ports, navigation rules and aids, and boating regulations. Next to one of the rows of books were rolled up charts and a navigation kit. Nate had taught himself how to navigate and routinely took *Speculation* out overnight.

Brooke arrived at Nate's desk and refilled his coffee mug. "Are we rich?" she asked looking at the coin.

"Very funny," Nate said, "I found this on our beach this morning."

"Is that gold?" Brooke asked, more serious now that she had a better look at the coin.

"Maybe. I don't recognize any of these marks or the language that is engraved on it." He put the coin and magnifying glass down and pointed to the bookshelf. "Hand me that book."

Brooke reached up to the top shelf and grabbed a heavy, hardcover book. She looked at the title—*The Golden Age of Piracy*—and tried to hide a grin.

Nate knew her expression meant: *only you would have a book like this, Nate.* "Thanks," he said, laughing at himself with her. "I'm glad to see that I'm still a cheap source of entertainment for you."

She giggled back, and then kissed him on the cheek.

Nate began to leaf through the book.

Brooke set the coffee pot down and picked up the coin and magnifying glass.

After checking the appropriate pages, he closed the book and looked up at Brooke. "Nothing in here that resembles the markings on this coin." He took a drink of his coffee.

Brooke passed the coin and magnifying glass back to Nate. "I can't make out anything on it either." She picked up the coffee pot. "Well, I'm going in to take a shower and then head out to do a little shopping. Your breakfast is cold, but it's on the table if you still want it," she said. "I looked down the beach this morning and I think the Gibsons are up."

Nate was once more absorbed in the mystery of the coin and only grunted in reply.

"I wonder if anyone will make us an offer on our place this summer," Brooke wondered aloud.

A few Hampstead locals had hung on to their homes, repeatedly declining offers that were made for their property. In some cases, it was enough money to bankroll them for a decade. The ink on the paperwork transferring ownership of the house from his mother to Brooke and him hadn't even dried yet when they had been approached. It was over Easter weekend, and they were at the beach house furnishing it with some of their own things. The doorbell had rung, and after five minutes of polite conversation, Nate and Brooke had said no; the prospective buyer and his trophy wife had stormed off.

Some of the mansion owners had even tried to sue the cottage owners, claiming that the cottages detracted from the beachfront's beauty. They wanted the locals out. Most of the locals wanted the castles bulldozed.

Nate set the coin and magnifying glass aside for a moment. "You think that the local kids have all the lawn jobs sewn up yet?" His father had once told him of an unofficial lottery held at the town barbershop to determine who would be allowed to apply for the summer mansion mowing jobs. It had been one of their last conversations.

"Probably," said Brooke. "I've felt stares at the dime store from Judge Hopkins and Sheriff Walker. I know they're wishing we would just sell our cottage already."

"How wrong is that?" Nate said. "The town leaders turning on the townspeople."

"What do they gain by us selling?"

"New mansions mean more opportunities for their sons or daughters to mow a summer resident's lawn," Nate said. "And if their kid does a good job, then maybe, just maybe, they'll get invited out for a summer party."

"Funny how some people get fooled into thinking they're moving up in the world," she said.

"If they only knew that they look like the person who walks behind a horse and picks up its droppings."

He couldn't help but laugh at the scene he was now picturing.

"What?" Brooke said.

He continued to laugh.

"Naaayyyyte," she said, poking him with her finger.

He gathered himself. "I started to envision some of the people we know who want to break into that circle walking behind the Budweiser Clydesdales at the Fourth of the July parade picking up piles of shit and waving to the crowd. Agree?"

"One hundred percent. Oh, the pictures you paint, Mr. Martin," Brooke said.

"You're the only one that can see the pictures I describe, sweetie."

"When are we getting our internet connection?" Nate said.

"They can't make it out until next week."

"Damned cable company. We're supposed to have cell phone reception out here next summer too. I'll believe it when I see it."

She kissed him and then left the garage.

He picked up the coin again and then looked out the window at the spot on the beach where he had found it. Where had it come from? Were there more? He put the magnifying glass and coin in the top drawer of his desk and reshelved the book. He stood with his hand resting on the dive gear for a moment. *Let's have a look.*

He entered the house through the sliding glass door and could hear the shower running as he walked down the hallway and grabbed a towel from the linen closet. He exited the house and as he stepped off the deck, he noticed that the blinds were now open on the lakeside windows of a house two down from them. No doubt the owner had his binoculars out and was watching to see what Nate was up to. The man spent more time prying into other people's lives than living his own. The beach mansion owners had one complaint that held weight: the locals were nosey.

Nate passed by the stack of unused wood in the sand and made his way to the water. The lake was placid and the sun had risen far enough to see the sandy bottom. He positioned himself at the approximate point where he had found the coin. He looked back toward the house to make sure it had been found on his property. It had.

After strapping the knife to his right calf, he pulled the mask down past his face so that it hung by its strap around his neck and rested on his upper chest. He entered the water holding the fins above the surface and probed the bottom with his toes for more coins as he walked out up to his waist. Feeling none, he put his fins on and pulled the mask over his head. He spit into the faceplate, rubbing warm saliva all over, and then dipped the mask into the cold water. After securing it to his face, Nate verified his alignment with the spot on the beach where he'd found the coin and dove under.

The water's temperature was probably in the high fifties, and Nate kicked to warm his body, seeing nothing on the bottom at first. Then, his own anchor auger, wire, and buoy appeared. He surfaced next to *Speculation*, took a deep breath, and dove to the bottom to test the auger. Holding onto the steel pole, he pulled from side to side, then up and down. Neither motion moved the mooring. He checked the wire which ran through the auger's eye to the buoy and back to the eye: they were secure.

A few summers back, he had applied for a job as a navigator on a yacht out of Shelby's. The local paper had advertised that a crew was needed for the vessel's summer voyage up Lake Huron to Mackinac Island, down Lake Michigan to Chicago, and then back to Hampstead. Perhaps "applied" was too strong a word. Thinking that mailing an item like a resume would be too formal, he had shown up at Shelby's to inquire about the job. The marina owner, Kevin Shelby, had finally opened his office door after Nate's third stream of knocking. Shelby had a cigarette and cup of coffee in one hand and was running the other hand through his greasy hair. There had been an open bottle of Baileys on his small desk.

After hearing Nate out, Shelby had said, "Fuck if I know. I've never even heard about the cruise, you sure you've got the right marina?"

And that was the end of his career as a navigator—and possibly berthing his boat there.

Nate swam under *Speculation* and after seeing that the hull was fine, he surfaced and kicked further out until the water was approximately ten feet deep. He took a deep breath and dove.

He traced the bottom and swam in a zigzag pattern out to a depth of twenty-five feet. Odds-and-ends were scattered across the sand: rocks, a tire, a rusted can but no coins. He surfaced. The sun hid behind a cloud making the water darker as Nate treaded. A breeze had started and *Speculation* wandered around her mooring. Where did the coin come from? Nate rotated in a slow circle watching the waves and hearing the distant cry of a seagull.

The sun came out from behind the cloud and the khaki colored bottom illuminated under his black fins. He dove and kicked back toward shore while hugging the lake bed. Had he hoped to find something? Sure. Did he really think that he would? No. At least he knew the boat wasn't going anywhere.

As he dried off on the beach, Brooke emerged from the house.

3

"I'm heading out now," she said, "What were you doing?"

"Checking the mooring," Nate shouted back, "everything's fine."

"All right, I'll be back in about an hour."

Nate gave her the thumbs up sign and watched as she stepped off the deck and disappeared around the side of the house. When she got back, he had his own errands to run.

Beecher Hardware looked gloomy when Nate showed up in the late afternoon. The morning's promising sunshine had faded, leaving an overcast rainy day. So much for the weather report. Brooke had arrived home after shopping and was reading her new book on the couch when Nate had left for town.

The front door chimed as he entered, smelling fresh lumber and paint. The owner, Tyee Beecher, was at his usual post behind the front counter, reading the paper for probably the third time just to make sure he had all the local gossip memorized. He was fifty-two and had taken over from his father twenty-eight years ago.

"Hi, Tyee," Nate said.

Tyee lowered the paper and stared. "You up for the summer or just the weekend?"

"The summer. We got in yesterday," said Nate, "I'm here to pick up a new lock for my boat. How are things?"

"Aisle five," Tyee said and went back to reading the paper.

Nate walked over to aisle five and picked up a master lock. The locks were wedged between half-a-dozen metal detectors and two columns of flashlights. He picked up a metal detector and felt the weight while swinging it in slow arcs above the floor. In the waters off Florida, there were literally millions, maybe billions in lost treasure from sunken galleons waiting to be discovered. There existed the slim possibility that the treasure would roll in toward the coast and wash up on the beach. On a spring break when he was in high school, he had taken an early morning run on Daytona Beach with his father and seen dozens of people tacking metal detectors back and forth.

Nate hung the detector back up. He wasn't that crazy, even though he had donned a mask and fins less than two hours ago and swum around looking for a trail of gold coins in Lake Huron.

When he returned to the counter, Tyee had left his paper and was rustling around in the back room. There was no one else in the store. Nate wasn't in a hurry. He had a haircut appointment in half an hour but the barber shop was only a block away. He always started the summer off with a flattop, low maintenance and kept him cool. Brooke loved to rub her hand from the base of his neck up to the top. He kept it trimmed until a month before school started.

Tyee's six-foot five frame came through the doorway, his mess of black and gray hair nearly hitting the top.

"That all you need?" Tyee's voice was sharp and deep.

"I think so," Nate hesitated while Tyee rang up the master lock, "unless you could tell me anything about this." Nate took the gold coin out of his pocket and placed it on the counter.

"So that's why you were eyein' the metal detectors," Tyee said as he regarded the coin. "Well, it's French."

For the first nine years of his life, his name had simply been Beecher. His people held the tradition that one did not receive his name until performing a distinguishing act. When he saved his older sister from drowning at the beach, while other children and a few nearby adults panicked, he was given the name of Tyee, meaning Chief. Beecher came from his Chippewa ancestors who had intermarried with French explorers—a fact that still did not sit well with him. Hence, he could read and speak French, but rarely did or needed to. Tyee had tried college but didn't care much for school. On essay questions where he was required to write two-page responses, he answered them in two or three sentences, claiming that he had gotten to the point and didn't need to write more. After one semester, he dropped out and came back to work at the hardware store.

"French?" Nate asked.

"Appears to be," said Tyee, "Look here." Tyee picked up the coin and pointed to the date 1643. "King Louis the Fourteenth began his reign in that year, which would match the child's portrait displayed on the front face."

"I was wondering why anyone would put a kid on a coin," Nate said.

"Well, in those days it didn't matter how old you were. When your predecessor kicked the bucket, you were king. I think Louis the Fourteenth was around four or five when his old man croaked."

"Looks like I came to the right man," Nate said.

"Not really," said Tyee, "I only know that date and Louis's reign because my mother made me memorize it. She thought it was important for me to know my ancestry."

"You're part French?"

"We're all part somethin'," Tyee said. "Why do you think my goddamn eyes are green?"

Nate looked up at Tyee's eyes, but quickly averted his gaze out of embarrassment. Nate knew that Tyee had been the unfortunate victim of a quick marriage that had ended badly with no kids, but he had no idea that Tyee had French lineage. Tyee was back to looking at the coin. "What else do you know about Louis the Fourteenth?" Nate asked.

"Not much. He ruled for a helluva long time," Tyee paused, searching for more information and then grunted, "well, that's all I can remember. Education is pathetic isn't it?"

Nate wondered if some of his students would one day say something similar, needing knowledge that he was supposed to have provided.

Tyee continued. "And it's not for certain that this is from France. I'm just matching the date to the one I know and the fact that Louis took the throne early." Tyee flipped the coin to Nate.

"Think it's worth anything?" Nate said.

"Gotta be worth somethin' if it's genuine, but who knows how much."

"Do you know anyone around here who would?" Nate said. "My internet isn't working yet."

"The hell with technology," Tyee said. "Where'd you get this from?"

"I found it on the beach in front of my cottage this morning."

Tyee raised an eyebrow.

"No kidding," Nate defended.

"It looks like it's made out of gold, but I suppose you can never be sure with all of the fakes these days. I know one person who might know something about this," said Tyee, "but he doesn't like people too much."

"Who is he?" Nate said. "I wouldn't take much of his time."

"An old friend of mine named Abner Hutch. Lives out past the bight."

"The bight?"

Tyee grinned. "It's another name for the bend in the coast north of where you live. You've never heard it called that before?"

Nate shook his head no.

"Hutch lives out on the tip."

"Can I phone him?"

"No phone line at his place. I'll call him on my radio and tell him you're comin' out. He'll probably mess with ya."

"Mess with me how?"

"You'll see," Tyee shrugged.

"Anything else I need to know about this guy?" Nate said.

"Bring a bicycle with you. It's the only way you can get to his house other than walking the blasted mile past Mrs. Hawthorne's."

"He doesn't have a driveway?" Nate said.

"He parks his truck at Mrs. Hawthorne's. He hardly ever leaves his place anyway, and if he does, he just takes his boat."

"Who is Mrs. Hawthorne?"

"She kinda looks after him, since his wife passed away."

"Recently?"

"Eleven years ago. Don't ask him about it. Not much of a talker anyways. Mrs. H has a phone, so I could get ahold of him that way, but radio's quicker. Got one at his house and one on his boat."

"Any kids?" Nate said, trying to ascertain as much about Hutch as possible before meeting him.

"You sure are askin' a lot of questions."

"Well, it's unusual for anyone to not have a driveway or a phone. It doesn't sound like a person who would be able to tell me anything about this coin."

"He's a retired Coast Guard Chief Warrant Officer. After his wife passed away, he's kinda become an unofficial Great Lakes historian and wreck diver.

I'm not sayin' he can tell you anything about that coin, but if it's got somethin' to do with the lakes, then he's your best bet."

The door chimed and two men entered carrying a Styrofoam cooler.

"Hey, you sell bait?" one of the men asked.

"No. You'll have to go next door to Mickey's," Tyee said, and the men left. Nate looked puzzled.

"What?" Tyee said.

"Tyee, you sell *everything* in this hardware store. It's like a mix of Cabellas, West Marine, a well-stocked dive shop, and Dick's sporting goods. Why don't you sell bait?"

"You don't understand how a small town works do ya?" Tyee said and didn't wait for an answer. "I purposely don't carry bait 'cause Mickey Leif is my friend. I don't compete with friends, so I refer all of my customers to Mickey. He doesn't carry the stuff I do, so he refers his customers to me. That way we both stay in business."

Nate tilted his head back in understanding, feeling stupid for not figuring it out before he let the question slip out of his mouth. "You said Hutch dives."

"I did," Tyee said.

"Does he get all of his stuff from you?"

"Mostly. On some wrecks though, he needs special equipment so I have to order it for him. When it comes in, he just drives over in his boat and picks it up out back," Tyee said while motioning his thumb toward the store's rear window. The hardware store was on the water with a dock out back. At the end of the dock was a large wooden shed painted red with white trim and a black shingled roof. A boat was tied up to one side.

Another customer entered, and Nate picked up the master lock from the counter. "How much did the lock come to, Tyee?"

Tyee winked, "What lock?" and put the lock in Nate's hand with no receipt.

"I should really pay for—"

"Forget it. Your father was a good man. You seem to take after him," said Tyee.

"Thanks."

"Remember, Hutch doesn't like meeting new people."

"I can handle an old man myself," Nate said.

"Don't say I didn't warn you."

Nate arrived home just after three o'clock. Brooke was eased back in a lawn chair wearing a yellow swimsuit and reading her new copy of *Appointment in Samarra* by John O'Hara. The sun had come back out, no surprise to Nate. The weather in Michigan could change over a bathroom break.

"Any good so far?" Nate said.

Brooke looked up from her book. "Not bad."

His interest in reading had started during one of the first summer visits to this beach house when he was ten. His grandmother had placed a well-thumbed copy of *Twenty-Thousand Leagues Under the Sea* on his bed in the guest bedroom along with a bucket containing two cans of Vernors, a bag of M&M's, and a bag of popcorn. It was raining when his parents had dropped him off and his grandmother had told him that the blow-up raft, sunscreen, Kool-Aid, and beach towel would have to wait until tomorrow. His grandmother began to unpack his suitcase while he cracked open a can of Vernors and took a long drink. After shoveling a handful of popcorn into his mouth, he propped himself up on the bed and began to read.

Page by page his surroundings transformed from a day bed nestled into the corner of a small room with a wooden floor into an underwater world full of mystery, adventure, sea creatures, and danger aboard a submarine.

"Thought that might keep you company while it rains today," she had said.

From that summer on, he had read one Jules Verne novel a year at his grandparents' house during his week-long summer stay.

When he had read everything by Verne except for *Mysterious Island* (he had heard that Captain Nemo reappeared in it), he put the book in a box and swore it would be the last book he ever read—a journey through literature bookended by a Captain whose last name meant "no one." He kept the box in the bottom drawer of his nightstand back at their two-story house in the woods a few miles from the town where they taught.

"A candidate for our annual exchange?" Nate said.

"Too early to tell," Brooke said.

They made deals with each other. He would suggest a book to her and he read a book that she chose. Some of the books ended up being more interesting than their own.

He got closer. "Love the haircut," she added.

"Thanks," Nate said, stopping at the foot of her chair.

"Come closer and let me feel."

He leaned over, smelling her suntan oil. Brooke moved her fingers up the back of his head. "Very sexy," she said.

Nate tilted back his head and blew her a kiss, then held up the master lock. "I'm going to lock the boat and then head north out to the point," he motioned at the shoreline in the distance.

Brooke's eyes followed Nate's pointing finger to the area where the shore hooked out into the water, making a small bay. "What's out there?"

"Someone who might be able to tell me more about this," he said, pulling the coin from his pocket.

"I didn't know anyone lived out there. From the water, it looks like the only part of Michigan the loggers never got to."

"Tyee told me. The guy I'm going to see is a retired Coastie who knows about the lakes."

"What's a *Coastie?*" she said.

"Coast Guard," Nate said.

"Why would this guy know anything about that coin?"

"It's worth a shot, babe," he said, flipping the coin in the air, catching it, and looking out at the water.

"I'm planning dinner for five thirty."

"I should be back well before then." He moved behind her and began to rub her shoulders.

Brooke put down her book and closed her eyes. "Mmmmm, you're hired," she said. "Are we still on for tonight, Casanova?"

"Think we can top last night?" Nate asked.

"Have we ever backed away from a challenge?"

He kissed her on the cheek, moved to her ear, "Be ready," he whispered.

He started to walk away, but then turned around and kneeled down in front of her. "I haven't said this enough," he took her hand, "but I *am* excited to have a baby with you."

She hugged him. "Where did that come from?"

"I just needed to say it," he said, feeling the warmth of her body.

5

The point was no more than four square miles of land jutting out from the coast, the curving crest creating a natural bay, or bight, of water. From the air, it looked like a giant whitecap wave on its side. The area was carpeted with oak trees and contained only two houses.

Nate veered his Jeep off US-23 and took Old Point Road for a quarter of a mile to where it turned from asphalt to dirt. The Beatles' song "A Day in the Life" started to play and he turned up the volume and began to sing. The Beatles were not his favorite group but they had been his father's. He missed a line, hummed to fill in his mistake, and picked up the lyrics on the next stanza. Another half-mile and the road dead-ended in a cul-de-sac with a gate blocking the entrance to a narrow dirt driveway that curved off into the woods. Nate shut off the Jeep and removed his bike from the trunk. Next to the gate were two mailboxes. The top said, Hawthorne, the bottom, Hutch. The sun was behind a patch of clouds and a warm wind whistled through the trees. After locking the Jeep, he walked his bike around the gate, hopped on, and pedaled off into the woods. He glanced at his watch: he didn't want to be late for his evening with Brooke.

The driveway bent to the right, and it seemed to be taking him back toward the cul-de-sac when it curved left and then straightened out. Nate peddled, listening to the hisses, buzzing, and other sounds coming from the green foliage that bordered the path. The sun was back out and casting shadows across the ground. At the end of the straight line, the driveway banked right again, and the woods opened to a circular dirt plot.

Nate stopped. Directly across the circle, maybe twenty yards away, was a wooden post marking a bicycle path going off into the woods. A rusted-out pick-up sat quietly in the weeds to the left of the post. To Nate's right stood a two-story white house with navy shutters, a red door, and an enormous porch. A dark green Suburban was parked in front. Nate began walking his bike toward the house when the front door opened and a small gray-haired lady stepped onto the porch. She was carrying a tray with a pitcher and two glasses.

"You must be Nate," the woman said in a voice that would calm enemies on a battlefield.

"Yes, ma'am," Nate said.

"I'm Lucille Hawthorne. Tyee called me and said you might be out this way today. Come and have a glass of lemonade before you head up to Abner's."

Nate went to put the kickstand down on his bike, but his shoe hit nothing but air as he looked down and remembered that he hadn't put the new stand on it yet. He went to lay it down on the dirt, when Mrs. Hawthorne said, "You can prop it up against the porch."

Nate obeyed, albeit embarrassed, and walked his bike over to the porch.

"Nice to meet you, Mrs. Hawthorne," Nate said while extending his hand, "Nate Martin."

"Call me Lucille and sit."

Nate sat down on a wicker chair and watched as Lucille filled both glasses. She passed one to him and he took a long drink. Ice cold. He finished the glass. The bicycle ride had made him thirstier than he thought. He set the glass down on the wicker table and Lucille refilled.

"After Tyee called me, I spoke with Abner. He was out on the water but said he should be back soon and would call me when I could send you up."

"I thought he didn't have a phone," Nate said.

"Oh, he doesn't. He'll radio me on VHF. I have a set inside the house."

Nate took another drink of lemonade. As he tilted his head back to drink he could feel the porch's ceiling fan blow on his face. He set the glass down and motioned toward the wooden post on the dirt circle. "Is that the path to his place?"

"Yes. It's a little less than a mile back. You can take your bike but be careful, lots of hills and sharp turns—night and day from the path you took from the gate to here. One moment of not concentrating and you're likely to get bent up in the trees," she grinned.

Nate smiled back but thought it would be anything but humorous to be carried out in a stretcher and spend the rest of the summer cooped up inside the cottage counting down the minutes until school started again. "So, how long have you lived out here, Lucille?"

"Ever since my husband passed away—lovely man, heart attack, fifty-three, went way too young. I sold the family fishing business and our restaurant to buy the land out here. I planned for my sons and daughters to build houses by me so I could see them more often and help with the grandchildren, but they don't care too much for the Michigan winters. They'll be up for the Fourth of July, though."

Nate thought about asking the question again, but chose not to interrupt.

Lucille could read his expression. "Sorry, Nate. I'm getting off track. When you get to be sixty-four, it happens. I've been out here fifteen years."

Sixty-four? No way, Nate thought. If she dyed her hair, she'd pass for a couple of decades younger, but it would somehow take away from her beauty.

When they had shook hands, he estimated her height to be around five feet. Her frame was slender. "How old is Abner?"

"He's just a spring chicken, sixty-two. Got as much energy as anyone I've ever known, includin' me, and that's sayin' a lot because I still consider myself busy," she said and downed her lemonade.

Nate grinned. "He's only two years younger than you."

"After sixty, getting two years older can sometimes feel like ten," she said. "I've tried to tell Abner that, but the man still thinks he can do the stuff he did when he was around your age. Early thirties, if I'm not prying too much?"

"Thirty-two," Nate said.

"Haven't lost my touch," she said, and hit his leg. "Anyways, I've known Abner for thirteen years. He was going to retire from the Coast Guard and was looking for a place for him and his wife to live once he got out. I was hesitant at first because I wanted family living by me, but he and his wife were such kind and good-hearted people, I couldn't say no. When his wife passed away—"

She was cut off by the radio inside the house.

"Excuse me, Nate. That's him."

Lucille went inside and returned a minute later. "He's ready for you."

Nate finished the rest of his lemonade and rose to leave. For a moment, he thought about asking Lucille more about Abner Hutch, but decided to shelve it for later.

"If you come out again, call ahead and I'll make sure the gate is open so you don't have to ride your bike to this point. Don't bring your own bike either, I've got one you can borrow," she said and handed him a piece of paper with her phone number.

"Thanks for the drink." Nate descended the porch steps and wheeled his bike over to the path. When he turned around to wave goodbye to Lucille, she was already inside the house.

* * *

Brooke Martin faded in and out of sleep as the clouds covered and uncovered the sun above. From behind her beach recliner a voice said, "Mrs. Martin, you're looking splendid today."

Brooke turned around and saw the owner of the voice, Tim Gibson, walking across the back lawn toward her. She rose with a grin.

6

"I've been trying your doorbell for the past thirty seconds with no luck, so I thought you might be out back," Tim Gibson said.

"Thirty seconds? I thought you'd figure it out faster than that," she flirted. She and Nate had met Tim and his wife Jane at the end of last summer. They lived four houses down the beach in a sizable two-story compared to the Martins'.

Gibson put his arms out in front of him and shrugged as if to say *you got me*. They hugged and Brooke offered him a chair.

Gibson spotted Brooke's novel lying on the chair. An index card was sticking out about half-way through the book. "It's nice you don't turn down the corners of the page to hold your place," he said.

"I would feel like I was abusing the book if I did that," Brooke said.

"*Exactly* how I feel," Gibson said. "Nate around?"

"No, he's out right now. And Jane?"

"Back at the house unpacking. We got here this morning and just made a grocery run. I saw that your grass was cut and thought I'd stop by to say hello. When did you guys get here?"

"Yesterday," said Brooke. "Want a drink?"

"Sure."

Brooke headed inside and returned with two icy beers.

"Thanks," said Gibson as she handed him his beer, "I see you've got the boat in."

"Yeah, Nate put it in yesterday," Brooke said. "How long are you guys up for?" *Up for* was a relative term. People traveled to Lake Huron from all over Michigan to enjoy the white sandy beaches and water activities, but most of the people that Nate and Brooke knew were from south of Hampstead. The Gibsons were from Ann Arbor. Tim was a professor of finance at the University of Michigan's Business School, and Jane taught yoga at an upscale fitness club.

"Probably until just after the fourth," Gibson said. "I'm teaching the second summer semester. How about you and Nate?"

Something looked different about Gibson to Brooke. He was almost the spitting image of her husband but a few inches taller. He had parted black hair that was graying at the temples; the gray stated he was old enough to know how to do things, the black stated that he could still do them. Hair. That was it; his beard was gone, admittedly taking his age down from forty-two to the mid-thirties. His white teeth sparkled in contrast to his already tanned face. "Probably the whole summer," she said.

"Sounds great," Gibson said. "Do you and Nate have plans for tonight?"

Brooke was in the middle of a swig and held it a little longer to think of her response. She lowered the bottle and saw that it was already half gone, but it was hot outside and tasted good. "Nothing officially scheduled." Except trying to conceive a child, but she couldn't tell him that.

"The four of us should get together," Gibson said. "When should Nate be back?"

"I planned dinner for five-thirty."

33

He brought the beer up slowly, tapped the top on his lips a few times, and then took a sip. "I wonder—" his voice trailed off.

He's trying to figure out how to invite us over for dinner and not spoil what I might have already prepared at the same time. I have enough food for the four of us. It might be fun. "I have an idea."

"Oh, I love those," he joked.

Brooke laughed back. "Would you and Jane be up for dinner here and then some drinks on the beach?"

"Sounds lovely, but I feel as if I've invited us over."

"Don't be silly," she said. "One of the joys of summer, letting plans come together." Where was Nate when she needed him? *Letting plans come together*; he would be so proud—and still making love to her tonight.

"Let me run it by her when I get home, but I don't foresee it being a problem." Gibson paused finishing his own beer. "Have we known each other long enough for me to give you a personal compliment?"

"Go for it," she said.

"You look very nice today. Do you and Nate still work out?"

She had lost five of the ten pounds that she wanted to take off but didn't think it was noticeable. "That was sweet, and yes, we still do. It's easier over the summer. More time, you know?"

"I do. Our kids are away at camp, so we're getting used to having time to ourselves again." He turned his attention away from her and to the water. "Looks like Leonard is up, too."

Brooke stood up next to Gibson and saw Shaw's mega-yacht, *Triumph*, slowly heading up the coast. "Do you know him?"

"Not personally," said Gibson, "Big Baltimore businessman who grew up in Michigan. He summers here."

The yacht was sleek and beautiful as it cut the waves. A breeze kicked up and Brooke could smell Gibson's mellow cologne.

"I better head out," he said, "hopefully see you later, and thanks for the beer."

The woods parted and Nate's bicycle fishtailed in the loose sand as he struggled to maintain control. He braked hard with both handles and took his feet off the pedals, spreading his legs. The bike reached the bottom of the hill and slowed as it went up a rise, eventually coming to a rest in front of a log cabin. The cabin had two peaks with a flat area of roof in between. A man sat in a rocker on the porch, but his features were hidden by the shade. The rocker creaked back and forth as Nate set his bike on the dirt and approached.

"Mr. Hutch?" Nate asked.

"Pretty sure," Hutch replied in a coarse voice.

"I'm Nate Martin—"

"I know who you are. Let's see the yellow boy," Hutch interrupted.

Nate climbed onto the porch—there were no steps—and pulled the coin out of his pocket. Hutch sat barefoot in a pair of trousers smeared with blood and tiny bits of what looked like fish guts. He had on no shirt, exposing a thin layer of chest hair on a stocky frame that was clearly being cooked darker by the sun each day. His hair and beard were shorter than Nate's flattop and completely gray. Nate handed him the coin.

Hutch rocked forward and turned it over a few times in his hand, feeling the coin's weight. On his right bicep was a tattoo of an anchor with a mermaid wrapped around it. The mermaid's hair spiraled into the name 'Sherry' above the anchor. The texture of Hutch's hands and feet resembled an oiled baseball glove, the fingernails and toenails cut short.

"So, you found this on your beach, huh?"

"How do you know that, Mr. Hutch?"

"Don't call me that."

"Abner, then?"

"Don't call me that either. I go by Hutch, but it doesn't make a damn bit a difference, because I won't be seein' you after today anyways."

"Why do you say that?" Nate said.

Hutch rubbed the coin in his right hand. "It's like this: you bring me one coin that may or may not be genuine. The question you have for me is, how in the hell did it show up on the beach in front of your house? I don't know and neither do you. If I had to guess, some rich fuck was visiting one of the palaces down your way and it fell out of his pocket while he was trying to lay one of the summer maids from Hampstead High School on the beach. Either way, one coin don't mean shit to me or you. It didn't come from the Lakes, because we never had any gold travel on them. The exchange rate for gold is about twenty-two dollars per gram; some days more, some days less. Let's say that coin weighs about ten grams. So, you've got yourself about two-hundred and twenty dollars, enough to put gas in a car for a month. For me, a whole year. Now, let's say that it is genuine and from France—"

Nate jumped in. "How can you tell if it is, and how did you know I found it on my bea—" Nate stopped, wondering how he could be so stupid. Obviously, Tyee had told Hutch about everything they had talked about in the hardware store when he called to let Hutch know that Nate was coming out to visit him.

"Looks like you figured it out," said Hutch. "Thinking before you speak avoids dumb questions. Mind if I continue?" Hutch waited for eye contact and then started up again. "So, if it is one of King Louis's original gold pieces, a *louis d'or*, it would range from about two-hundred and fifty dollars in very good condition to around one-thousand dollars in extra fine condition. Again, gas for a month, or gas for a few months."

Nate stared at the coin and then looked up into Hutch's dark eyes.

"Wonderin' how I know that?" Hutch said.

Nate nodded, having figured out it was best not to speak.

"I've got a somewhat dated version of the *Standard Catalog of World Gold Coins* inside. Bought it when I got out of the service and thought I was going to start collecting," said Hutch.

"I'm surprised," said Nate. "I would have thought because it's so old that it would be worth more."

"Common misconception. Non-collectors assume coins are antiques, but they aren't. For a coin to be worth somethin', the number minted and grade are what counts," said Hutch as he brought the coin close to his eye. "To the naked eye this looks to be at least a fine grade, but I wonder—" and he brought it closer "—did you clean this before bringing it over?"

"Sure. I wanted to—"

"Damn fool. You may have permanently damaged the surface and reduced its value by half. Now you're looking at only a week full of gas," Hutch laughed.

Embarrassed, Nate answered back, "I only used warm water and some dish soap."

"So now you know all about coins, huh?" said Hutch. "You should never clean a coin. A collector who knows what he's doin' might use a diluted citric acid like lemon juice to clean a gold coin, but not us."

"I don't think I did any damage. Besides, maybe there are more coins."

"Not likely. Sorry you wasted your time coming out here. If that's all you've got, I've got some fish to clean for supper." Hutch flipped him the coin.

"Yeah, but it would be a shame if there were more," Nate said while turning to leave. "I've heard it all before about the ships that traveled the Great Lakes not carrying gold, and I don't believe it. Have a fine Navy day, or however the hell you Coasties sign off." Nate took a few paces and then stopped. He turned around to see Hutch standing and leaning against one of the front porch's posts. "Listen, I'm sorry. That came out wrong."

Hutch interrupted, "No it didn't. What do you do for a living, son?"

"I'm a teacher."

"A teacher of what?"

"High school science." Where is this going?

"So, you're here for the summer?"

Nate nodded.

"How long you been comin' to Hampstead?"

"Since I was a kid," Nate stated. "Does it matter?"

Hutch remained silent for a few seconds. "Let's go inside."

7

The inside of Hutch's was as rough as the outside. Black sheets were nailed into the logs above the windows serving as blinds. The house was clean but sparse. On level ground now, Hutch stood an inch taller and was perhaps ten pounds heavier than Nate, but it was all muscle. Would he look this cut in thirty years? Hutch led the way from the entrance into the kitchen. The kitchen table was made of dark wood that had been varnished to a shine and seating was on two long benches. An empty wine rack was at the end of the counter and the floor was linoleum. They exited into a narrow hallway. On the walls were a few photographs, but Hutch walked too fast for Nate to get a look at them. At the end of the hallway Hutch opened a door and ushered Nate in.

Nate stood awe-struck. The vaulted ceiling must have been over twenty feet high at the peak. Two walls were filled with large windows, and the other walls were built in bookshelves containing what must have been thousands of books. A massive oak slab of a desk with charts strewn across the top sat in the middle of the room. Matching leather chairs with accompanying ottomans were positioned on either side of a fireplace that one of the bookshelves was built around. Before Nate could take in any more of the room, Hutch had opened a door to the outside.

"C'mon out back," said Hutch, "I've got to finish cleaning the fish I caught and then we'll talk some more about that coin."

Nate stepped out onto a gargantuan deck that was stained the same color as the log house. Hutch headed toward the edge and slowly disappeared down what must have been a flight of stairs. From the deck, Nate could see the blue water and sandy bottom below. A few points to the right and about a thousand yards offshore was a raised mass of rock called Diamond Crag. To the left of Diamond Crag and further out were the Sannistey Islands that locals called the Twin Sisters or Double Bitch. The two islands were separated by no more than fifty yards, and the larger of the islands was home to Sannistey Light, which had been unmanned for over a century.

Nate walked to the edge of the deck and saw Hutch thirty feet below at the bottom of a stairway built into the side of the hill sloping away from the deck. Hutch stepped onto a long dock that extended out into Lake Huron. Moored to one side was a power yacht and tied up to the other was a Rigid-Hulled Inflatable Boat (RHIB). Hutch continued walking down the deck but raised his hand and waved Nate down. Nate reached the bottom of the steps and found himself on a platform over the water. He turned around facing the stairway. To the right was a standard sized metal garage door with a heavy-duty padlock run through a stainless-steel eye that was anchored in concrete. Above the door was a long row of floodlights facing the dock. Nate guessed that when turned on, the entire area of water encompassing the boats and dock would be illuminated.

Nate turned back around and walked out on the dock past the boats to the end where Hutch was bending down to clean a stack of fish.

"Quite the place, Hutch."

Hutch nodded as he picked up a carving knife from the dock, pulled back the gills from one of the fish, and sliced the head off. Next, he cut the top fin and both side fins off. Holding the tail, he made a full-length longitudinal slit and scooped out the guts and threw them in the bucket. Lastly, he cut off the tail and quickly scaled the fish. He grabbed another fish and started cleaning again.

"Are those perch?"

"You know much about fish?"

"Not really, memories of my dad and me mostly."

"Yeah, they're perch. Can't catch 'em like I used to. Supply is down. Hell, when I was a young boy we'd haul 'em in as fast you could bait the line and stick it back in the water. Never had to worry about bait either. I use minnows nowadays from Mickey's, but back then as soon as you caught one you could poke out his eye and put it on your hook. The little bastards would go after it. Not anymore though. Only reason I can catch this many is because I know my spots," Hutch said, hands never stopping. In a few minutes, he was done cleaning.

"My father and I used to come up and fish for whitefish in the fall, steelhead and lake trout in the summer, and sometimes walleye," Nate said. "I guess you could say we fished for perch year-round too."

"Grab me a newspaper," Hutch said gesturing to a stack sitting on a folding chair nearby, while picking up a pair of khaki shorts.

Nate did and as he turned to grab a paper, heard a splash behind him. The water flattened out where Hutch had entered and thirty seconds later he emerged by the end of the dock with his trousers in hand and the khaki shorts on. Hutch climbed the ladder which had been welded to the end of the pier. Nate watched water drip from Hutch's soaked khaki shorts.

"Be dry in less than an hour," Hutch said.

After slinging the trousers over his shoulder, he took the newspaper from Nate and began to wrap the fish into small packages.

"Hope they don't do away with newspapers because of the goddamn internet," Hutch said. "I get a lot of miles out of my papers."

"I think it's inevitable," Nate said.

Hutch shook his head. "Not sure all change is for the better. Don't even get me started on cell phones. You watch, we'll have a buncha fuckin' zombies walkin' around this planet in another ten years."

When he was done packaging, he dumped the fish guts into the lake and then dipped the bucket in to clean it out. Holding the bucket, he motioned for Nate to place the packages in.

As he placed the last one in, Nate looked over the side into the water. It seemed deeper than usual this close to shore.

"How deep is this area around your dock, Hutch?"

"Twenty feet."

"Why is it so deep?"

"Some white-collar prick had dredging equipment brought in a few summers ago just to create a slip large enough for his yacht at the marina. So, I borrowed the dredging service for a day when the guy was out of town. The draft on *Queen*," said Hutch pointing at his sixty-foot yacht, "is less than five feet, but I like to have room when I dive to wipe the shit off her bottom."

They started walking back toward the staircase. "I take it these are both your boats."

"Nifty deduction," Hutch laughed. "Yeah, they're mine. Got the RHIB as a special retirement deal and I just finished paying off *Queen* last year."

"How did you get a Coast Guard RHIB, don't they inventory those things?" Nate said.

"That one had major problems and it was going to take more money to fix her than to buy a new one. I knew I'd have time in retirement to work on her, so I swung a deal."

"Looks brand new," Nate observed, looking at the twenty-four-foot boat. He'd always wanted to ride in a RHIB and even contemplated buying one. When Brooke looked at a model that Nate had researched at a boat show, she ran her hands along the RHIB and asked, "Where is the cabin with the cushions?" That was the end of the boat show. Two months later, they bought *Speculation.*

"It took me a couple of years to get the right parts and redo the engine, but she runs as smooth as silk now. As you can see, I refinished her in all black."

"Top speed?"

"Over forty knots."

"Runs on?"

"Diesel. Could have gone to jets, or even modified the hull to carry two big outboards, but I know more about diesels. Plus, I get my fuel delivered here."

"You get diesel fuel brought to your dock?"

"Yep. Gasoline too," said Hutch. "I've got a friend at Shelby's Marina who runs a quiet refueling business. He's got two tanks on board his boat. Got a pump too. Our business is usually done in about a half hour. I pay him and he's gone."

"I don't get it," said Nate. "Why don't you just drive your boat over to the marina and fuel up there?"

"Because he's cheaper. I get it for about half-price."

"Why would he do that? He's losing money, not to mention the fuel he has to use for his own boat traveling back and forth from your place. It's out of his way."

"Got it all figured out don't ya? Of course, I never said whether he actually pays the marina for the fuel now did I?" Hutch said raising his brow.

8

Nate looked back at the two boats.

"I'm not sure what exactly goes on and I don't want to know. None of my business. But, I'm pretty sure that dickweed of an owner, what's his name—"

"Kevin Shelby," Nate aided, remembering his lone encounter in Shelby's office attempting to sign up as navigator on a yacht leaving out of the marina, which Shelby knew nothing about.

"Yeah, he's in a little bit of debt to my friend. Hell, even if he wasn't, he probably wouldn't know the fuel was missing. He's usually drunk or high most of the day, and I got no use for fuck-ups like that. The only reason the marina hasn't gone under is because he's sellin' the stuff he's doin'."

They reached the end of the dock and Hutch saw Nate looking at the garage door beside the staircase.

"Gear locker," Hutch said and then headed up the stairs.

As they entered Hutch's library, Nate checked his watch.

5:00

He would have to leave. Damn. Even if he did leave right now, he'd be a few minutes late. But, how could he leave now after apparently gaining some cursory level of trust with Hutch?

"Hutch, I've got to head out. Wife's got dinner, and—"

"No need to explain, I remember it well," said Hutch. "Let me see if I can spot a mint mark on your coin before you go."

Nate stood, looking at Hutch.

"I admit. You've got me a little interested," Hutch said.

Nate passed him the coin, and Hutch walked over and sat down on the folding chair behind the desk.

"What would the mint mark tell you?" Nate said.

"Where the coin was made," Hutch said as he dug around in the desk drawer and finally pulled out a velvet bag with the end tied off in string. "If this coin is from France and made in 1643, we're looking for an 'A'."

"Why an 'A'?"

"Letters were assigned to different cities where coins were made. In 1643, French coins were produced in Paris, whose mint mark was 'A'. I read before you came over that newer coins contain more distinguishing marks. Most coins manufactured by the French Mints contain two small markings that represent the person responsible for the dyes which struck the coins. The first mark lists the Engraver General and the second lists the Mint Director. I couldn't find any coins listed that had an Engraver General marked before 1726, and any that had a Mint Director before 1768. So, the only distinguishing mark that there could be on your coin would be the mint mark." Hutch untied the string and pulled a magnifying glass out of the velvet bag.

"What power is that hand magnifier?" Nate said.

"This one's five-times and I've got another one in my bottom drawer that is twenty-times."

"Really? Doesn't seem powerful enough. I've got three fifty-times microscopes back in my lab at school."

Hutch inspected the coin while answering. "Anything beyond forty-times is useless unless you're an expert. Five-times to twenty-times is ideal for identifying the grade. If we really wanna get specific, I've got a stereo-microscope with a zoom feature in a cabinet by the bookshelf with a range up to forty-times. It's the most expensive thing I have inside the house," Hutch said.

Nate watched as Hutch moved the coin close to the magnifying glass and then away. "Get me the other glass out of the drawer," Hutch said.

With the more powerful glass, Hutch concentrated and then held the glass steady. "Well, it looks like your washing didn't hose up the grade, and if you take a peek right now you'll see that you've got something genuine."

Nate looked over Hutch's shoulder and saw the letter 'A' through the glass.

Hutch set the glass on the table. "We've got a gold French coin over three-hundred years old. Not somethin' you find every day." Hutch rubbed his chin with his thumb and index finger. "For speculation sake, let's say that it wasn't carelessly left on the beach in front of your house. It's probably the only one, but because it's gold, it is a bit peculiar that it was on your beach or that no one came looking for it. If you permit me to make a rubbing of your coin, I'll see if I can find out where it might have come from. If I do find anything, I'll call you tomorrow. Just leave your phone number with Lucille."

Nate nodded his head in agreement and allowed a wave of excitement to rise in him. Hutch left the room and returned with a piece of wax paper, which he laid on top of the coin. From the top drawer of his desk, he brought out a set of graphite sticks. After three rubbings, Hutch had the desired accuracy and made a final rub of both sides, then handed the coin back to Nate.

"You remember the way out?" Hutch said.

"Yes," Nate said as he turned to leave.

"Wait a minute," Hutch said as he moved swiftly to the deck and returned with two of the newspaper packages of fish. "Here's one for Lucille and one for you. Should be pretty good eats."

"Thanks," Nate said while catching the packages from Hutch. "Talk to you tomorrow."

"Maybe," Hutch said and then sat down to look at his rubbing of the coin.

9

Nate arrived home just before six. Lucille had offered him another glass of lemonade, which he couldn't pass up. Brooke stood in the driveway. Her hair was pulled back giving him a profile shot from forehead to sunglasses to nose to lips to chin to neck to bare shoulders, turquoise tube top stretched tight, short white skirt, smooth legs, and sandals.

Nate turned off the engine and exited the vehicle, ready to apologize for being late.

Brooke Scarlett Martin was a high school English teacher and had taken him to task in a chess game on the first day they had met. He was the sponsor for the after-school chess club, and he'd underestimated her when she walked into his classroom, heels clicking on the hard floor, and said, "I was told I could find a good game of chess in here."

He had replied with, "Step right up."

His queen had come off the board in ten moves, and he had never recovered. She was an attractive woman and had distracted him. A craftier player? That too.

After the game, he tried using humor to hide his embarrassment. "So, who blindsided me by letting you know where my room was?"

She had stood, straightened her skirt, and said, "Oh, a friend."

His students had stopped their games long ago, preferring to watch him match wits with Brooke.

"Friend got a name?" he had said.

"Of course, but I'll make a deal with you."

"I'm listening."

"My friend's name will remain secret, but I'll allow you a rematch."

He had wanted to ask her to dinner right there, but instead had acted like he was pondering her offer. The quiet seconds seemed to be filled with his students' thoughts: "C'mon, Mr. Martin, kick her ass!" or "He who hesitates is lost, Mr. M—you're done."

Finally, he had stood up, shook her hand, and said, "Deal."

Only three months later did she tell him that she hadn't asked anyone who he was or where his room was located. She had seen him at the first faculty meeting of the year and had watched where he went afterward.

He approached with caution but before he could speak, Brooke gave him a quick hug. "The Gibsons will be here for dinner any minute. Tim dropped by earlier and I thought it would be fun."

"Works for me," Nate said. "Sorry I was late."

"You can make it up to me later," she winked. "Now, get inside and clean up." She noticed the newspaper package he was carrying. "What's in the paper?"

"Fresh fish from the guy I went to see. Should last us a few dinners," Nate said.

"That was nice. I'll put them in the freezer while you get ready," she said. "Was he any help?"

"He's going to do some research and call me if he comes up with anything."

In ten minutes he had shaved, showered, and put on a pair of jeans with a tight fitting long sleeved white t-shirt. He put the coin in his pocket—he liked knowing it was on him—contemplated splashing on some cologne, but decided he was clean enough and headed to the kitchen. No one was there. Looking out the living room window, he saw Brooke outside on the deck. No Gibsons.

The deck table was set with cloth napkins, Pfaltzgraff plates, and both a water and wine glass at each setting. In the middle were two ice-buckets. A bottle of chardonnay chilled in one and a bottle of cabernet chilled in the other. As Brooke set a pitcher of water next to the ice buckets, Nate opened the screen door.

"You should go into business," he said.

"I thought it would be nice to get out our dishes and napkins and actually use them," she replied and worked on straightening the white table cloth. They mostly ate off paper plates during the summer months—less hassle.

"Why are we chilling the red wine?" Nate asked.

"I read that it should be served between sixty and sixty-five degrees, so I brought out the other chiller."

Nate had never had a cold glass of red wine in his life. "Anything I can do to help?"

She shook her head 'no' and went into the house. He followed her.

"What are we having tonight?" he said, entering the kitchen.

"Potato casserole, barbeque chicken, and salad," she said.

Nate approached her from behind and put his arms around her. She was bent over looking in the oven to see if the casserole was done. He smelled her perfume. "Are you sure we didn't get stood up?"

She playfully brushed him off. "Behave yourself."

He held her again, stronger this time, and started kissing her neck. "You're looking a little too good for me to behave."

"Naaayyytte," she said shivering as he nibbled on her ear.

There was knocking at the back door. "Later," Brooke said and started toward the door with Nate following. "I'll get the door," she said, "could you check on the chicken?"

Nate reversed his steps and went outside. He raised the grill cover and flipped the chicken. Soon, he heard laughter followed by the screen door opening. Tim and Jane Gibson stepped out. Gibson was dressed in chinos and a black collared shirt. Jane was in a summer dress that exposed her sinewy tanned legs. She was almost as tall as Nate with blonde hair past her shoulders. She was attractive, and *knew* she was attractive. It was hard to believe that she had two children. Of the four of them, she was the oldest at forty-three.

"Nate, good to see you again," Gibson said shaking Nate's hand.

"Likewise," Nate said back.

Gibson moved aside and Jane leaned in to give Nate a careful hug so their chests didn't touch. "It's been too long," she said.

Nate offered them a seat while he worked on the chicken and Brooke entered with drinks for everyone. She had a martini containing a toothpick with three olives for Gibson and a sea breeze for Jane. After passing them out, she brought Nate over a can of Busch and then took a sip of her own sea breeze.

Gibson took a drink. "Nate, how was the school year?"

"Fine," he lied. He didn't mind talking about teaching; he just didn't want to talk about how his father's death had affected him the past year. Nate closed the grill and motioned to Brooke that the chicken was ready. She headed indoors. "And yours?"

"Nothing to complain about. The usual university politics, committees, subcommittees, audits, senate hearings, arrogant grad students, you know."

"I'm afraid I wouldn't, but it sounds like a hassle."

"Probably just a larger scale of the bells and whistles you deal with at the high school level," Gibson said and slid an olive off the toothpick and into his mouth.

Nate cracked open his beer. "I see you've lost the beard."

Gibson paused to register the shift in topic. "Oh yeah, it got to be a pain in the ass last fall."

Nate turned to Jane. "Enjoying vacation?"

"Much better now that I'm having this," she said, raising her glass. "Your wife can make a mean drink."

"Yes she can," Nate said.

"Here we are," Brooke said as she emerged from the house with the casserole. She handed Nate a plate to put the chicken on.

Gibson rose. "This looks fantastic, Brooke," he said grabbing the tray from her. "Where may I set it for you, ma'am?"

"On the hot pad next to the red wine," Brooke said.

"Is that your boat out there?" Jane asked Nate.

"Yep," Nate said bringing over the chicken. "I put it in yesterday."

"Got it augered in?" Gibson said.

Nate nodded, picking up their corkscrew and opening the bottle of red.

"Think it'll stay put in heavy weather?" Gibson said.

"It should," Nate said. He was sure that the Gibsons had a boat, but he couldn't remember if he had asked Tim last summer. He didn't think that he had. "Do you have a boat, Tim?"

"We have a fifty-foot yacht we keep berthed at Shelby's."

"Nice," Nate said.

"Yeah, but we're thinking about selling it," said Gibson.

"Why?" Brooke asked, pouring wine into everyone's glasses.

"Tim hasn't been getting much use out of our toys lately," Jane said.

"What toys?" Brooke said.

"For one, we thought it would be fun to have our Porsche up here to cruise around in, but have rarely used it," said Jane, "We like the roominess of our Escalade too much."

"Do you have an All-Terrain Vehicle, Nate?" Gibson asked.

"Don't have one of those," Nate said.

"I saw some kids riding them around on the beach a few summers ago and it looked like a blast. Bought one last summer, and the first few rides were okay, but it got boring. One night, I decided to take a zip down the beach and almost ran over a couple half-dressed, rolling around in the sand."

"I've seen some people using them to haul wood or make runs down to the party store," said Nate.

"I thought about using mine for that," said Gibson, then he drained the last of his martini. "Bottom line is that it hasn't been worth it."

"So, you met my new friend?" Hutch said.

"I did. He seems like a nice young man," Lucille said. "Chances are, he is, so you should be *nice* to him."

Hutch scratched his beard. "Sounds like you think I won't be?"

"I was born at night, Abner, but not last night." She sipped her coffee. Deciding, she leaned toward him. "You haven't had anyone out your way in some time. Having Nate around might be good for you."

Hutch began to say something but drifted back into the wicker chair on the porch. He looked down into his empty coffee cup.

"Watch your hands," Lucille said, pouring coffee from a thermos into his cup.

"I can't figure out why that coin washed up on his beach."

"Sounds to me like you want to."

"I still have your assurance that you don't tell anyone that I allow you to call me out on things, right?"

53

"Now, why on earth would I want to see your reputation as a tough old salt be tattered? Not even a little. You should be ashamed, needing to ask."

"Well, things change. Never noticed that, Lucille?"

"Plenty do. But some don't. And a man that's been alive as long as you ought to be able to tell the difference."

Hutch frowned. "That makes twice you putting me down over a single cup of coffee."

"That's your *second* cup you're finishing, Abner." She smiled.

Hutch stared at his cup, looked back at her.

"That's better," she said. "When you smile, you don't look near as mean as usual."

Hutch got up. "Fish weren't too bad tonight," he said stretching his arms.

"Mighty tasty if you ask me," she said.

"You staying for a brandy and our rematch in Cribbage?"

"Not tonight. I've got some papers to look over that might tell me more about that coin," Hutch said.

"So, you *are* interested."

"I said *might*."

"Well, off you go then. I've got the dishes tonight."

"You sure?" said Hutch.

"Yes. I'll see you for coffee tomorrow morning."

Hutch left from the porch and was a few steps onto the dirt when Lucille said, "Abner, your daughter called me today."

Hutch stopped, staring into the darkness of the woods.

"You need to call her," Lucille said.

Hutch lowered his head for a moment, raised it, stared some more, and began to walk again. Instead of heading to the wooden post marking the bike path, he walked around the side of the house and into the back yard. The thick grass felt refreshing on his calloused feet. In the far corner of the lawn was a path Nate had not seen earlier in the day.

10

After a dessert of chocolate brownie and ice cream topped with raspberry sauce and macadamia nuts, Nate excused himself to start the bonfire. He dropped down the steps from the backyard to the beach and began positioning wood in the fire pit. He heard footsteps behind him.

"What do you do to keep in such good shape?" Jane said.

Jane? He turned around to see her with a glass of white wine—they had killed the red over dinner and Brooke must have opened the other bottle in the chiller. "I try to run every day," said Nate, "and touch the weights a few times during the week."

"As a yoga instructor, I'm always interested to hear how other people do it," Jane said.

"Well, I doubt I could do what you do," Nate said, continuing to get the pit ready.

Jane grinned and then sipped on her wine, her eyes watching Nate. "You were a collegiate athlete, right?"

"I played baseball," Nate said.

"I remember," Jane said. "For Michigan *State*."

"The enemy," Nate said.

"I won't hold it against you," Jane said. "It's not polite to pick a fight with one's host."

"I know a little bit about fighting," he said.

"Please, fill me in."

"My coach mandated that we boxed at least once a week during the season."

"What for?"

"He called it 'inspiration.' Something about nothing prepares a man to be mean and tough more than connecting a punch into another man's face." Nate paused. "Seems silly now."

"Well, you won't have to worry about fighting me," Jane laughed.

"So, I'm off the hook?"

Jane took a drink and then said, "Yeah, but I'm going to keep my eyes on you."

"Let's hope I can build a fire that meets with your approval," he said.

She finished her wine. "I'm on empty. Time to refill," she said. "Want me to grab you another beer?"

"Might as well. Thanks." He took a section of newspaper and crinkled it up into a cone and placed it under the tee-pee of kindling wood he had built in the pit. Grabbing a lighter, he lit the paper.

Brooke entered the kitchen with the last of the dishes: two Collins glasses. Gibson was at the sink washing the plates and glasses she had brought in on the last trip. She thought that he had just come in to use the bathroom. "Tim, you don't have to do that," she said. "Go outside and relax."

"It's the least I can do to say thank you for such a marvelous dinner," Gibson said. "You keep an excellent table and are even better company."

She watched as he moved his hands in the soapy water, taking his time with each plate and glass. Nate would power rinse dishes and then jam them into the dishwasher. The dishes got cleaned either way, but this was different—more gentle. After running them under the faucet, Gibson wiped the rinsed pieces with the fresh towel she had left out. After inspecting, he put them carefully on another towel that was spread on the counter, put the drying towel on his shoulder, and then dipped his hands into the water again. As she approached, she noticed he was wearing different cologne from the afternoon. They both suited him well, but this one was more vibrant and hung in the air longer when passing by.

"Looks like you have some experience," she said.

"With what?" he said.

She made eye contact and he concentrated on her, not moving a muscle in his face for a few seconds, then grinned.

"With washing dishes," she said.

"Part of my job description growing up with my father," he said, starting to lather a plate.

"What about your mother?" Brooke asked.

Gibson held the plate still. "She left us when I was a kid."

"I'm sorry," Brooke said. "How did she pass away?"

"Oh, she's still alive," Gibson said. "She ran away with some guy when I was eleven. Tore everything apart."

She felt even worse. "I—"

"Don't worry. It was a long time ago," he said. "Besides," his grin returned, "I turned out okay."

"Yes, you did," she said.

He went back to washing the plate. "I've found over the years, that washing dishes by hand with someone is an opportunity for conversation. It's calm."

"Calm?" Brooke said. "It was always work to me."

"Dishwashers make things easier, but there's something to washing dishes in a sink. Warm water moving over your hands, the sound of it lapping up against the sides of the sink when you remove a dish—like when you rise from the tub after a long-awaited bath. The task starts out as work, but there are hidden opportunities in every task." He took a Collins glass from her and began washing it.

She waited until he was done, watching him, but saying nothing. His forearm muscles flexed as he dried the glass. When he was done, he put his hands out to receive the other Collins glass she was holding. Their hands touched as he took the glass from her.

"I'm talking too much," he said.

"No, you're not," she said and took out another towel to dry her hands. "I like what you said." She took a bottle of Merlot out of the wine rack above the sink and began to open it.

He rinsed the glass and took the towel off his shoulder. "Probably not moving fast enough for you, am I?" he said, wiping the glass and then setting it on the counter.

She held up the bottle and said, "Fast enough to want some more of this, I'm sure."

"Wine does make the job more enjoyable," he said. "I wouldn't say no to another glass."

"Another glass it is," she said.

"I must warn you, though, it may slow me down even more."

She poured them both a glass. "I think you have proven to me tonight that slowing down isn't necessarily bad."

"I'm not in as much of a rush to do things as I used to be. Savoring each opportunity adds up to a more fulfilled whole." He let the water out, rinsed the sink clean with the nozzle, and then dried his hands.

"Sounds like a good line to drink to," Brooke said.

They raised their glasses and then drank. Brooke looked out the window and saw Jane walking toward the house on the back lawn.

"Need any more help in here before we head out to the fire?" Gibson said.

"No, you've done enough already," Brooke said. "Thank you, Tim."

Jane stopped at the table outside and refilled her glass of wine. Brooke and Gibson stepped onto the deck, and after Jane grabbed a beer for Nate out of the cooler, they headed for the bonfire.

11

They all sat barefoot in beach chairs, circled around the fire. In between the chairs, Nate had anchored four tiki torches into the sand. Mosquitoes could be a problem at night, which the Martins and other beachfront owners dealt with by burning citronella.

Gibson took a drink from his glass of wine and then kicked a log back on the pile that had fallen off. "Nate, what high school teachers do is extremely important, but I was wondering the other day if some of them are as serious as they need to be."

Nate looked at Gibson. "What made you think of that?"

"I know I said earlier that I had nothing to complain about this year, but there is one thing that sticks in my mind," said Gibson. "I get students year after year who don't know their ass from a hole in the ground in terms of writing, research, critical thinking, and, heaven forbid, responsibility. I can't teach 'em. Most freshmen failed my class last year. Some from not showing up, some from not completing assignments." Gibson took a slow, measured sip.

"I thought you were at the business school and didn't teach freshman," Nate said.

Gibson hesitated, clearing his throat. "Usually I don't. I had to fill a freshman intro course vacancy for a grad student who had a baby over last summer and didn't return to school."

Brooke entered the conversation. "It's odd that they didn't hire someone new. I would have thought U of M had a number of professors waiting in the wings, trying to angle their way into a position."

"Oh there are!" Gibson laughed. "Not to toot our own horn, but it's a lengthy screening process, which we take immense pride in."

"Back to your freshman," said Nate, "You attribute their failures to high school teachers?"

Gibson spun his wine glass's stem making the red wine spiral inside. "Yes, I do. I imagine that there are some students who have teachers like you and Brooke," Gibson pointed at them, "that do care, and I'm sure those are the kids who are passing. But, on average, most kids are failing because their prior schooling prepared them to fail. To be honest, most K through twelve teachers aren't intellectuals."

"I can see that on some level," Nate said. "I also once heard someone say that the definition of an intellectual was someone who didn't know that he didn't know anything." Nate paused; Gibson stared at him. "Let me ask you a question, though. How do you feel when your students fail?"

Gibson smiled, "Feel? That may be one area where we're different. In college," he paused, attempting to add weight to the level of school he was instructing at, "I can't feel for a kid who's too incompetent to pass my course. It's still teaching, but it's also a business. When they show their grades to their parents—" another measured sip, "—that is, if their parents even care, maybe it wakes them up to the fact that they're not going to be coddled like they were in high school. So, when they pay or their *parents* pay for them to take my course again, maybe they'll try harder. Maybe they won't. That's where my caring *has* to stop."

"Interesting," said Nate.

"Why interesting?" said Gibson.

"Interesting because this doesn't sound like the typical liberal view of education that is promoted to the public, but it does sound like the reality of an ivory tower liberal. Ever heard the phrases: Liberal until a leader, or, Liberal as long as I have mine?"

Gibson was silent. He sat forward, "Well, I am in the business school."

Jane said, "Between research, tenure meetings, departmental bureaucracy, and grading student work, I don't know how Tim can do it all—and still find time for the kids and me."

"Our hosts go through the same routine, Jane," Gibson said.

"Oh, of course," said Jane.

"Well, didn't mean to nickel and dime," Gibson said. "I respect your opinions and after ruminating, I would love to follow up on this conversation sometime. From the university side, I know we don't always provide the exhilarating experience that is expected of us. I should have started out with that tonight."

"Food, water, shelter," Nate said. "After that, human beings made up the rest."

Brooke raised her hand as if to say 'no problem, we're all friends here.'

"At least we're all still employed," Gibson said. With his glass of wine, he motioned down the beach. "Jeff Sawyer lost his job a month ago."

"That's horrible news," Brooke said.

Jane spoke up. "Yes, Stacy called me right after it happened. Jeff is devastated; he'd been an architect with the company for over a decade. I guess no one is safe in this lousy economy."

Nate thought about asking what had happened. Was Sawyer laid off? Or had he been fired? Did it matter? The Sawyers were around the same age as the Gibsons and owned a three-story Nantucket style house sided in cedar-shake. They had all gone on a day cruise last summer in Sawyer's sailboat.

"No one is building a damn thing around here," Gibson said. "Jeff has applied to more than a dozen firms and the half that weren't going under said they had barely enough work to keep the staff they had busy."

"Stacy told me that they can last until the end of the summer, but that they're already eating up their savings," Jane added. "They will have to short sell their house if he can't get a job."

"Have they thought about selling their boat?" Nate said.

"Actually, they got rid of it at the end of last summer," Gibson said. "A couple of weeks after we went on that day sail, if I remember right."

"How can they be doing *that* badly?" Brooke said.

"I feel like I've said too much," Jane said.

"You haven't, darling," Gibson said. "Jeff and Stacy are a fine couple, but they stretched themselves too thin—leveling their old cottage and building that manor—unfortunately, it's now coming around to bite them."

The fire crackled and popped. "I hope they'll be okay," Brooke said.

Nate looked over her shoulder. A couple walking hand-in-hand were making their way along the water's edge. He didn't recognize them, but waved as they passed by. Tim and Jane sat looking at the fire.

"Switch of subject?" Brooke said.

"Welcomed," Gibson said with a wink.

"Nate found a coin this morning on our beach," Brooke said.

"What kind of coin?" Gibson said.

"I visited someone today who believes it's an authentic gold coin from France," Nate said.

"Do you have it with you?" Gibson said.

Nate fished around in his pocket and pulled out the coin. He handed it to Gibson.

Gibson wedged his drink in the sand and eyed the coin, bending forward in his chair to use the light from the fire to aid his inspection. He rubbed the coin between his hands, tapped it, held it close to his face, then far away, and finally read the date out loud, "Sixteen Forty-Three."

"Jesus. Is that when it was made?" Jane asked.

"I'm no gold expert," said Gibson, "but it looks authentic." He passed the coin back to Nate and picked up his drink.

"I wonder how much it's worth," Brooke added.

"Let's ask the finance major," Jane proudly stated looking at Gibson. "How's gold doing on the market these days?"

Gibson twirled his wine glass. "On the rise. For pure gold value, the coin is probably a couple hundred bucks. If it's part of a private collection, a limited piece, or lost by someone and a finder's fee is out there—a lot more."

"What if there's a lost treasure out there?" Jane said pointing at the water. "In the Keys last winter, we were told about all of the shipwrecks off Florida and the treasure that's on the ocean floor waiting to be found." She turned to Gibson, "Isn't that what that guide said on our snorkeling trip?"

Gibson was looking out at the dark water. In the distance, a green light marking Buoy #1 blinked.

Nate answered for him. "What he told you is true, Jane. As for the Great Lakes, any historian will tell you that there's no gold in them."

"Do you believe that?" Jane asked.

"Nothing has proven otherwise," Nate said. "This coin probably fell out of someone's pocket while they were taking a walk."

12

It was nearly midnight as Nate pulled off his t-shirt and jeans and threw them into a laundry basket in the corner of the bedroom. The clothes smelled like the bonfire. He moved to the bathroom and stood in front of the mirror in his under shorts. Cupping his hands under the faucet, he turned it on and brought the cold water to his face twice then dried off with a towel. He turned off the bathroom light and headed toward the bed, ready to sleep like a log.

Brooke was still awake, reading a magazine by her bedside lamp. The rest of the room was dark and waves could be heard crashing on the beach through the screen. They hadn't made love yet, but it hadn't been brought up either. Nate climbed into bed and turned on his side, facing the water. He closed his eyes.

"You okay?" Brooke said.

He opened his eyes. "Yeah, why?"

"Seemed to get a little testy between you and Tim tonight."

"Oh, he's harmless," Nate said. "Take the guilt card off the table and his arguments crumble. He knows it, and I know it."

"I think he's charming."

"*Insecure* is a better word."

"Said the high school teacher to the PhD," Brooke sneered.

Nate laughed. "Oh, Christ. Those three letters breed self-doubt."

She rolled her eyes. "He seemed interested in the coin."

"Yep." He closed his eyes.

Brooke set her magazine down. "So, no early retirement for us, huh?"

"Probably not," Nate said. Not the question he was expecting. He opened his eyes again. "But—"

"But what?" she said playing along.

He turned toward her. "Can't rule it entirely out."

"Why?" she said.

"Too many 'What Ifs' in my opinion."

She turned off her lamp and snuggled up. "Let's hear them."

Was this going to be the prelude to their lovemaking? Getting him to talk about something he was interested in, and then jumping his bones. "We haven't made love yet tonight. Do you want to before I get into this?"

"A woman can think about two things at once," she said, kissing his arm. "So, let's have it, Jacques Cousteau."

He sat up. "Over fifteen thousand ships have traveled on the Great Lakes. Of those, around six thousand never made it to their destination."

Brooke cut in, "We have six thousand shipwrecks?"

"Approximately, yes. Of those six thousand, less than one-quarter have been found. And those are the shipwrecks that we *know* of. Who knows how many there really are. Now, let's say that we have complete faith in the ship registers, which clearly list all cargo carried. The overwhelming trend says lumber, coal, iron ore, grain, and beaver pelts—which were as good as gold in the seventeenth century. Boring, right? Now, let's say that people over the past three and a half centuries are not always honest. Might there be something in these ships that was not listed?"

"Makes me wonder," Brooke said.

"As long as greed exists, we'd be foolish to look the other way," Nate said. "It's presumptuous to say there *is* sunken treasure in the Great Lakes, but I believe it's also presumptuous to say there isn't." He felt the excitement rise from deep within. He was no longer tired.

"What would it mean for gold to be discovered on the Great Lakes, babe?" Brooke asked.

He got out of bed. "I don't know. Depends on how much," Nate said. "If there was a lot, wealth for whoever found it and a place in history." He started to dress.

"Where are you going?"

"To the garage, I just thought of something I could look at."

"Have you forgotten about making love?" she said.

"Not at all," Nate said, "but to your point, I can't think of two things at once."

"What do you think of her?"

"Brooke?" Jane was riffling through the pages of the latest *People*. She glanced at Tim, back at the page.

"Yeah," Gibson said.

Jane shrugged. "Ordinary." She went back to *People*.

Gibson lifted his glasses out of his shirt pocket and put them on. He reached for their copy of *The Hampstead Record*. "Just ordinary?"

Jane lowered her magazine until her eyes broke the glossy paper horizon. "Precisely. Ordinary *is* just ordinary. You notice anything about her that surpasses ordinary?"

Gibson opened the paper but kept it on his lap. His eyes tiptoed across the room. "No. Can't remember you ever describing another woman as ordinary."

"I didn't *describe* her. I categorized her." She raised the magazine back up.

"Interesting way to spin it."

"What's the interest?" Jane said.

"Collecting data."

Her eyes on her magazine, she missed his smile, one he meant her to see.

"I don't see us spending much time with her or her husband," Jane said. "That Jennifer Lopez still has one prime ass."

"She's not the only one." This time she caught his smile. Inclined her head thanks.

"We've only had dinner with them once," he said.

Not so easily swayed. "Right."

"What's the turn off?"

"What's the turn on?" The only thing she was reading now was his face.

"The old philosophy of being around younger people keeping you younger."

Jane flipped a page. "Ah. But there may be a hiccup in that theory."

"Enlighten me," Gibson said.

"They couldn't keep up with us."

"How do you know?"

She flipped a page. "I know."

Gibson lifted his paper and started reading an article about a Hampstead high school football hero from the 70's who thought that qualified him to run for County Commissioner. Two paragraphs in, he tossed the paper aside, reached for his wine glass, took a sip, another. He let the second one linger in his mouth. "How about we test your theory?"

Jane put the magazine down. "Tim, tonight was boring. There's nothing to test. If you want some action, let's invite Stacy Sawyer back over. She was fun."

"Having Stacy over again would be like chewing on yesterday's breakfast," Gibson said. "C'mon, let's invite Nate and Brooke over for dinner and drinks and see what happens." He smiled, one he saved for persuasion.

Jane shook her head. "I can answer that for you right now: nothing—the same thing that happened tonight. You know you get bored even more quickly than I do." She leaned forward. "And why have Nate over? I could see that he pissed you off tonight with the intellectual swipe."

"No, he had a point. Most of my colleagues *are* owned by their ideologies. He just hasn't figured out the rules of the game we play by."

"And what are those?" Jane said.

"Activist by day, capitalist by night," Gibson grinned. "And don't ever let your students see your five thousand square foot house."

Jane looked around the room.

"Do you know how many times I've heard friends tell me how they *better* be compensated at a competitive salary or else they'll go to a more prestigious university that *wants* them and pays more? Or, how about the campaign to become the number one public university in the country? If those two statements don't reek of competition, then I don't know what does."

She smirked.

"All that aside, Brooke's a Democrat and Nate's an Independent. I checked."

Jane laughed at him. "You're so paranoid."

"No, just an academic who does his research."

He stood, came up behind her chair, and stroked her shoulders. "We won't be bored. You won't be."

"You can't guarantee that," she said. But she didn't shake off his hands.

"Remember, *the lifestyle* requires complete dedication and constant communication. We have options. Soft swap, Full swap, and our favorite: anything goes. The kids are away at camp for another ten days. Until then...be neighborly. Tonight could have been an off night. They could surprise us and up the ante on our play time, you know."

"Do I have to cook?" Jane said.

"Something–nothing fancy. The piece de resistance will be you, in something new I'm going to buy you to wear that evening."

"Black?"

"Absolutely."

She nodded. "Do I get to pick it?"

Slowly, he lowered his hands to her large breasts. "We do that together. The way we do everything that's fun." He could feel her nipples hardening. "Tomorrow afternoon?"

She nodded. "Okay, why not? And when," she asked, her breath quickening, "will we be having the scintillating pair over?"

"The next night. Or maybe Christmas," he said, laughing as he picked her up and headed upstairs.

13

The sun peeked through the garage window and Nate stirred nearly knocking the bottle of Jack Daniels off his desk. As he rose, his head thanked him that the bottle had only opened once last night. Nate's weekend voyages with hard liquor were behind him, but there was the occasional cool night in the summer when the bottle beckoned to provide him with a stiff belt while watching the sun set. And then there had been the nights on the back deck with his father sipping on scotch talking about life's finer points.

What time was it? He remembered looking through a magazine on wreck diving, sipping whiskey. Then? That was it, he must have fallen asleep.

Nate looked at the clock on the wall above his workbench and it said 9:00. He couldn't remember the last time he'd slept in that late. He grabbed the bottle of whiskey and placed it back on top of the fridge and headed out of the garage.

A breezy morning greeted him as he moved toward the house. The Jeep was gone from the driveway. Probably best considering how he had not come back in the house last night. Would she be mad? He'd apologize as soon as he saw her.

Nate entered the kitchen and saw that there was a fresh pot of coffee brewed. He grabbed a mug from the cupboard and then noticed the piece of paper next to the coffee pot as he filled his cup. It was a note from Brooke letting him know that she was at the store and that there was a message for him on the answering machine. Nate looked over at the machine and saw that there was 1 message. The '1' was not blinking so Brooke had listened to at least some of the message. Nate pushed play. The message was received at 8:02 A.M.

HI, NATE. THIS IS LUCILLE HAWTHORNE. ABNER CAME BY THIS MORNING AND WANTED ME TO CALL AND LET YOU KNOW THAT HE'D LIKE YOU TO COME OUT THIS MORNING WHEN YOU'RE UP. HE SAID TO BRING YOUR BATHING SUIT. HOPE TO SEE YOU. BYE.

Nate took a gulp of coffee and went to the bedroom. In the closet, he grabbed his leather rucksack—a rarity because he had bought it brand-new and paid full price—and put on a clean t-shirt, shorts, and hiking boots. He put his swimsuit and a towel in the bag and donned his Detroit Tigers baseball cap. In the kitchen he filled a thermos with ice water and placed it in his backpack. He began munching on a snack bar as he left the house. The bike ride to Hutch's would substitute for his morning run.

As he wheeled the bike to the end of the driveway he wondered if he should go back and wear the safety helmet that Brooke had made him buy but decided if it was his time to go while riding a bike on the shoulder of US-23, then a helmet would make little difference. Maybe it would, but he'd survived almost three decades of riding his bike in Hampstead without a helmet. He realized that he had forgotten to leave a note for Brooke. No problem, she would check the answering machine if she hadn't listened to the whole message the first time.

* * *

Bike rides with his father had lasted forever when he was a child. The turnaround point on their route was a hill that led up to the highway from the road that they lived on. For most of the summer, Nate could not make it to the top. At first, his father would stop next to him and together they would walk their bikes to the top, enjoying the fast ride down—coasting for blocks with their feet out to the side. Later, however, his father would not stop to wait for Nate. He would shout words of encouragement over his shoulder as his legs pumped up and down propelling his bike to the top.

Nate would try to stay with him but wasn't strong enough to keep going. A few times he cried. His father would always patiently wait at the top, and they would then fly down together. One day, his father was pleasantly surprised when he reached the top of the hill and found Nate a few bike lengths behind, eyes wide open, little grunts of exertion coming out as he made a final push. He ended in his father's arms.

The ride down the hill and the cool iced tea waiting for them had never been better. Recently, he had driven by the house. The hill was hardly a mountain anymore, and it was less than half-a-mile from the house.

The tire tracks from his bike ride the day before were still visible in the loose dirt as Nate rode through the woods. Lucille hadn't been outside when he had entered the clearing, so he had pressed on to the trail that led to Hutch's.

The path continually veered to the right. The hills were challenging as he pedaled fast downhill letting the momentum carry him as far up the next rise as possible until he had to pump for the remainder. Nate eased around another tight curve to the right and at the bottom of the hill, saw the loose sand open up into Hutch's front yard. The ride seemed to take less time than yesterday.

Hutch was on the porch with a book in his hand as Nate brought the bike to a stop and leaned it against the wooden post at the edge of the clearing.

"Mornin'," Nate said. He walked up the slope to Hutch's porch and removed the backpack. His shirt stuck to his back.

"Mornin' was a few hours ago," said Hutch. "When do you cottage folk get up?"

Nate pulled the thermos from his backpack and drank. He was thirsty and it gave him time to think of a response.

Hutch started again. "Thermos, huh? At least there's somebody else in this world who hasn't succumbed to buying goddamn bottled water."

Nate swallowed and recapped the thermos. "Tap water and ice cubes from the tray in my freezer haven't killed me yet," he said.

Hutch couldn't hide his smile, but quickly recovered. "Amen," said Hutch. "C'mon up here and have a seat."

Nate took a seat next to Hutch. Hutch had a beer in his hand.

"What did you find?" Nate said.

"It's more about what I didn't find."

14

Brooke arrived home at half-past noon. She had been to Family Video (Netflix had yet to run it out of business), a department store, the post office to pick up their withheld mail and arrange to have it start coming to their mailbox again, and finally the grocery store to get the things she had missed yesterday.

Brooke shut the door to the Jeep and peered around. Her husband was nowhere to be seen. He should have been back from his run already. Was he still asleep in the garage? She stopped and opened the door. Everything was where it had been, but there was no Nate and his bike was gone. She shut the door and headed indoors. Since she had left him a message earlier explaining where she was, maybe he had left one inside the house for her.

She set her sacks down on the kitchen table and looked around for a note but only found the one she had left for him. With his bike gone, there was little possibility that he was inside, but she called his name and checked each room anyway—to no avail. She retuned and put the groceries away, then, she remembered the message on the answering machine. She played the entire recording this time.

At least now she had a good idea where Nate might be. However, not knowing when he would be back and the disappointment of not making love last night had her feeling edgy. She remembered trying to stay up when he went to the garage, but hadn't made it long. Today and tomorrow were still in the window, so instead of exerting negative energy wondering when he would be home, she poured a glass of iced tea and sank into the couch with her book. The sun hid behind a cloud and the room went gray. A box fan was pointed at her, making the condensation drops on the outside of her glass shiver. She tried to get back into the book, but the fan felt good and her thoughts turned to an early night in their relationship a few years ago.

It was October and their house sat quietly, surrounded by a forest of trees with their leaves in full color. Nate had cut the lawn, now a thick carpet of green, and the last rays of sunlight were fading into the purple sky. They had returned from taking a walk in the woods and were sitting on the back deck drinking hot apple cider.

"I thought we handled the situation well," Nate said.

He was referring to the stupid fight they had had earlier over him not showing much appreciation for the gift she had picked up for him yesterday. There was no special occasion, she had been in JC Penny's picking up a pair of pants for herself when she spotted a polo shirt she thought he would look good in. When she returned home, he was in the closet taking off his shoes, and she handed him the bag. He took the shirt out and held it up to eyeball the fit. After realizing it would work, he said "Thanks," and put the shirt in the laundry basket.

"I think we learned a lot about each other," Brooke said.

On the walk, they had discussed that next to someone spending quality time with her, she felt love and showed love through gifts. When Nate asked her why she hadn't discussed this with him earlier (it could have prevented the argument), she didn't know why. As they talked it out they agreed that after only being married for six months, they were still adjusting to the communication and compromises that marriage requires.

"I spoke to my mom about it," Brooke said.

Nate took a sip of cider. "What did she have to say?"

"Typical mom. She dismissed it as me just getting worked up over nothing."

Nate laughed.

"What?" Brooke said.

"Your mom is a hoot. She can double-barrel you sometimes," Nate said.

"Like I said—typical mom," Brooke said.

"Did the conversation end there?" Nate said.

Brooke shook her head. "I tried to change tactics and asked what the secret to her marriage was."

"Oh, I can't wait for this," said Nate.

Brooke couldn't hide her smile. "She said, 'Oh, he's just my best friend.'"

"Now *that's* philosophical," Nate said.

"Hold on, because she did end up making one good point," said Brooke.

"Which was?"

"She looked at me after I asked her about her marriage and said, 'You and Nate starting to bump into each other's edges?'"

"What did you say to that?" Nate said.

"I told her that we were," Brooke said.

"I guess we don't know it all yet," Nate said.

"Think we ever will?" Brooke said.

Nate stood up, finished with his cider. "I don't think anyone ever knows it all. I'm just glad that we have our parents to talk to, because they've seen more than we have."

"Promise you'll always be open to talk like we did today," she said.

"I promise," said Nate, "Now, how about going inside and getting the chess board out? I've got a big rematch with my father over Thanksgiving."

"You're on," Brooke said.

Within minutes the board was set up on the kitchen table, the pieces in place, and Nate was back from his pre-game ritual of changing into an old pair of running shoes. "Black or white?" he asked.

"You can pick," Brooke said. He chose black.

Three moves in, Brooke brought out her queen and Nate lost his focus.

"You never bring your queen out this soon," Nate said.

"You want to play or chat?" Brooke asked.

An hour later, Nate was done, and Brooke was doing her best to hide her own smile by refilling her water glass at the sink. "Want some water?" she asked him.

"Only if it's deep enough to drown in," he said. "Why did I ever suggest we bring out the board? My father is going to destroy me next month." But he was grinning, and patted her tush as she returned to the table.

"What now?" she said, setting the game aside.

The clock on the wall confirmed that the first game of the World Series was starting soon. Besides, it was barely eight o'clock. Still, she knew the answer she wanted. They had made love every night for the past week—minus last night because of the argument—and, according to her, were still on their honeymoon.

He walked out of the kitchen and sat down on the couch. "How about watching the Series?"

She followed him and sat on the other end of the couch. "Need a break from me tonight, babe?"

"How about after the first three innings?" He grinned at her.

She slid over and fit into his waiting arm. "I can work with that," she said and kissed his cheek.

15

N ate sat in his swimsuit on the gunwale of *Queen* as Hutch secured the anchor. They were in fifty feet of water directly north and approximately five hundred yards offshore from Big Sanisstey Island.

Little Sanisstey was five square miles smaller and lay south of its larger sister. The two islands had no more than fifty yards of water separating them. There was a sandbar that nearly ran the coastline in the middle of the canal separating them, and in years when the lake level was down, the sandbar broke the surface of the water giving the canal a Mohawk. The Sanisstey islands had been uninhabited since Sanisstey Light went from having a lightkeeper stationed on the big island with his family, to being an automated light in 1895. In 1930, the light was abandoned due to the construction of a new light nearby, rendering Sanisstey Light unnecessary. The lighthouse still stood along with a ramshackle series of small houses.

The sun beat down on Nate's neck and *Queen*'s varnished teak. The temperature was over 80 degrees and now that the boat was anchored there was no breeze for relief. Sanisstey Light was off the stern as the boat rested in the water.

"Want a beer?" Hutch asked as he came down from the helm console on the top level.

Nate nodded yes.

Hutch hopped down onto the deck and went into the wheelhouse. He emerged with two cans and threw one to Nate.

"So, you didn't find anything out about the coin, but you think there is some connection to the Sanisstey Islands?" Nate said, recapping their brief talk at Hutch's house before they loaded up *Queen* and left the dock. Hutch hadn't said much on the ride out, just the information about the islands.

"Sort of," Hutch said.

Nate waited.

Hutch pulled a packet of papers out from the backpack he had brought aboard and handed them to Nate. "Take a look at these."

On the top of one of the pages was the date July 7, 1859. "Looks like some sort of diary," he said.

"Wait until you get to the last four pages," Hutch said.

By habit, or impatience, Nate flipped to the end. The last page was blank. So was the second and third to last pages.

"Don't get ahead of yourself," Hutch said. "Start at the beginning. Helps you get a feel of the whole thing."

Nate started over and read. Hutch disappeared into the wheelhouse and soon sounds of charts being shuffled and cabinets being opened and closed could be heard.

When Nate reached the fourth to last page, he brought it close to his face and held it steady. The top three-quarters of the page was filled with cursive writing under an entry dated July 28, 1859. Under the writing was a sketch—a sketch of the exact coin that he had found.

"Look familiar?" Hutch said, entering the stern.

"It's my coin," said Nate. "Whose diary is this?"

"Have you ever heard that that place is haunted?" Hutch said pointing at the lighthouse.

"Haunted?"

"I don't believe it, but that's what's been said."

"I'm confused. You told me that you wanted me to come out today because of what you didn't find," said Nate, "and why didn't you show me these papers back at your house?"

"Because that's how I work," Hutch said. "I think more clearly out here than I do back on shore. It's true; I didn't find anything out about the mystery owner of your coin, but I've got Tyee getting some books for me that might help. They should be here tomorrow."

"And the papers?" Nate cut in.

"From my library. I have various ship logs, records, memoirs, articles, and artifacts from shipwrecks and lighthouses on the Great Lakes. After I gave up on my coin collecting hobby, I became a Great Lakes history nut. I've got a network of friends who alert me when somethin' new is up or been discovered. The papers you're holding are an example. When Sanisstey Light became automated, all the records were brought ashore. Lighthouses originally fell under the responsibility of the Treasury Department and later the United States Lighthouse Service, so the records were shifted from department to department until the decision was made for lighthouses to be maintained by the U.S. Coast Guard. So, the records for Sanisstey Light eventually ended up in a back room at the old Hampstead Coast Guard Station where they did nothing but collect dust. When the station was shut down a decade ago, a friend of mine discovered these and asked me if I wanted them because they were going in the trash otherwise. The stuff he brought me is a stack about four feet tall that I have piled in one of the closets in my library. After you left last night, I looked at the rubbing and started thinking that I had seen something similar to it somewhere—maybe it was the fact that I was looking at the rubbing on a piece of paper. Anyways, I started to dig through the stack and around two a.m. I found that drawing."

"These are diary entries from a lighthouse keeper on Sanisstey Island?" Nate said.

"Correct. They're from the very first keeper," said Hutch. "The lighthouse was finished in 1858, and the first keeper's name was Captain Stuart Daniels."

"Captain?"

"Being a lightkeeper was a prestigious profession and much sought-after. When applying, one had a better chance of getting the job if he was a Captain or a war veteran. Of course, having political connections always helped. Hence, Captain Stuart Daniels was hired to keep the Sanisstey Light. Daniels was a recluse though. Had no family and preferred solitude, probably why no one knew something was wrong for awhile."

"What do you mean, wrong for awhile?" Nate said.

"Well, that's where all of this haunted shit comes in. The original lighthouse settlement on the island was just the tower and the keeper's house. As you see now," Hutch pointed again to the lighthouse, "other buildings were built later: a boathouse, workshop, carpenter's shop, smokehouse, and generator house. In fact, the original keeper's house was torn down and the boathouse was built in its place. The keeper's house that was constructed after the old one had been destroyed eventually became a rendezvous for Hampstead high schoolers to come out and screw, suck down liquor, and God knows what else."

"Do they still come out here?"

"Not anymore. It's been vandalized and graffitied so much over the years that no one bothers. Plus, if kids wanna mess around nowadays, they just do it in their own homes."

"True," Nate said.

"Back in those days, it was almost tradition for the keeper of a light to be passed down from generation to generation. Granted, it was a hard job to get, but if you did, and had children, then they took over the light when you died. Some lighthouse keepers were provided with an assistant. But when it became a family business, the wife served as the unpaid assistant. As I said before, Daniels worked the light alone and didn't want an assistant. Since he was alone, some of his duties would have been more time consuming, like hauling the heavy barrels of fuel, probably still sperm whale oil at that time, up to the lantern room. Then one day he disappears."

Nate looked back down at the paper with the sketch of the coin. "Looks like this was his last entry."

"Read it," Hutch said.

July 28, 1859

Followed daily routine. Rose before dawn and made coffee. Running low on sugar. Extinguished light at sunrise. Morning weather. Winds: NE 10kts. Sky: clear. Seas: calm. Temperature: 60. Barometer: 30.04 and steady. No ships in sight of the station. Morning hours dusted, swept. Rowed around the sisters. Took one of the chickens last night, grilled at mid-day. Should provide meals for this week. Afternoon weather. Winds: E-NE 15 kts. Sky: cumulonimbus/foreboding. Seas: 2-4 feet. Temperature: 75. Barometer: 29.96 and falling. No ships in sight of the station. Checked security anticipating coming storm. Painted for three hours in the afternoon, then carried two barrels of oil up to lantern room and filled. Lantern should be good for three nights. Trimmed wicks, oiled clockwork, and cleaned and polished glass and metal in lantern room. Finished just before dinner. Chicken for dinner with port. Stormed all afternoon. Checked fittings and security again. Read until 1 hour before sunset. Lit light. Evening weather. Winds: NE 15-20 kts. Sky: cumulonimbus, thunderstorms. Seas: 6-8 feet and heavy. Temperature: 55. Barometer: 29.94 and steady. 1 ship on horizon heading south. No contact made. Have found coins. Picture below.

-S.D.

16

Nate pulled out his coin. It glistened in the sunlight as he compared it to Daniels's drawing below the July 28 entry. Water was lapping against *Queen*'s hull, and Hutch was now sitting in the fighting chair with his legs crossed, drinking another beer. "Why would he add the part about the coins in the lightkeeper's log?" Nate said.

"Technically, he shouldn't have. Lighthouse logs were official records. Lighthouse inspectors hated when lightkeepers added their personal junk to the logs," Hutch said.

Nate flipped back through the other pages of the log. They all mirrored the last entry with respect to routine, weather, and shipping traffic. None of the others seemed to mention personal observations. "I don't get it. You said he disappeared?"

"After I found that log, I looked at what little there was about Captain Stuart Daniels's disappearance. A week after Daniels's last entry, someone in Hampstead noticed that Sanisstey Light was not being lit. The local police took a boat out and Daniels was gone. They read his log, searched the lighthouse, keeper's house, and both islands, but no Daniels."

"Did they find any coins?" Nate said.

"There's no record of it, and no documents ever mentioning a search for any coins on the islands. I'm sure after they didn't find anything in their initial search it was forgotten about."

"Could he have drowned?" Nate said.

"That's what the authorities concluded, but it's not likely. The rowboat that Daniels used for his daily exercise was gone, but it could have blown away in the storm. Plus, a body never washed up anywhere."

"Could he have split and left on a ship that was passing by?"

"All of his personal effects were still at the lighthouse and nothing was missing except his nightgown, nightcap, and the lamp he would have used to move around the lighthouse at night. His working clothes were laid out on a chair next to his bed, which was made. That's what's got me stumped."

"But why would he write down in the official lighthouse log that he had found coins?" Nate thought further, "Why not keep that in a personal diary?"

"Not sure," said Hutch. "The only thing I can think of is that if he did find something then he was trying to lay claim to it in an official record."

"Sounds more like a mystery than a haunted lighthouse," Nate said.

"Call it what you want. I already told you I don't believe it's haunted, but it's safe to say that anytime a person disappears from a place and is never found, someone's gonna cook somethin' up about it."

Nate looked away from Hutch and toward the lighthouse. When they had rounded the two islands earlier, Nate noticed that there weren't any docks or coves for a boat to put in at. "If Daniels found any coins like mine, where do you think they'd be?"

Hutch grunted, "Who knows? But it's too much of a coincidence for us not to check out."

"What do you mean?"

Hutch stood up and slipped below. He returned with two sets of fins, mask, and booties. He handed Nate a set and sat down on the opposite gunwale. "We'll swim over and peek around a bit," he said and pointed at the booties. "They've got hard rubber soles so we can walk around on the islands once we get there. Might be a bit snug, but I figured they'd work since we're close to the same size."

"Can't we get closer?"

"This is as close as I like to get. There's a series of sandbars, most with sharp rocks, that would slit *Queen*'s hull clean and then we'd be done."

"Don't you have a dinghy?"

"I do."

"Why don't we use it in case we find something?"

"It's not here."

Nate leaned over the gunwale to look forward where the dinghy had been secured when he first saw *Queen*. The place where it had been was empty. "Why don't you have it out here?" Nate said.

"It's in my storage cave behind the dock. I did some touch up work on her between looking through that mountain of papers in my closet yesterday and this morning. Don't worry, if we do find something, she'll be ready by tomorrow."

The men began to put on their gear. The booties Hutch had given Nate were a little loose rather than tight.

"We don't have much time," Hutch said as he pushed his right bootie into the fin's opening and then pulled the ankle strap around and snapped it in. His back was to the sea.

Nate looked past Hutch at the color of the sky further out to sea. A granite sheet was moving toward shore as if the sky was transposed into Microsoft Paintbrush and someone was dragging the line of gray across a light blue background. Nate snapped his fins into place and joined Hutch on the port gunwale. Both men sat with their masks strapped on but temporarily pulled up onto their foreheads. "How much time do you think we have?"

"Maybe an hour, maybe less," Hutch said. "Follow me."

Hutch pulled his mask down and performed a backward roll into the water. Nate did the same and was soon kicking toward Big Sanisstey. The water felt cold at first but Nate warmed as he kicked alongside Hutch. Nate came up for a breath after a moment and looked behind them. *Queen* had settled after rocking from the men going over the side and was resting at anchor. Hutch's head broke the surface a few yards away.

"Did you think she was going to leave us?" Hutch said.

Nate was going to respond, but Hutch had already gone underwater. Nate took a deep breath and went under. Hutch kept their pace fast. They swam four or five feet beneath the surface, coming up only for short breaths. For as much as Nate ran—and prided himself on being in shape—he was struggling to keep up. How much did Hutch swim?

Nate couldn't see the bottom at first, but after a few more breath stops, it came into view. It angled up sharply ahead, eventually ending in the first sandbar, which was only six feet below the surface.

The men swam over the sandbar and the depth below them dropped to around twenty feet. They came up for another breath and instead of resuming toward shore, Hutch did a surface dive to the bottom. Nate did the same as if playing follow the leader. Hutch was looking at a glass bottle partially submerged in the sand. He pulled the bottle up. Miller Lite. He shook his head and then swam along the bottom with the bottle in his right hand. Nate's lungs began to ache and he surfaced for a breath. When he submerged, Hutch was still swimming on the bottom and a few moments later, the men were at the second sandbar which was all jagged rocks. Hutch came up a few yards short of the bar and waited for Nate to join him.

"Go over this bitch carefully. It's only two feet below the surface," Hutch said.

Nate obeyed and they floated on the surface above the rocks, giving a few short kicks to put them past. The water deepened until the next bar, which was as rocky as the last, and after passing over it Hutch stood up and they were in water up to their chests about twenty yards from the shore. They removed their fins and waded the rest of the way.

The lighthouse was surrounded by rocks that sloped down into the surf. Hutch and Nate walked down the coast until the rocks ended and the ground became dirt with weeds popping up all over. They set their fins and masks down along with the bottle and started walking up the slope.

The brush was thick, obscuring their view of the small houses positioned around the tower. In fact, only the tower could be seen until they stepped out of the brush onto what was once a path from the tower through the rocks sloping away to the water.

"What do you plan to do, Hutch?"

"Let's start with the tower."

All that was left of the immense door that had once been at the entrance were two hinges. Nate and Hutch walked through the doorway. With the exception of a collapsed wooden table, they were greeted by a bare room. A stone staircase wound its way up along the wall.

"Looks like a solid job," Nate said.

"Fifty-five feet tall and all made of limestone except for the lantern room, which is made out of granite to support the weight of the iron, copper, and glass," said Hutch as they began to climb the steps. Hutch was in the lead.

"When was the lighthouse shut down again?" Nate said.

"When Shauna Shoal Light was built in 1930, they didn't need this one anymore. We should be able to see Shauna Shoal from the lantern room."

"Is it on an island like this one?" Nate said.

"No. It was made to be an automated remote station. It's simply a seventy-foot tower made of concrete reinforced by steel that sits on a concrete foundation," Hutch said.

Nate could see light above as they neared the lantern room. He paused on the steps and looked down. The wooden table was a little more than a speck on the floor, and for a second it seemed to rise toward him and then shoot away—he felt like Jimmy Stewart looking down the bell tower staircase in *Vertigo*. The steps were at least four feet wide, but there was no railing anymore. Nate moved away from the edge and hugged the wall the rest of the way up.

17

There was still a wooden hatch at the top of the stairs that led up into the lantern room. Hutch pushed it open and they climbed up onto the granite floor. As Nate stood up, he felt the wind whip across his face. A ratty blanket was left in the corner with half-a-dozen rusted beer cans. There was no lens left in the center and the glass around the room had been shattered and swept away long ago. They had a 360-degree view. The seas were starting to churn below, and in the distance *Queen* was bobbing up and down while rocking side to side as each wave rolled against her hull. The storm would be on them soon. "Impressive view," Nate said.

"Do you see Shauna Shoal Light?"

Nate looked to the north and then east. His eyes settled on a sliver of silver rising up from the blue water. He concentrated on it and then a green light flashed twice, went dark for six seconds, and then flashed twice again. He swiveled his head past *Queen* and located the rock formation of Diamond Crag offset against the shoreline of the mainland.

"How high is the peak on Diamond Crag?" Nate said and continued looking around.

"About fifty feet. Looks small from here doesn't it?" Hutch said.

"Yeah," said Nate. He glanced once more at the Crag, then began to study the terrain and vegetation on the islands below. Rock surrounded the lighthouse and other buildings. The whole settlement was on a plateau. The shoreline bent inward in one spot, a wedge of water that disappeared into the rock underneath one of the houses. The groves of towering trees inland thinned to bushes, then patches of weeds and dirt, eventually becoming bare rock at the coast. The Little Sister had the same inhospitable terrain.

"The lake level is down again this year. In fact, this is the lowest I've ever seen it. Even lower than it used to be before it rose over twenty years ago and caused everyone to spend a fortune in goddamn seawalls."

Nate had been almost a teenager when two houses had caved into the lake because water had eroded the ground beneath them. His father and the rest of the beachfront owners in Hampstead had to put up seawalls to save their houses. Now, most of the seawalls were rotted and needed to be rebuilt or torn down.

Nate pointed down at the building where the water seemed to run underneath it. "What was that place used for?"

Hutch walked over by him. "That was the boathouse."

"The place that was built over the old keeper's house?"

"Right," said Hutch. He looked out at the sea and then down at the boathouse. The roof sagged on both sides of the peak and the side closest to the lighthouse had a section missing. Hutch faced Nate. "It's a safe bet that there's nothing in the lighthouse. No real place for Daniels to stow anything. The masonry in this beast was solid; it would have taken him time to carve out space to hold anything." He swiveled his head to the oncoming clouds and then back to Nate. "We can check out the boathouse quickly before we swim back out."

They headed down the steps and made their way across the rocks. Like the lighthouse, there was no door to the boathouse. The room was dark and wind poured through the missing section of roof.

"There's nothing in here," Nate said and started walking into the room.

"Stop!" Hutch yelled and grabbed Nate's arm.

Nate shot a look at his arm and felt Hutch squeeze harder, pulling him back. "What?"

"Look up."

Nate did and saw a wheel at the end of a metal beam. An identical metal beam was positioned approximately six feet away and parallel to the first beam. A boat hoist. He looked down.

"Figure it out yet?" Hutch said.

Nate inched toward the opening in the floor. The iron gray water lay more than thirty feet below. "Thanks," Nate said. "Where's the boat?"

"Who knows? Somebody probably swiped it," Hutch said.

"That water is at least thirty feet below us. A hoist doesn't lower a boat that far."

"Usually true, but see those chains?" Hutch pointed to two chains hanging from wire on the metal beams. "Since we're only talking about lowering a dinghy—probably didn't even have a motor—the wire was cut to around twenty feet. The chains could then be used to lower the beams according to the water level."

Hutch walked over to the corner of the lift by the wheel where he pushed a toggle switch on a metal box. Nothing happened. He traced the box's wiring back to a corner of the boathouse and dusted off the top of a gas generator. The gas can next to it was empty. He tipped the generator up and then let it back down. No gas in it either.

Nate walked along the wall until he was at the corner opposite of Hutch. Rain began to tap on the roof. He pulled back a wooden set of shutters exposing a window with glass still in it. His eyes followed the narrow waterway out to the lake. The sky was a mix of gray and violet. The whine of metal turned his attention back to the lift. Hutch was turning the wheel and the lift bars were lowering.

"Take the wheel for a sec," Hutch said.

Nate walked to the wheel and Hutch approached the closest lift bar. Then he grabbed on and pulled down on the bar, eventually hanging on it.

"What in the hell are you doing?" Nate said.

Hutch put his feet back on the ground and then peered down into the hole. He moved his head from one side to the other and then knelt down. "I wonder how far inland the water goes." He checked the wire connection to the chain and the chain to the lift bar. Then he walked around the opening to the other side and did the same. Feeling satisfied, he walked back and hung from the lift bar. "Lower me."

"You're kidding me."

"Lower me, goddamnit."

"Hutch, if this thing goes," Nate said pointing at the lift, "you've got a big drop and who knows how deep that water is down there."

"It's deep enough. You don't have to pull me back up. I'll take a look and then swim out and meet you at the opening."

Hutch's eyes were firm.

"You sure?" Nate said.

"Do I look sure?"

Nate lowered the chain.

18

The lift jammed and Hutch hung fully extended from the lift bars.

"That's as far as she'll go," Nate called down. "The wire is stuck. How much of a drop to the water do you have?"

Hutch looked down. The shaft was dark and it was difficult to judge how far away his feet were from the water. Hutch gathered a throat full of phlegm, and spit. The light splash echoed in the cave below. "Call it ten feet, maybe less," Hutch yelled back up. He moved his hands so his body was facing into the cave. The light from the opening above cast a few shadows, but not enough to tell how deep the cave went.

"I can still raise you I think," Nate said.

"Piece of shit lift," Hutch said.

Nate moved away from the wheel and watched as Hutch held on to the beam far below. "Let me try to raise you," Nate said.

"Forget it," Hutch said. He kicked his legs, swinging the lift bars over the center of the water, and dropped.

Nate heard the *sploosh* as Hutch entered the water. His eyes searched for any movement, but the surface was flat.

"I'm not sure how far it goes back," Hutch's voice echoed up a few seconds later.

"Where are you?" Nate said.

"I'm past the opening toward the interior."

"Did you hit bottom when you dropped?" Nate said.

"No," said Hutch, "It's at least fifteen feet deep. I'm going to swim in and see if there's anything."

Hutch began breast stroking further into the cave. His eyes were adjusting as light from the entrance allowed him to see the ceiling, which was higher than he expected, rising around ten feet above the water. Thunder echoed through the cave. Hutch treaded water. Ahead, the cave bent to the right and narrowed.

It was hard to distinguish the surface of the water from the background now, and he was kicking slower and going more on feel than sight. He kept his arms on the surface to alert him of anything in front. He thought he heard Nate yell something down to him but the wind had blown the words apart. He was surrounded by darkness.

Hutch's feet hit something. It wasn't the bottom, so he moved over it and was soon swimming forward again. He tried to stand up but sank a few feet below the water. The depth was shallower—no more than eight feet—and after a few more strokes, his feet found the bottom. His head was the only thing that cleared the water for a few steps, but stepping further, more of his body emerged. The air was cool and Hutch kept his hands out in front of him, anticipating the back of the cave. The water was at his waist, no longer getting shallower.

His hands touched rock in front of him. He followed the surface up and just above his head he could feel it level off. He pulled himself up and crouched on a plateau. Putting his hands above his head, he rose carefully searching by feel for the ceiling above. His legs locked and his arms stretched all the way above him—still no ceiling. He put his arms in front of him and walked forward. Five paces in, his hands did not hit rock; they touched what felt like dirt. He grabbed a handful and it fell to the ground out of both sides of his hand as he rubbed his fingers and thumb together. He bent down and started working his hands up from the bottom.

The dirt pile was angled in to the interior of the cave as he rose. He walked side to side on the plateau. The dirt pile ran the entire breadth, which was about three paces wide. Feeling he could do no more without a light, Hutch lowered himself off the plateau. The cold water gave his body a jolt as he pushed off and began swimming toward the opening.

When he arrived at the point directly below the lift, he called up to Nate but heard no response. The sound of splashing came from the cave's opening. He swam toward it and soon saw Nate coming toward him.

"Thinkin' ahead, huh?" Hutch said.

"Figured I wouldn't be hoisting you back up so I decided to join you," Nate said. "I brought the bottle and your fins and mask; they're out at the opening."

"That'll work," said Hutch.

"Find anything?" Nate said while lifting the mask off of his face and resting it on his forehead.

"Not sure," said Hutch. "I'll tell you about it on the boat."

"Do you think we should head back with the weather this way?" Nate said.

Hutch looked up at the sky through the hole in the boathouse roof. It was black above them and just as black in the distance. He started to answer but the boom of thunder cut him off. When it subsided, Hutch said, "Normally, I'd say we wait it out. Summer rains beat the shit out of you for about ten minutes and then pass. But this baby isn't passin' for a while. It came up on us quicker than I thought it would."

The two men swam the remaining twenty yards out of the cave. A bolt of lightning shot down from the sky on the horizon, soon followed by an eruption of thunder. The rain needled the water around them. Whitecaps were assaulting the shore as Nate swam over to the ledge where he had put Hutch's fins and mask and the bottle. He handed them to Hutch and soon they were kicking away from the shore.

The boat bucked as Nate pulled himself over the transom. The deck was slick and the chilly rain was pelting him as he pulled off his fins and mask. Hutch's gear was already bunched up in a corner. *Queen* rocked as waves lifted the boat up and down. Nate made his way toward the wheelhouse and saw Hutch up forward, pulling in the last few feet of the anchor line before the anchor itself appeared and Hutch worked the windlass to secure it. Nate was standing at the door to the wheelhouse when Hutch jumped down on the deck in front of him.

"Let's go," Hutch said and pushed past Nate.

When both men were inside, Hutch closed the hatch behind them and started the engine. He turned on *Queen's* running lights and flipped a row of switches that started the wipers on the wheelhouse's windows. Hutch throttled forward and *Queen* began to cut the waves as they headed away from the Twin Sisters and toward shore.

"If I'm right, we haven't seen the heavy stuff yet. I think we can beat it in," Hutch said and pushed the throttle further forward. He looked back at Nate, who was shivering. They were still in their bathing suits and boots. Hutch grabbed a towel from a locker under the wheel and threw it to Nate.

"Thanks," Nate said. He dried off and put his t-shirt back on, which was still warm from the sun hitting it earlier.

Hutch did not dry off, but threw on a t-shirt with the Coast Guard crest on the front from the same locker. Then, he grabbed a thermos and handed it to Nate. "Pour two cups for us," he said.

Nate looked around, "Where are the cups?"

Hutch kept his head forward and pointed with his thumb at the bulkhead behind him. On two nails left of the hatch hung ceramic mugs.

Nate set them down and unscrewed the top of the thermos. Into the mugs poured coffee as black as the sky above them. He handed a mug to Hutch.

Hutch lifted it and downed the coffee.

"Want some more?" Nate said.

"Nope," Hutch said.

Nate took a sip and nearly burned his tongue off. "What did you find in the cave?"

Hutch told him the rough topography that he had been able to feel.

"Do you think we should go back?" Nate said.

"I think it's worth another look," Hutch said.

The rain started to let up and the seas evened. Nate walked over and tapped on a blue tarp in the corner of the wheelhouse adjacent to the helm console. "What's under here?"

"Take it off and see for yourself," Hutch said.

Nate pulled off the tarp, exposing a rectangular machine the size of a laser printer. The outer frame was littered with knobs and buttons and the inner frame was the size of a computer screen and made of paper. A metallic arm extended from under the outer frame, with the end elbowing down ninety degrees, its ink tip resting on the paper. "What is this, Hutch?"

"It's a plotter for my wide-scan beam and sidescan sonar," said Hutch.

"May I turn it on?"

"Sure."

Nate turned the machine on and nothing happened. After thirty seconds he looked at Hutch. "I don't think it's working."

Hutch exhaled a laugh. "Probably because I'm not operating either one of my sonars. There's nothing to print out."

"Why didn't you tell me that?"

"All you asked is if you could turn it on."

"Do you like needling people?"

"It amuses me," said Hutch.

Nate turned the machine off and covered it back up. Hutch looked at him and shifted his eyes back at the water. He throttled the boat down, but not enough for the seas to take over.

"Take the wheel," Hutch said.

19

Nate came over and grabbed two of the mahogany spindles. Hutch stepped aside and pointed down at the binnacle. The amber glow made his hand look yellow. "Keep her on two-seven-six," said Hutch as he turned away from the helm.

Nate watched as the ship's heading went to two-seven-zero. "Shit," Nate said.

Hutch turned back around and looked at the binnacle. "She's only a single screw, so her ass naturally swings to starboard. Keep the wheel a bit over to starboard to compensate and she'll drive pretty straight," Hutch said and then walked over and took the blue tarp off again.

"What are you doing?" Nate said as he steadied the boat back up on two-seven-six.

"Showing you how this damned thing works."

"You said that you had more than one sonar."

"Do you know anything about sidescan sonar?" Hutch said.

"A little," said Nate.

Hutch turned the plotter back on and energized another piece of equipment next to it. "I use sidescan sonar to view the seabed and any structures or objects laying on it, hopefully wrecks or a shit-ton of fish."

"What do the wrecks look like?" Nate asked.

"You'd be surprised," Hutch said. "Since they're in cold fresh water, the hulls stay preserved. That's the big difference between diving on shipwrecks in the Great Lakes versus the warm waters of the tropics; the shipwrecks on the Great Lakes still look somewhat like ships. The ocean's saltwater corrodes wood and metal, and after time all that's left of a wreck is a pile of ballast rocks. So, if I cross over a wreck out here, and the equipment is working properly, the plotter will draw something that actually looks like a ship."

"Neat," Nate said and kept fighting with the wheel.

"Indeed," Hutch said. "The term 'sidescan' usually refers to using a 'fish', also called a 'towfish', which looks like this." Hutch opened a locker beneath the plotter and pulled out a device that was around four feet long and looked like a torpedo. "When I'm using my sidescan sonar, I tow this behind my boat with around two-hundred feet of coaxial cable. I lower it to a certain depth and it gives me a picture of the bottom." Hutch held the fish over the plotter with one hand, treating the plotter like the sea bottom, and moved his free hand from the fish down to the plotter. When his hand hit the plotter, he bounced it back up toward the fish. "The fish transmits small pulses of sound which are absorbed and reflected back by the bottom and any other underwater objects. The strength of each returned pulse together with the time that the pulse traveled provides an underwater picture."

Nate watched as Hutch put the fish back in the locker. "So, the piece of equipment you turned on next to the plotter is for the fish?"

"No. What I turned on is my other sonar. It's hull-mounted and instead of being called sidescan, it's called a wide-scan beam. It basically works on the same principles but is a lot less accurate than my fish because as the boat goes, so goes it. You pretty much have to have dead-calm seas to operate it. I prefer using the fish, but sometimes I don't feel like fussing with the cable. The hull-mounted takes the flip of a switch and a little adjusting. Since you wanted to see something, I fired it up."

Nate now noticed that the mechanical arm on the plotter was moving back and forth slowly across the paper. "Where is your hookup for the fish?" Nate said.

"It's a piece of cake. I'm against computers, but I do own a cheap laptop. The coaxial cable from the fish hooks into my laptop through a USB connector. Simple as that. Mrs. Hawthorne installed the software on the laptop. The program draws a picture like this old plotter, except it's digital and on the screen. The only pain in operating it is that I've got to set up my towing winch in the stern to run the cable out. And, of course, make sure I've got the cable deep enough so some dip-shit boater doesn't cross my wake too close to the boat and get his screw all tangled up in my cable."

The plotter completed its first drawing and the paper advanced. Hutch stopped the machine and studied it for a minute. He took out a pencil and recorded the latitude and longitude from the GPS monitor mounted on the bulkhead above the forward set of windows.

"See something?" Nate said.

"Probably not. Like I said, the equipment acts squirrelly in bad weather, although we're not rolling too much. We're over a drop-off and it doesn't always like that either."

"But we're getting closer to shore."

"Ever heard of a blue hole?" said Hutch.

"A blue hole?"

"I'll take that as a no," Hutch said. "It's created when the ceiling to an ancient cave system collapses. Dean's Hole off Long Island in the Bahamas is probably the deepest. When you snorkel there, the sand goes from five to six-hundred feet deep in just a few kicks. The drop off we're over is the closest thing we've got to a blue hole. The depth drops from thirty to three-hundred feet and then rises back up to fifty-feet again. It's like a crater. The gradual drop-off doesn't occur until you get past the Twin Sisters." Hutch shut down the machines and threw the tarp back on. "Throttle us back up."

Nate did and then asked, "How much do the sonars cost?"

Hutch exhaled a laugh again. "Why is everything with your generation cost-related? Most of you just run things up on a credit card anyways. Don't have the discipline to save enough to buy things that are important. You don't live within your means. Instead, you live in the moment and think it's all owed to you."

"I don't," said Nate. "My father taught me the value of a dollar a long time ago."

"Then your pops is a smart man," Hutch said.

"He *was* a smart man," said Nate. "Why do you make so many assumptions about me, Hutch?"

Hutch was silent.

"It wouldn't be fair if I made assumptions about you, would it?" Nate said.

"Try me," Hutch said.

"Let's start off with something that isn't an assumption: you steal fuel from that local marina—"

"That owner is a—"

"Fuck-up. I know. But that doesn't mean it's right for you to do it. Now, assumptions. I could assume that since you don't pay for fuel, you probably didn't pay for your sonar systems. If I had to guess, one of your old Coast Guard buddies swung a deal for you. Then, it wouldn't be a long shot to assume that you're not only a thief from the local town, you're a thief from the service that provided for you and your fami—"

He heard the door to the wheelhouse open and then slam shut behind him. Nate stared back at the binnacle. The only sound he could hear now was the wipers.

20

The rain did not let up and Nate arrived home, soaked, at six p.m. The Jeep was in the driveway. He parked his bike in the garage and ran through the rain toward the house. He opened the screen door and saw another note from Brooke taped to it.

The Sawyers had invited Brooke and the Gibsons for drinks at a pub called McCleod's and he was invited too if he felt up to it. If not, there was taco salad in the fridge. The time she had written the note was 5:15 p.m. He took off his clothes in the kitchen and walked naked down the hallway to the utility room. He threw the wet clothes in the washer and headed for the bathroom to shower.

Nate kept returning to Hutch's exit from the wheelhouse. For an instant, Hutch had lost his composure. Hutch had left Nate alone in the wheelhouse the rest of the trip, and when he had returned to bring the boat next to the dock, he was solemn. The anger had left, replaced with a blank, distant look. When he had shut off *Queen*'s engine, he had put his hand on Nate's shoulder and said, "Sorry about gettin' pissy. You made your point."

"I was out of line," Nate said.

"Maybe, maybe not," Hutch said. Then, they had shook hands.

* * *

Randall McCleod stood behind three feet of mahogany at his rightful place in the bar that he had named after himself. It was quarter after nine and the summer folk had started to pile in waiting for him to help them get sloshed before getting into their expensive vehicles and driving drunk back to their beach estates.

"Randy, I need six shooters for table three, and three long-neck Millers for table two," said Christina Allen, McCleod's only waitress and, at some point, the servicer of almost every McCleod's regular.

McCleod wiped the sweat off his forehead, couldn't afford air conditioning—which didn't keep the crowd away—and tipped his head back to acknowledge the order. His shoulder length grey ponytail bounced on his neck. He should have fired her awhile back. She ended her shift early every night because she was drunk and leaving with a customer, but it was usually around one a.m. and he could manage the last hour himself. Plus it was summer, and some help was better than no help. She was hanging on to her one-time nomination to the Homecoming Court during high school, and ever since— beyond the sex McCleod couldn't understand why—people still lined up to kiss her ass.

McCleod filled Christina's tray with the drinks and gave her the same wink he gave her whenever they chose to rekindle their own romance, which was usually in the middle of winter when all anyone in Hampstead ever did on the weekends was drink. And why shouldn't bartender and barmaid hook-up? McCleod was once a high school standout in football with plans to attend college on a scholarship, make the NFL, and come back and save everyone in Hampstead. For one semester, he was on track. Then his grades went in the toilet, and he'd been in Hampstead tending bar ever since. He was six-two, two-forty, but the flooring was elevated behind the bar making him look closer to six-eight to customers. And for non-locals, that's what he told them his height was when they asked. And why shouldn't he?

Christina shook her ass at him and disappeared into the growing crowd. He wondered how many she had had already.

"Randy, can a guy get a fuckin' drink around here?"

McCleod didn't need to look where the voice was coming from. He simply went to the tap, poured a stout, and shoved it down the bar. His brother raised the new glass and said, "Many thanks."

Most people considered Randall McCleod a shining star compared to his brother. At thirty-five, Troy McCleod was fourteen years younger than Randall, and his birth was rumored to be an *oops*. Seventeen years removed now from blowing out his ACL and blowing up his life, Troy was a local fisherman, fishing but mostly drinking in the summer and collecting unemployment during the winter. Ice fishing was too cold.

Randall McCleod had established a fine bar and grill. Over one hundred beers on tap, fantastic soup, and an expansive deck out back with a bonfire pit in the middle made McCleod's the preferred watering hole in Hampstead. The location was a two-minute walk from Shelby's Marina and another ten minutes from the beach mansions, which kept the money rolling in. If he got in a bind over the summer, he'd simply arrange for one of the millionaire drunks to be pulled over after leaving the bar, have the cop take a payoff for not arresting the rich pinhead, and then split the money with the cop. And why shouldn't he?

A group of five customers were steadily making their way to the bar; in the lead were the Sawyers. Jeff Sawyer had been a little *too* regular lately, drinking like there was no bottom to his glass, told McCleod everything: job lost, boat sold, in deep deep do-do, blah, blah, blah. Sawyer had also left a few nights with Christine. The threesome in tow McCleod had never seen before. Unfamiliar people did not make Randall McCleod nervous. Sooner or later they would take their place on McCleod's picture wall—a wall filled with photos of customers with Randall, and sometimes Christine and Troy. No, unfamiliar people were an opportunity. To call a customer by his or her first name after a few drinks was to up one's tip. McCleod knew Sawyer was on board for at least fifty bucks, but could he get the rest to follow suit? Such are the thoughts of a successful bartender.

Sawyer's wife peeled off for the restroom and Sawyer continued to lead the unknown trio toward McCleod. The man approaching with Sawyer was athletic and so were the two women. His guess was these were new summer folk. The brunette seemed to be out of bar-going practice as she said 'excuse me' or 'I'm sorry' to everyone she bumped into. The blonde moved with confidence. Maybe they weren't summer folk. The brunette was dressed to fit in, but the clothes looked too new—not her regular garb. Randall McCleod smiled. This would be easy.

Nate lay in bed watching the Tigers bat in the bottom of the ninth while eating peanuts and drinking Vernors. The rain had stopped after dinner and he had the windows cranked all the way open. He could hear waves beating on the beach. Succumbing to the chilly air, he had put on a sweatshirt. Brooke was still not home and a part of him began to worry. When was the last time she had been out this late? He yawned.

The game ended—three up, three down, fourth loss in a row—and he turned off the lights. Music could be heard from somewhere down the beach as Nate drifted off to sleep. He did not hear Brooke enter when she got home. Nor did he hear her getting sick in the bathroom. Nor had he seen the way Gibson traced the curve of her ass as he conscientiously walked her to the door.

21

Hutch sat on Lucille Hawthorne's living room davenport. The cushions were a plaid pattern of brown, tan, and green; the arms at both ends were wood. A cream-colored phone with a cord sat on the coffee table in front of him. Hutch looked at his watch: 11:30 p.m., meaning 8:30 p.m. in California where his daughter Melanie lived. Lucille was sitting across the room in a rocking chair, moving slowly back and forth. A Frank Sinatra record was playing on a turntable in the corner, noticeable enough to be heard but not enough to interfere with a conversation—or a phone call.

"I haven't spoken to her in a year," Hutch said.

"You don't have to tell me," said Lucille, "I've been marking off the days on my kitchen calendar."

"Where do I begin?" Hutch said.

"Where I told you to: with an apology."

Hutch went to take a sip of the brandy Lucille had brought out.

"Not until you're done with the call," Lucille said.

Hutch put the brandy down. From his shirt pocket, he removed a wrinkled piece of paper with Melanie's phone number on it. He looked over at Lucille and then put on his glasses.

Picking up the receiver like he was sneaking in a phone call that he didn't want his parents to hear, he pushed each button. When the line began to ring, he set the paper down on the coffee table.

"Hello," a man's voice answered.

Hutch recognized it as the voice of Melanie's husband. "Oh, hello there—" he began waving at Lucille for the husband's name.

"Jim." Lucille said.

"—Jim," said Hutch.

"Who is this?" Jim said.

"It's," he paused.

Lucille gave him a reassuring look.

"Melanie's father," he said. "May I speak with her?"

"Oh," said Jim. "Just a moment."

Hutch covered the handle. "He's going to get her," he said to Lucille.

"You can do this, Abner," she said.

"Hello?" came Melanie's voice from the phone.

"Hi," Hutch said.

"What do you want?" she said.

He heard a baby cry in the background. "Is that Michael?" Hutch said.

"Yes," Melanie said.

Hutch was silent. His grandson had been born three months ago.

"Are you still there?" Melanie said.

"I am," he said.

"If you're not going to talk, then we should end this call," she said.

Hutch took a deep breath. "I have some things I'd like to say, and I—" he searched for the words.

"Need you to listen," Lucille whispered.

"—need you to listen," Hutch finished.

"The last time we spoke, I did nothing *but* listen," Melanie said. "You didn't let me get in a word. I don't know how many times I left messages at Lucille's that you never returned."

"Twenty-seven," he said in a low tone.

"So, why should I listen now?"

"You have every right not to," said Hutch. "But I want to ask for your forgiveness."

"My forgiveness?" she said.

Hutch let out another breath.

"I—"

She cut him off. "You haven't even seen your new grandson! And your four-year old granddaughter doesn't even know her grandfather. Sound familiar?"

He'd missed too much. The years had gone too fast. Before his wife died, he'd told her that he wanted them back—all of them. "I can't change the past, Melanie. But I want to change where the future is headed."

"I can't take this right now," she said. "It's too—" and her voice broke, "painful."

The line went dead.

Hutch put the receiver down, and his head down with it.

Lucille came over and sat next to him. "We'll try again. I'm very proud of you."

Hutch shook his head.

22

At six-thirty, Nate awoke to a cold shadowy bedroom. The breeze from last night remained, and he lay in his briefs. At some point he must have taken off his sweatshirt but didn't remember. Brooke was on her side facing away from him and snoring almost as loudly as the box fan she had evidently turned on when she got home. Nate sat up. The lake was as flat as a pancake, and the sun was just above the horizon. He saw a large glass of water placed on top of Brooke's nightstand and also a garbage can next to the bed. Must have tied one on last night.

The last time he had seen a trashcan by the bed was at the hotel where they were staying for Brooke's best friend's wedding. On the way back to their hotel after the reception, Brooke had come on to him in the parking lot and they had intoxicated sex as soon as they made it to their room. He was stirred awake by the sound of Brooke getting sick in the bathroom. He had offered his help, but had the bathroom door slammed in his face. The next morning, there was a trashcan on Brooke's side of the hotel bed. He was still naked; she was in a pair of sweatpants and a t-shirt.

Nate stood up and stretched. His arms and legs were tight from the swim yesterday. The weather forecast for the day was the same as yesterday, starting out nice and then thundershowers. It was supposed to clear up by late evening and be perfect the next few days, sunny and briefly spiking up to ninety before leveling off at around eighty. Nate walked around the bed and gave Brooke a sympathy kiss on her forehead. The garbage can was empty. He went into the bathroom and noticed that the rug that usually was underneath the toilet was gone; she must have missed a little.

Nate shaved, showered, and put on coffee. He walked to the end of the driveway to pick up the paper and had started the sports section when the phone rang. It was almost seven.

Nate picked up the phone. It was Hutch.

"I know it's six-fifty, but I waited as long as I could. You up?" Hutch said.

"Yeah, I'm up. What do you mean you waited?"

"I've been up since four-thirty, like I am every morning. Already taken my run, swam, read the paper, and I'm on my second pot of coffee."

Nate wondered if he'd still be going even a percentage of that strong when he was sixty-two. "Anything new?"

"Tyee called me on my radio an hour ago and says the books he's got for me will be at his store around eight. I'm taking' *Queen* over. You interested?"

Nate walked to the bedroom and peeked in on Brooke. She was still snoring and lying motionless. "Yeah, I'm game."

"I'll bring *Queen* in as close as I can, but you'll have to swim out to me. I checked the dinghy this morning and the paint's not dry yet. Damn humidity does that sometimes."

Nate agreed. Back home, he'd had some bookshelves custom made out of pine and stained. When he ordered them, he asked when they would be done. The owner had replied, "Three weeks, but if it rains nothin' around here gets done." Nate had asked him what he meant. "I mean that the wood don't take no stain 'cause of the humidity." It rained one day in the allotted three weeks. The bookshelves were delivered two months later.

"I'll be ready," Nate said.

23

Leonard Shaw sat in his robe on the balcony of his third floor master bedroom overlooking the water, drinking an espresso and checking the stock market on a laptop. His wife was still in bed, sleeping off a hangover from last night. It was hard to notice if she was still in bed on most days since she slept with the covers over her head and her five-feet, ninety-pound body hardly gave the king-size more than the appearance of the covers needing to be straightened. At fifty-one, she was ten years his junior and they had been married for twenty years. He had been in the petite brunette phase at that time and had never left it.

Shaw listened as two sets of footsteps grew louder on the outdoor stairs that led up to the balcony. Balcony was the proper term for an extension from a second or third story room, but this was more the size of a deck and was furnished with Adirondack chairs, glass tables, wooden benches with cushions, and a wet bar. Shaw set his computer aside, walked over, and closed the sliding glass door to the bedroom.

"Good morning, gentlemen," Shaw said.

The shorter, heavier set man took a seat across from Shaw at the glass table. The other man remained standing. Shaw poured the seated man, his lawyer Joshua Bagley, a cup of coffee.

"Why did you fly me in this morning, Leonard?" Bagley asked.

Bagley had arrived in a seaplane less than an hour ago, and a speedboat had taken him from the water to Shaw's beach.

"I've gotten wind of something and wanted to ask your advice."

"And I couldn't have given it to you over the phone?" Bagley said.

"No," Shaw said.

Bagley moved the chair back far enough to cross his right leg over his left knee. It was getting harder to do this because of his weight. "I'm not sure I like this, Leonard."

Shaw had hired Bagley twenty-one years ago to draft his prenuptial with his soon-to-be wife. Six years prior to that, Shaw had become the youngest CEO in Grauman Enterprise's history at thirty-four and was worth millions on his wedding day. Now, he was worth multi-millions. A few more buyouts and it would be billions. Bagley had ridden on Shaw's coattails and was now one of the most connected lawyers in Baltimore, where Grauman's main office was located. In fact, he had been labeled the unofficial Mayor of Baltimore. Shaw stared into Bagley's sunken eyes and guessed he was running through the possibilities of what Shaw would have had him come in person to talk about.

Bagley had narrowed the possibilities down to three.

One: Shaw was again contemplating retirement. The subject always seemed to come up over the summer when Shaw was away from Baltimore, either relaxing at his beach house in Hampstead or touring the Great Lakes on his mega-yacht, *Triumph*. The eighty-hour work-weeks were beginning to catch up. As CEO, he began at five a.m. and worked to seven p.m. Monday through

Friday and came in from seven a.m. until late afternoon on Saturdays. Except for vacations, he had kept to the schedule for twenty-seven years.

Now sixty-one, his goal was to retire in 4 years at sixty-five after forty-one years with the company—the last thirty as CEO. The final four years would preserve the $250,000 sliver of his pension that would be taken away if he retired any sooner. Even after that many years of service, Grauman would be expecting that his dedication to the company would endure beyond retirement and that he would bequeath a generous amount to the company in his will. Both he and Bagley knew that it was never coming. At the root, Leonard Shaw was frugal. He had learned as a young working-class paper pusher to save what he made and live below his means in case anything ever happened. It had sounded fine, until he was making more in a month than his parents had ever made. But he never broke character. The toys that he and his wife were surrounded with were all her doing, and he monitored her closely.

The truth was that almost half of his wealth was going to go to his alma mater, Duke University, upon his retirement. The truth of Shaw's intentions entertained Bagley as he watched Shaw at Grauman benefactor appreciation lunches and dinners, where Shaw would kiss ass and stress the importance of donations and loyalty.

Two: Shaw had heard of Bagley's recent indiscretion and was contemplating severing ties before he got dragged in with the newspaper and media sensationalism that threatened. Shaw felt that as powerful and influential as Bagley had become, he somehow could not escape his roots. Bagley had bullied his way to the top, nothing more, nothing less.

In Baltimore and Washington D.C.'s inner corridors of power, Bagley was known as a man who got things done—and got them done quickly. Bribe any politician, lobby for influence, and seal any deal. Need to disappear for six months with no questions asked, see Bagley. Need a judge in your pocket, Bagley. Need an invite to a White House State Dinner, yep, Bagley. With a thick stomach from everyday power lunches, slicked back gray hair with puppy brown eyes, charismatic charm, and a smile that could make anyone believe that their daughter was safe in his presence at night, Bagley ran Baltimore by day and chased skirt by night, only to come home and have breakfast with a loving wife (his third) and their two children before they left for school. A morning of sleep, and the cycle started over again.

Until recently, it had never gotten out of control. There were always rumors (never confirmed) of Bagley being sighted at the Playboy Mansion and at a Catholic Church in the same day on west coast trips. In Baltimore, his unofficial office was in a downtown bar called "The Advocate." Bagley would lure lawyers, brokers, and senators away from the hustle and bustle of Baltimore and D.C.'s core and treat them to a day of booze, boobs, and promises. Lunch was always on him. The joy juice usually kicked in by Happy Hour, and then Bagley would lay out his case, and before dessert was served by strippers and call girls, he had his guests signing ludicrous deals. After paperwork was signed and handshakes exchanged (sometimes high fives), Bagley sent his boys back to their offices in cabs. After all, he didn't want them to get a DUI, did he? Sometimes he even sent *a nightcap* back with one of his newly acquired friends. And that is where the recent trouble had started.

A politician he had sent back last week had had a guest waiting outside the man's office. The politician's wife had watched as her husband struggled to get out of the cab, laughing while a hot number wearing knee high red boots and little else pulled on his tie with both hands. When the politician had finally freed himself, he had turned around just in time to have his wife's purse clothesline him. Normally, this wouldn't have been a problem and Bagley would have denied everything. But this time he had been in the back of the cab, and the wife had taken pictures. Now there was an investigation starting at "The Advocate," and Bagley was fighting to keep his spin on every story that was being reported, which was why he was so pissed off at Shaw for flying him out here.

Three: Somehow (and Bagley felt a chill at the possibility) the events of last summer had resurfaced, which would be the worst-case scenario. That might be the reason Shaw had his head of security, Jackson Floyd, present at the meeting. Floyd was an immense physical presence, standing six-foot eight weighing two-fifty. He had been an Australian spear fishing champion before becoming somewhat of a mercenary for hire. Bagley had found him during the events and Shaw had hired him—and now trusted him with his life. If something new had come to light in regard to last summer, Bagley was uneasy of being within arms reach of Floyd.

"No worries, Joshua," said Shaw. "I have some interesting news. Floyd here informed me last night that a cottage owner down the beach has found a gold French coin from the sixteen hundreds."

Bagley pulled out a pack of cigarettes and lit one. He took a long drag and chased it with a sip of coffee. "And?"

"I'm wondering if this is something we could get in on if there's more."

"That's what you called me here for?"

"There is also the issue of last summer, which Floyd tells me may present a problem."

"What problem?" Bagley said leaning forward.

"Let's not focus on that aspect right now. Let's stay with the first. I want you to find out how much I would need to offset the penalty I would take if I retired this summer. If there is more gold, it might be worth it."

"When do you need this? I'm kind of busy putting out a fire at the moment," Bagley said and inhaled on his cigarette again.

"I know you are," said Shaw, "but that's not my problem. You got yourself into that mess and you're going to have to pull yourself out of it. I want you to stay here until we have a working number."

Bagley raised both hands in a "What?" gesture, the way he began every cross-examination after hearing damaging testimony against a client.

Shaw stared at him. "You're staying. I've got Floyd keeping his eyes open. He'll let us know."

The sound of a powerboat caught Shaw's attention. He motioned for the binoculars around Floyd's neck.

Floyd handed them over, and Shaw brought the binoculars to his eyes. Down the beach he could see a boat approaching the shore and then backing down to remain about fifty yards out. His attention was then caught by a man jogging down to the water with a pair of flippers in his hand. The man took off his shirt and put it in a large Ziploc bag along with his flip-flops, wallet, and a set of keys. Then, he put on his flippers and swam with the bag floating on the water until he reached the boat. An older man reached over the gunwale and helped pull him aboard. Then the boat turned and headed along the coast. Shaw dropped the binoculars and with his eyes motioned for Floyd to leave.

Floyd descended the stairs and was gone. Bagley turned his attention from the boat back to Shaw.

"Is that the guy who found the coin?" Bagley said pointing back with his thumb toward the lake while taking another drink of coffee.

"Yes," said Shaw. "He lives in the brown-sided out-of-date cottage with the small deck. Why don't those people just sell? It disgusts me to look down that stretch of beach and see those shacks lined up one after another."

"How did Floyd find out about the coin?" Bagley said.

"That would be where last summer comes in. Can you have some rough numbers for me later?"

"Sure," Bagley said.

"One more thing," said Shaw.

"Yes?"

"See if you can find out if any other gold has ever been discovered on the Great Lakes."

24

Queen rounded Hampstead Point and Nate could see the line of buildings along the coast. Hutch turned the boat to starboard and steadied up on a course. They were seated in two chairs bolted to the deck on the level above the wheelhouse at the fair-weather control panel.

"I line up with the Hampstead Water Tower once I round the point. It takes you right into Tyee's place," Hutch said. The sky was already starting to darken on the horizon, promising a storm like the day before.

Nate picked up the pair of binoculars that were resting on the console in front of him. "So, we're picking up some books?" he said, scanning the Hampstead coastline. He found the water tower and then moved down until he saw the back of Beecher Hardware. A long dock came straight out the back steps and ended with a large shed over the water.

"A couple on Louis the Fourteenth," Hutch said, "which reminds me, I found something going back through Captain Daniels's log entries last night."

Nate put the binoculars down.

"Well, it wasn't really in his logbook. It was on an order form that he had sent to the mainland. Lighthouse keepers were only supplied a few times a year, if that. One week before his last log entry he had included a requisition for a book on how to write and speak the French language."

"Why would he need that?" Nate said.

"It's got me puzzled too," said Hutch. "He wouldn't need it to read a coin."

Nate had left the coin at home but tried to remember if there was any writing on it. One side was a picture of King Louis the Fourteenth with the date 1643 and the other side had a fleur de lis. Was that all? He was sure it was. So, what would Daniels need a book on French for? He ended his thought with a shrug.

"Well, the only thing I can think of is that there was something along with the coins," said Hutch.

"And you think that these books on King Louis will have any kind of answers?" Nate said.

"Maybe, maybe not. But they'll at least give us an idea of the time period and how your coin might have made it over here."

"Hutch, don't you think we're starting to stretch this thing a little thin?"

"So the optimist has become a doubting Thomas, huh?"

"I'm trying to be a realist," Nate said.

"It's still too much of a coincidence that the coin that rolled up on your beach is exactly like the one that Daniels drew in his logbook. And now we find out that he wanted a French book," Hutch eyed him, "Nate—"

It was the first time he had heard Hutch refer to him by his first name.

"—when was the last time you believed in anything?"

'Believing in anything' could mean a variety of things. However, Nate was sure what Hutch meant: When was the last time he had passion for something? Something that drove him, gave him purpose no matter how absurd, enticed him, motivated him, focused him. Maybe ten years ago, in his last at bat. Maybe the last time his dad told him a sea story.

"Well, it's been a helluva a long time for me," Hutch said.

* * *

After tying up to Tyee's dock, Hutch and Nate entered the hardware store. The door jingled and Tyee came back to greet them. Hutch and Tyee shook hands, and then Tyee extended his huge hand to Nate. When they shook, Nate's hand felt like it was in a vise grip.

"Let me ring these last few customers out and then I'll meet you downstairs," said Tyee, "your books are on the table in the lounge."

Hutch and Nate left Tyee at the front counter and headed down a flight of stairs.

"Doesn't Tyee have any employees?" Nate said.

"He's got a few, but on slow days he lets 'em go. Might even still pay 'em. He likes his quiet."

The storeroom, which served as the employee lounge, took up the entire basement. Stock boxes had been piled up and moved over to accommodate two leather chairs and a coffee maker with two burners, which sat on top of a crate. Hutch smiled while looking at the coffee pots.

"What?" Nate said.

"Well, those coffee pots are a rite of passage here. Tyee plays a prank on the new employees he hires. He figures if they can withstand it, then they're worth keepin'. If not, then it weeds 'em out." Hutch pointed to the pots. "The pot on the bottom burner is for brewing, and the pot on the top burner stopped working years ago. Instead of fixing it, Tyee started using it as a deposit for used coffee grounds—he reuses filters at least once—and the bottom pot's last remains before a fresh one gets brewed. On a new guy's first day of work, Tyee hands him a Beecher Hardware mug at the counter and then takes him downstairs to have a cup of coffee and show him the work lounge. He always has his cup already filled before they come down here. When they arrive, he fills the new guy's cup from the top pot and toasts with him to the new job.

The results are usually different for the poor sonsabitches. Some spit immediately as the cold, floatie filled liquid enters, some vomit after swallowing a tiny bit, and one idiot actually dropped his mug, breaking the handle off when it hit the floor. If you take it in stride, from that point on you are family to Tyee, and he takes care of you."

Hutch walked over to the wall and pulled a stained mug with 'Hutch' stenciled on it from the rusty nail it hung on. Then, he filled his cup from the bottom pot.

Nate sat down in one of the leather chairs and felt like he had sunk to the floor. Hutch had picked up the books on the table and was leafing through one when heavy footsteps came down the stairs, and Tyee filed in through the doorway to the lounge.

"You find the books?" Tyee said to Hutch.

"Got 'em, thanks," Hutch said.

"Let me know if you need any more," said Tyee.

The light over the two chairs went out followed by a clap of thunder. The light came back on.

"We should head back," said Hutch.

The three men headed up the stairs and outside onto the dock. The sky was still light over their heads but dark in the direction they would be heading. A lightning bolt shot down by Hampstead Point, followed by a rumble of thunder.

"I thought that shit had all passed through yesterday," Tyee said.

"No way," Hutch replied. He tapped on the shed while passing by it. "How's my winch doing?"

"Fine," said Tyee. "You haven't used it in awhile."

"Haven't had a reason to," Hutch said as he hopped down onto *Queen*'s stern.

Tyee cast off the bow line, and Nate cast off the stern line before stepping on board. Hutch started the engine and they waved goodbye to Tyee.

By the time they had rounded Hampstead Point, it was sprinkling.

"We'll anchor more north of the island tomorrow and take the dinghy into the cave with floodlights and scuba gear," Hutch said.

"If there's nothing in the cave, where do we go from there?" Nate said.

"I guess we'll start checking the other buildings, but the cave is our best bet," Hutch said.

"Why?" Nate said.

"Because it was under the building that Daniels would have stayed in. With the water level being so low, it will let us go back into parts of the cave that were underwater before."

"What time do you need me out at your place?" Nate said.

"I'm going fishing tomorrow morning so I'll be out until around nine. I was pretty sure that you'd be comin' tomorrow when I was talking with Lucille this morning—"

"But you called me before seven," Nate interrupted.

"I know I did. We have coffee on her porch at five-thirty."

"Oh," Nate said.

"She wants me to tell you that you're invited for breakfast tomorrow at eight. When you're done, come over and meet me on the dock."

"Agreed," said Nate. "What are you going to do for the rest of the day?"

Hutch lifted one hand from the wheel and put it on the stack of books. "I'm gonna read these to see if anything raises an eyebrow. I might take a look at the logs again too." Hutch brought his hand back to the wheel and began to turn it. "You're more than welcome to come out and read, but I don't wanna zap your vacation. Like you said, we may be stretchin' this a bit thin."

Nate wanted to go. In fact, there was nothing more that he wanted to do than go and load up the dinghy—dry or not—and head out to Sanisstey Island to search the cave. Hell, even if he had never found the coin, he would have liked to have spent an afternoon in Hutch's library looking through the high-powered scope at ships passing by in the distance, studying the wreck dioramas Hutch had built, talking with Hutch about diving and Great Lakes history, maybe even having a glass or two of the dark rum Hutch had in a decanter on his desk. Could Hutch see through him and know this? He thought of Brooke. Would she be feeling better? What had happened last night?

"I'll have to pass this afternoon, but I'll be out to Lucille's in the morning," Nate said.

Hutch brought the boat in closer. As they drove down the shoreline, a man was taking down a beach umbrella in front of his house. They passed by Leonard Shaw's and noticed that one of Shaw's three jet skis was barely in its hoist. The weather had probably snuck up on whoever had used it last, and they didn't feel like standing in the rain to raise it up far enough to prevent it from floating away. At least one did every summer.

They passed the Gibson's and Hutch brought the boat to an idle as Nate threw on his flippers and put his belongings back in the Ziploc bag he had brought out.

"See you tomorrow around nine," Nate said as he swung his feet over the gunwale to where his flippers were touching the water. Two lightning bolts came down over the trees behind the cottage next to the Martin's.

"Better paddle fast," said Hutch, "that lightning is close."

Nate gave a short wave and then entered the water. The rain picked up as Hutch entered the wheelhouse and headed for the bight.

25

Brooke was still asleep when Nate entered the bedroom. He could tell that she had been up at some point because the glass of water on her nightstand was now filled with Gatorade and the blinds were closed. Nate slipped off his swim trunks and went down the hall into the utility room. He opened the washer and saw the light blue rug from the bathroom covered in orange bits. The smell of dried vomit hit him and he felt bile rise in his throat. He hurried into the living room sucking in breaths of fresh air. Once his throat and stomach felt normal again, he held in a deep breath and returned to the washer, poured in detergent, started it, and hurried out again.

In the bedroom, he crept to the dresser and pulled out a pair of gym shorts. After giving Brooke a soft kiss on the cheek he headed for the kitchen where he heaped roast beef, ham, and turkey onto a piece of bread and laid two pieces of Swiss cheese on top. After melting the cheese in the microwave, he poured ranch dressing on before laying the other piece of bread on top. From the refrigerator he grabbed a Vernors and then plopped some sweet pickles on his plate.

Rain splattered against the living room windows and the room became dark. Nate ate on the couch in peace as bursts of thunder rumbled overhead and the box fan blew a steady stream of air on him.

An hour later, a knock at the door woke him from a nap.

Joshua Bagley sat in his stateroom aboard his host's yacht, *Triumph*. The ship was in its slip at Shelby's Marina and it had been raining for the past few hours. He had opened a bottle of Gentleman Jack and was on his second drink as he continued to trudge through the chore Leonard Shaw had given him. Bagley had just gotten off the phone with the last museum on his list that dealt with maritime disasters and shipwrecks on the Great Lakes. They all had told him the same thing: no gold had ever been found on the Great Lakes, and some curators would give an annoyed sigh before adding, "because gold was never *carried* on the Great Lakes." He had listened to the first curator list what the Great Lakes ships had carried, but then hung up on the rest when they started the same spiel.

Bagley took a sip. Wasn't he above this petty shit? Shaw obviously needed him more than he needed Shaw. On a few occasions, he'd actually told friends that Shaw reported to him, which should have been true.

What else was it Shaw had wanted him to do? Right, find out how much treasure he would need so that the bastard could retire now instead of four years out. Fuck that. He'd make up a number and then quickly explain that it didn't matter because there was nothing buried beneath the waves anyways. Then, maybe he could get back to Baltimore and put out the fire with this politician's crazy wife. Anything to get out of this small Michigan town, where the pace of life was comparable to an eighty-year-old running two miles. But then again, someone had recently said that eighty was the new fifty. Fat chance. Eighty was eighty. Why didn't Shaw summer in the Hamptons or on the Vineyard like everyone else in his financial bracket? Bagley set his glass down and thought back to last summer. It would make more sense than ever for Shaw to sell his house, sell the yacht, and never come back here. *That* advice he could and had given to Shaw rather than this ridiculous daydreaming about gold.

Nate ushered Tim Gibson into the living room and gave him a towel to dry off with.

"What can I do for you, Tim?"

"I was just passing by and thought I'd say hello," Gibson said.

"In the pouring rain?"

Gibson laughed in embarrassment. "I thought it was over when I left the house but got caught in it right before I got to your place. Thanks for letting me in."

"No problem."

"How's Brooke doing?"

"Still resting," Nate said. "Looks like she had *a lot* of fun last night."

"We all had more than we should have. McCleod's bartender makes some strong drinks. We had to carry Jeff Sawyer out of the place last night."

"How's he doing?"

"A mess," Gibson said. "Sorry you couldn't join us, though, because we did have a good time."

"Can I give you a lift home? This storm doesn't seem to be quitting anytime soon, and Jane may be worried."

Gibson flicked his right wrist like he had just followed through after shooting a basketball. "Ah, she's fine. I appreciate the offer, but I think I'll walk back. How's that coin business going?" Gibson began to cough, louder and louder.

"Can I get you something?" Nate asked.

Gibson got his cough under control, got out "Something to drink," then started coughing again.

"A beer?" Nate said.

Gibson gave him a thumbs up.

Nate left for the kitchen and when he returned, Gibson was gone. The toilet flushed in the hallway bathroom and Gibson re-entered the living room and sat down on his towel as Nate passed him the beer.

"Thanks, Nate. I'll wash this cough down quickly and be out of your hair." Gibson took a swig and then added, "So, nothing new about the coin?"

"Not too much," Nate said.

"That guy out on the bight wasn't able to shed any light?"

"Not really. We're pretty sure the coin is authentic, but it's only one coin. I may just keep it and show the kids at school."

"Kind of a shame isn't it?" Gibson said pointing out the living room window at the lake, "no treasure beneath those whitecaps."

"Keeps the Great Lakes ordinary, I guess," Nate said.

"Good word choice," Gibson said and took the last of his beer in a big gulp—quick for a guy who said he'd had too much last night. Maybe he drank a lot or needed to steady up. Both men rose to their feet and walked to the back door.

Gibson turned to Nate before heading out. "We wanted to invite you both over for dinner tonight, but it looks like tomorrow night might be better."

"I don't think we have anything on tap for tomorrow," said Nate, "I'll check with Brooke when she gets up, and we'll give you a call."

"Great," said Gibson. He shook Nate's hand and then left across the front lawn.

Nate closed the door, stepped back into the living room, and lay back down on the couch. He closed his eyes and was soon out.

26

"I don't get to wear my black dress tonight?" Jane said.

Gibson was drying off from a shower. "Patience," he said. "I don't get to wear my favorite color either." Gibson was a lover of black cashmere sweaters and almost always dressed in black twill and black cord while teaching.

"She wasn't up when you went over there?" Jane took his towel and watched as he walked past into the closet.

"Still recovering," he said grabbing a terry-cloth robe.

"That's a shame," she said, "because I actually enjoyed her company last night."

"Willing to admit that I was right to give her a second chance?"

"I'll go so far as to say that I'm starting to see how it might work out with the three of us." She walked to her sink and gargled some Scope, then took a brush through her hair. She was wearing only a pair of running shorts.

Gibson watched her body, toned like a college cheerleader's. "If Nate keeps busy, it will be even easier," he said.

"Are you sure there's nothing about Brooke that you just want for yourself?"

Had he slipped up? He was sure that he had not made it obvious. When they had added a female student to their sex life a few years back, he had gotten greedy and had had his own sessions with the girl. He had tried to keep the girl's mouth shut by bribing her, but Jane had found out anyway. She had told him to never do anything like that again or else she'd throw him out. "Absolutely not," he said. "I want nothing more than to share her between us."

His zest was for power, where Jane's was needing to be desired. She had gone through a period in college, before she met him, when she thought she was a lesbian, and had experimented. She had ultimately decided that she preferred men, though she had told him that she was still attracted to women. *She* was the one who had first suggested a threesome.

"I'm glad to hear that," Jane said.

He admired her assertiveness and independence. She was like a drill sergeant when conducting her Yoga classes, and she was popular for it—the fitness club had to turn people away wanting to join her class because it filled up so fast. Health nut could not begin to describe her; she visited GNC more than the grocery store. She was also a dedicated mother to their children: she almost never missed an event, and a twelve-year-old boy and fourteen-year-old girl had a lot of events.

"Where did you get that?" she asked, seeing him take a gold watch out of a felt-lined box and put it on.

"From a jeweler in Ann Arbor before we left," he said.

"How much?" Jane asked.

"Just under two thousand," he said.

"Jesus Christ!" she said. "You *have* a watch. Aren't we supposed to be talking about large purchases?"

"Will you relax?" he said. "I talked him down from three grand."

"I can't believe this. Do you want to end up like the Sawyers?"

"That will never happen."

"I—"

"Listen." He said. "We have some money in reserve to buy nice things. We like *nice* things." He sat on the bed and pulled her down next to him. "Did I ever tell you about the bike I wanted when I was growing up?"

Jane shook her head no.

"It was a ten speed. My friends all had them, and I asked and asked why I couldn't have one. My parents told me that they didn't have enough money. So, I spent two summers wheeling around on a used one speed, my friends riding circles around me on their ten speeds. Then, my mom had her affair and left us. The summer after, my father and I were eating dinner—well, I was eating dinner, he was drinking his—and the doorbell rang. I opened it and there was a delivery man with a shiny ten speed. I couldn't believe it: my mom had bought it for me. My father signed the paperwork and I took off on the bike, showing it off to all of my friends. I returned home just before dark and parked my bike in the garage. The next morning, I opened the garage door and it was gone."

"What happened to it?" Jane said.

"After I had gone to bed, my father loaded it up in his truck and sold it to someone for booze money."

"Did you ever get it back?"

Gibson leaned in for a hug and Jane kissed the top of his head. "No," he said. They held each other for a minute, and then Gibson started to slide his hands underneath her shorts.

The rattling of pans woke Nate. The rain had stopped and the sky was lavender as he rose from the couch. He walked into the kitchen and saw Brooke in her robe putting a pot underneath the faucet.

"Good morning," Nate said.

"Don't start with me," Brooke said.

135

"I'm just kidding. It's good to see you're still alive."

"Barely. Could you get me a box of macaroni and cheese from the cupboard?"

Nate grabbed a box and opened it for her.

Brooke put the pot full of water on the stove. "I don't feel right," she said.

"Maybe you won't drink so much with them next time."

"Maybe I wouldn't have if you had been there," she said.

"So, I'm the reason you're hungover?"

"We've missed two nights that were in the zone," Brooke said, "and now we're going to miss another because I'm in no shape to make love tonight."

"I'll take the blame for the first night. I fell asleep on the damn desk in the garage," Nate said. "But I'm not taking the blame for last night."

"Neither am I," said Brooke. "You should have at least called or left a message from wherever you were."

He was starting to grind his teeth. Hold back. Don't do it.

"Don't you have anything to say?" Brooke said with her hands on her hips.

"I thought you could make out where I was from the message Lucille Hawthorne left on the machine. We have caller I.D. so if you needed me, you could have called her."

"That's not the point." Her voice was getting louder.

"Well, what *is* the point then?" Nate said.

"Oh, forget it!" Brooke said.

"Fine," Nate said.

She took a deep breath, then hunched over. A hand shot up to her mouth, she gagged, and ran out of the room.

Nate could hear her vomiting in the hallway bathroom. He shook his head and headed for the garage. Might as well prepare for tomorrow.

27

Nate entered the clearing to Lucille Hawthorne's just before eight a.m. She was already on the porch and waved at him while he walked his bike up.

"Good morning, Nate. I'm sorry I didn't have the gate open for you this morning like I said I would. I got a bit of a late start, but I'm glad you brought your bike."

Nate smiled. "Guess what, Lucille, I forgot you were going to. Packed my bike in the Jeep last night."

"C'mon up and grab a cup of coffee while I bring breakfast out."

He stepped up and filled his mug, then added creamer from a small china cup, scooped in two teaspoons of sugar and stirred. The front door opened and Lucille came out with omelets, French toast with powdered sugar on top, and a plate loaded with bacon. She went inside one more time and came out with a pitcher of orange juice and a basketful of toast.

"I appreciate the invite for breakfast this morning. This looks scrumptious."

"Such a polite man."

"Not always, I'm afraid," he said.

"None of us does the right thing always, Nate." She bowed her head and said grace.

"Has Abner told you about his nephew yet?" Lucille said.

"He hasn't," Nate said. "Is there a reason he would have?"

"He's coming up in another couple of weeks," Lucille said. "Sometimes Abner complains about him. Poor Henry, he was such a confused boy." She took a drink of coffee. "Better now though, compared to when he first came out here."

"He stays with Hutch?"

"Two weeks every summer. Henry's father ran out on Abner's sister when he was little, so she had to raise him alone. Fathers are important, and he didn't have any direction growing up. In high school, he was having himself a fine old time with not-so-good-girls and probably not-so-safe-drugs and God knows what other mischief."

"How did Hutch turn him around?" Nate said.

Lucille laughed to herself. "Finally, Abner's sister had enough and sent him out here one summer. Abner tells it better than I do, but I'll give you my version. The first night at Abner's, Henry snuck out, got drunk, and came back with some thirty-year-old local. Abner heard them come in and after some choice words, the woman left. After she was gone, he took Henry and threw him off the dock. Well, Henry started sinking because he didn't know how to swim. Can you imagine that? A high schooler who can't swim?"

"Abner jumped in after him and pulled him over to the dock. Henry ended up getting sick because he'd had too much to drink. The next morning, Abner woke him up and made him run five miles. Then he took Henry out on the boat and made him work all day. After a few weeks he came around. He's been coming back every summer since."

"I've had a few kids like Henry in school," Nate said.

"Must be sad to see."

"You want to be able to reach every kid you teach. But you know that you'll never be able to, so you make contracts with yourself."

"Like what?"

"Oh, I might say something along the lines of: if I can just help this one kid then my job is worth it."

"And is it?"

"In some ways. But it's never enough. I guess that's one of the reasons I keep coming back year after year, even though the ones that I didn't reach get older and farther away from me," Nate said.

"I think it's like that with anything in life," Lucille said. "You can't control everything, and sometimes you can't control anything."

"I don't know if I could have handled him coming out here year after year like Hutch does," Nate said.

"I think Abner sees a lot of himself in Henry," Lucille said.

"You think so?" Nate said.

"Abner was a terror to his mother and father while growing up. Barely passed high school and was headed for an early departure from life, when one day he left home and enlisted in the Coast Guard."

"How do you know all this?"

"He and I have grown to trust each other over the years. I tell him things. He tells me things. He'd be upset if he knew I was telling you all this, but the truth is I think he's takin' a liking to you. He does his best to mentor Henry every summer, and, sure, he dives with Tyee and talks to Mickey when he's over at the hardware store, but he's alone most of the year. You're the only one he's ever used my phone to call except his daughter, Henry, and Henry's mother. And if you ask me, Henry acts as a substitute for Abner's daughter."

"Hutch doesn't see his daughter much?" Nate asked.

"They had a nasty fight over the phone a year ago, and she still resents her childhood of him not being around and how her mother died."

"Is that what still eats at him?" Nate said.

"So, you've seen some of his temper I take it?"

"But I deserved it."

Lucille nodded. "When he enlisted in the Coast Guard, Abner was five feet six. When he came back home from his first duty station he had grown eight inches and his parents didn't even recognize him. Shortly after, he met Sherry and they got married. A year after that, Sherry had a complicated pregnancy that meant they would only be able to have the one child. Melanie was born at a time when the armed services did not make many special accommodations for weddings, childbirths, or deaths in the family. The old adage, 'if the military wanted you to have a family, then they would have issued you one,' held true. Abner was on a deployment in the Caribbean and wasn't allowed to come home for the birth of Melanie. As he advanced in rank—he eventually became a Chief Warrant Officer—the time spent away from his family increased over the years. He was never home, and Sherry basically raised Melanie alone. But he loved them both, and Sherry stayed loyal. He missed a lot of things that most parents and kids take for granted: birthdays, holidays, school plays, sporting events, and on and on. Abner did make Melanie's wedding, but it was like giving away a daughter he didn't know as well as he wanted to. He took it hard and has still not warmed up to Melanie's husband—felt that the young man took his little girl away. Before his last deployment they bought the lot here in Hampstead. Sherry lived in my upstairs bedroom while their house was being built. Abner would visit about once a month as his unit prepared for deployment. I enjoyed the company as my husband had passed away and my kids were all grown up. The house was Abner's present to her. He had promised that after that final deployment he was retiring and that they were going to make up for all the lost time together. They were going to play with their grandkids, travel, and most importantly, finally have a place to call home.

In Abner's thirty-year career, they had moved nineteen times. Sherry would never have to move again."

"What happened?" Nate said.

Lucille set her coffee cup down on the cream-colored saucer and stared past Nate into the woods that led to Hutch's, as if a screen had appeared and a projector was playing her answer on it.

28

"The house got finished just as Abner left on deployment. Sherry moved out of my spare room, but we would still have coffee every morning. After a while, however, she started coming over less. We had never made morning coffee on my porch an official date, so I didn't give it much thought. I figured she was busy getting the house together, and Melanie had come to visit a few times. Towards the end of Abner's deployment, I drove up to their place because I hadn't seen Sherry in close to a month—there used to be a driveway but Abner tore it up after Sherry died. Sherry looked so thin and sick. I asked her what was wrong and she told me that she had been diagnosed with terminal lung cancer. She had always been a heavy smoker. I asked if Abner knew and she said that he was due back in a week and wanted to tell him then. I urged her to tell him immediately, but she insisted she didn't want to worry him. Four months after Abner got home, she died."

Nate refilled his mug as Lucille ate more of her breakfast. Birds chirped in the woods next to the porch and the sun was at the top of the tree line casting narrow shadows onto the dirt. Nate eased back in the wicker chair, mulling over what had been said.

Lucille set her fork down and looked into Nate's eyes. "He's dealt with a lot of pain, but there's some that he's never dealt with—and may never deal with. It turns up now and again as anger towards the Coast Guard and sometimes he takes it out on other people. I used to worry a lot about him, but he's lightened up in the past few years. If you had found that coin five years ago, you could have forgotten about coming out here."

"He asked me yesterday when the last time was that I cared about something," Nate said.

"For him to ask you that tells me that what you and he are doing means something to him. All he could talk about over coffee this morning was getting to the bottom of the coin that you found. It's given him something to focus on, which takes away the pain."

Nate nodded.

"We fried some fish here for dinner last night and I turned on the porch lights while we read. He brought over a book that Tyee had gotten for him and I was settled into another one of my Agatha Christies. Around eleven I left him out here reading when I headed to bed. I got up this morning to have coffee at five-thirty, and he was still out here scribbling notes on a pad of paper."

"Did he say anything to you about what he had found?" Nate said.

"If and when he's ready to tell me, he will."

They finished their breakfast and Nate rose to leave.

Lucille had moved to her rocking chair with a full cup of coffee. "When do I get to meet Mrs. Martin?" she said while beginning to rock.

"Soon, hopefully," Nate said.

"You boys be careful out on that water today," Lucille said.

"Yes, ma'am," Nate said.

As he went down the steps and peddled across the clearing to the dirt trail, he wondered how many times she had said that to her husband before he had gone fishing.

* * *

It was a quarter before nine when Nate set foot on Hutch's dock. The RHIB was tied up in its usual place on the right-hand side. Before descending the stairs from the deck, Nate had seen *Queen* out on the water, but heading back in. He walked to the end of the dock where a cooler sat. On top was a piece of paper held down by a rock. Nate lifted the rock; the note said help yourself, be back soon. He opened the cooler. It was filled with beer, pop, and sandwiches in Ziploc bags. He first grabbed a pop and then put it back, choosing beer instead. Beer at nine in the morning. He laughed: just like his father.

He closed the cooler and sat down on top of it. The temperature was already nearing eighty so he removed his shirt and unzipped the duffel bag he had brought with him. Inside were his mask, fins, snorkel, dive knife, a towel, and a change of clothes. He placed the shirt inside and zipped up the bag, leaving him in his bathing suit and booties.

The beer was almost too cold, but refreshing. The lake water was clear and Nate could see a small school of fish swimming a few feet under the surface. He watched as the school angled under the dock and out of sight.

"Morning!" Hutch shouted from the fair-weather console above the wheelhouse. "Grab the bow line as I bring her past you, then hold her in place."

The boat was twenty yards from the dock. Hutch slowed *Queen*, and as the bow was just past the end of the dock, Nate grabbed the dangling line and checked the forward motion of the boat by holding on and then pulling back. Hutch shut off the engine and descended into the stern where he took the stern line and jumped onto the dock. There, he tied the line to a cleat.

"Okay, Nate, tie her up."

Nate secured his line to a cleat and *Queen* was motionless against the dock.

"Good breakfast?"

"Very good," Nate said. "How was the fishing?"

"Weren't biting on a damn thing today. Not a problem, though, because I had my books to keep me company," Hutch said, walking past Nate toward the stairs to the deck. "Let's get her loaded up."

The men walked to the end of the dock and Hutch went over to the metal door and crouched down to unlock the master lock. He pulled the lock out of the stainless-steel eye and lifted the door. The storage room was large with a high ceiling. Hutch entered and flipped on the lights.

The right wall was lined with half-a-dozen scuba tanks. Two complete sets of dive gear—regulator, wetsuit, booties, dive knife, yellow underwater light, fins, mask, and snorkel—hung on a rack above. Two spear guns were mounted on the wall like rifles over a fireplace. A metal ring loaded with spears hung from a hook. Resting on the floor in front of the scuba tanks was a compressor.

Hutch saw Nate looking at the compressor. "I keep that out here during the summer and bring it back to Tyee's shed for the rest of the year. Although, it might stay out here from now on. I got a brand-new winch that hooks up to the stern of _Queen_ for bringing heavy stuff up from the bottom. It takes up almost the whole damn shed."

Nate looked up at and saw a metallic winch hanging from the ceiling. "Why do you have two winches?"

"Oh, that," Hutch said looking at the winch. "That's just the little guy I use for deploying the towfish when I'm using my sidescan sonar. Not too strong."

On the left wall was more fishing gear than Nate had ever seen. Poles, reels, nets, vests, waders, tackle box upon tackle box, a fly-tying station, five-gallon buckets, and a few pieces of equipment Nate couldn't identify.

"A lot of that gear was just sitting in Lucille's garage, so she gave it to me," Hutch said.

Lying on the concrete floor in front of the fishing gear was an extra anchor, a set of floodlights, an adjustable metal tripod, and a welding torch with a helmet beside it.

The back wall was a workbench. Its counter was littered with drills, chisels, hammers, screwdrivers, and saws. There was a sink next to the bench with bottles of chemicals and test tubes in a wooden rack. A gas outlet was at the end of the workbench and a burner was connected to it with a rubber hose. An assortment of brooms—straw, nylon, big, and small—hung on the wall above the workbench along with two sledgehammers, shovels, nylon line, cable buoys, pipes, tubes, baskets, straps, and chain. Underneath the bench were coupling pieces, baskets of nails and bolts plus gallons of glue and rubber cement. Sheets of plywood and lumber were stacked in the corner.

The dinghy was in the middle of the room and rested on a pair of sawhorses, which Hutch had cut to conform to the keel so that they held the boat snug.

Hutch ran his hand along the dinghy's hull and then looked at it. "She's drier than a celebrity in rehab," he said. "Let's get her loaded first."

29

I t was near noon and *Queen* lay at anchor a few hundred yards out from the cave's opening. Hutch met him near the bow and they untied the dinghy and brought it to the stern. The sea was flat and the sky was cloudless. Nate could see the bottom thirty feet underneath the boat. Hutch went below and came back out dressed in an all black wetsuit. He was holding another one and gave it to Nate.

"If we were doing a short dive out here today," he said, "I'd say that we wouldn't need the suits. But the water in the cave will be colder and who knows how long we'll be in it."

Nate took the wetsuit and put it on. Both men strapped their dive knives to their calves and put their neoprene booties on.

"Let's lower her down in the water and then I'll hop aboard and you can hand me the gear," said Hutch.

Together, they lifted the dinghy and placed it in the water behind the stern. It was twelve feet long and had a seven-horsepower outboard motor. Hutch climbed into the craft and tied off the bow and stern to cleats on *Queen's* transom. Nate started to pass down gear: two tanks, two underwater lights, two weight belts, two sets of mask, fins, and snorkel, two shovels, a sledgehammer, two floodlights, a small anchor, and the adjustable tripod to put the floodlights on. When Hutch had everything positioned, he waved Nate into the boat.

Nate cast both lines off and the dinghy floated a few feet aft of the boat. Hutch pulled the ripcord on the motor. The smell of gas hit the air and the motor began to chug. Hutch twisted the throttle on the handle, and they headed toward the cave opening.

The cabin cruiser's engine turned off, and the boat drifted fifty yards off the smaller of the two Sanisstey Islands. Two men came up from below. Each threaded his dive knife's sheath through the belt in his canvas swim shorts. The helmsman radioed that they had reached their destination and then sat at the wheel and waited as each of the divers put on flippers and a mask. When they finished, they sat on the gunwale. The helmsman handed the taller of the two a waterproof bag that had the men's shoes, socks, and a pair of binoculars for each.

"Pick us up in two hours," the taller man said.

The helmsman nodded and the two men entered the water. Once they were clear of the stern, the helmsman started the engine and sped off.

At the cave entrance, Hutch turned off the motor and the dinghy coasted into the cave. He took out a paddle and steered the boat to one side.

"Nate, hold us in place."

Nate grabbed the wall of the cave and the boat came to a stop. Hutch took the tripod out. On the end of each leg was a clamp. He adjusted the legs and clamped one to the aft of the three benches where he had been sitting to operate the motor and clamped the other two on opposite rails. Then, he screwed in a floodlight on top of the tripod and fiddled with it until it was focused on the area of cave in front of the bow. He handed the second floodlight, a handheld version with a pistol grip, to Nate.

"The mounted light is good for a few hours, so use the handheld sparingly," said Hutch. "We'll adjust the mounted one as necessary when we get to the end and check out the dirt pile I found."

Nate nodded in agreement. They had discussed the plan on their way in. Hutch would dive and trace the bottom while Nate stayed on board and paddled into the cave, covering both areas in one sweep. If Hutch found anything, he would come up and they would anchor the boat and both dive.

Hutch strapped on a tank and put on his weight belt and fins. He spit into his mask's faceplate and rubbed the warm saliva all around. Then, he submerged it in the cool water and brought it back out, shaking it before putting it on.

Nate held the boat steady as Hutch eased his way over the side and then treaded water while gripping the boat's rail.

"I'll have a look around first and then we'll start," Hutch said.

Nate handed him an underwater light and Hutch slipped below the surface.

The light swung in a circle just beneath the water and then got smaller as Hutch descended. The smaller light circled once more, then got larger as it came near the surface. Hutch's head appeared a few feet away from the boat and he pulled the regulator out of his mouth.

"Twenty-two feet deep here. Mostly sand and rock on the bottom," said Hutch. "I'll tap on the hull three times if I want you to stop, otherwise let's just take it nice and easy."

"What if I see something?" Nate said.

"Just knock on the hull and I'll come up to see what's cookin'."

Hutch put the regulator back in his mouth and submerged. At the bottom, the light focused forward and Nate pushed away from the rock and began to paddle. He would go two or three strokes and then turn on the handheld floodlight for a few seconds, focusing the beam on the ceiling or at places where the mounted light didn't reach. He looked over the side and saw Hutch's light creeping along the bottom.

The cave's interior was slimy to a few feet above the current water level. The ceiling was a good twenty feet above the water. On the ninth or tenth cycle of paddle and sweep, they reached the boat lift. Nate tapped on the hull and Hutch was soon at the surface.

"We're below the lift," Nate said.

"Hold us steady for a minute," said Hutch. "Give me that handheld light."

Nate grabbed the side of the cave again and handed Hutch the light. Hutch turned it on and aimed the beam up the shaft at the lift bars part way down where he had swung out and dropped from. Then, he moved the light up the face of the cliff; there was graffiti all over the wall.

"Looks like some little shits used to have their friends lower them in the boat to spray-paint," Hutch said.

Hutch continued upward, past 'Jamie was here 1962' and 'John Olsen is a whore' until he reached the boathouse opening. He stopped the beam and squinted.

"What do you see?" Nate said.

Hutch swept the beam to the right and then back again.

"Thought I saw a person's shadow, but I guess not."

He swept the beam all around the opening once more and then directed it straight ahead. "Looks like the ceiling slants down. Watch the tripod," he said.

Hutch turned the floodlight off and lifted it for Nate to grab, but Nate was looking up into the opening.

"What you lookin' at?"

Nate eyed him. "Do you think anyone knows we're out here?"

"Who would care?" Hutch said.

"I don't know," Nate shrugged, "just wondering."

"Tyee and Lucille are the only ones on my end. Well, and probably Mickey. I'm sure Tyee told him, but he's not going to say anything. Hell, we haven't even found anything yet," Hutch said, and then looked back up at the opening. "Who have you told?"

"My wife. And a couple we had over for dinner a few nights ago," Nate said.

"Well then there's nothin' to worry about. Is there?"

His words echoed into the cave.

Hutch pulled his mask back over his face and flipped on his underwater light. "Let's get started again, shall we?"

The cave's ceiling lowered as they moved further in, and the underwater light appeared larger as the water became shallower. The cave started to bend to the right, and then the floodlight illuminated a wall of solid rock ahead. Nate tapped on the hull and Hutch appeared.

"What is it?" Hutch said.

Nate had the hand light trained on the wall a few boat lengths ahead of them and moved it down toward the water. There was no more than three feet of clearance, maybe less.

"We'll have to take down the tripod," said Hutch. "It was pitch black when I came through here. I had no idea that it dropped this low. Near the plateau though, it opens up. How high, I have no idea."

Hutch held the boat against the side of the cave while Nate unclamped the tripod and laid down flat on the boat with the handheld floodlight aimed forward.

"I'm ready," Nate said.

Hutch moved to the stern and kicked. The boat slid under the lowered ceiling and the sides of the cave narrowed to a few feet on either side of the boat. In a minute they were through and the ceiling began to slope up.

After resetting the tripod, Hutch said, "Hold us here. I'll dive and cover the area we missed."

Nate turned his body around and sat on the middle bench.

"Let me turn off the lights and get my eyes used to the dark before you go under, then I can watch you," Nate said as he steadied the boat in place.

"Okay," Hutch said, and Nate turned off the floodlights.

It took about thirty seconds for his eyes to adjust.

"All right, Hutch," he said.

He heard Hutch take a breath from his regulator and then the sound of bubbles as Hutch dove. Nate followed the light, but soon lost it as Hutch got into the tunnel portion. If Hutch had a problem, got snagged on the bottom or something, Nate would have no way of knowing. He could see nothing now, so he waited. The only sound was the echo of each breath he took.

The sides of the cave narrowed even more underwater and there was barely enough room to navigate. Hutch glided and moved his light from side to side. The floor of the tunnel was almost all rocks. He crouched on the bottom and then pushed off, reaching his hand upwards until he felt air, and then sank back down. He guessed he was in around ten feet of water. The bottom began to widen and he was out of the tunnel. He turned around and felt a surge of water behind him. He paid no attention to it, thinking his motion had caused the efflux. He started kicking back into the tunnel and toward Nate.

30

Nate saw the light appear and moments later Hutch was next to the boat.

"Nothing back there," Hutch said. "The plateau shouldn't be too far away."

Hutch went back under, and Nate pushed the boat out from the wall and began to paddle. The cave widened, and when he energized the handheld floodlight, he noticed that the ceiling had risen to at least twenty feet above the water. He turned off his floodlight and watched as the underwater light's beam moved from side to side.

He paddled three strokes, and the mounted floodlight's range reached the rock plateau Hutch had told him about. The cave narrowed, and he felt like he was in an auditorium moving toward a raised stage. He aimed the handheld at the plateau and followed it up. From this distance, there appeared to be a mass of dirt that rose from the back of the plateau. The ceiling curved down but it was difficult to discern where it went behind the pile. He turned off the light and paddled a few more strokes. They must be getting near the point where Hutch had told him the water depth became shallow. He could now see the back of the cave on both sides of the pile with the handheld light and estimated that in half a dozen strokes the boat would be there. Nate looked over the side but didn't see Hutch's underwater light. He turned around to see if Hutch was behind the boat. He wasn't. He paddled once more and the light reappeared up ahead. Nate moved the boat over Hutch and held on to the side of the cave. The light on the bottom wasn't moving. Nate knocked on the hull a few times. The light stayed fixed on the bottom. Nate knocked harder. A few seconds later, the light pulled back and came to the surface.

"We're almost to the plateau," Nate said, pointing at the rise ahead.

"Found somethin'," Hutch said.

"What?"

"I think it's a small boat, or used to be one. It's half buried and smashed up by a couple of boulders. Remember when I said my feet hit something close to the plateau the first time?"

Nate nodded.

"I think it was this boat. She appears to be split near her hind quarter with the front two thirds almost sticking straight up. There's a boulder on the other side that she's propped up against. I went past her and all the way to the back wall. The bottom slopes up in another boat length or two. On the slope I found an oar."

"Where do you think this boat came from?" Nate said.

"Don't know. She's been here awhile though," Hutch said.

"Do you want to look at it further or head to the plateau?"

"We can come back to it, let's go to the plateau."

Hutch stayed on the surface and when he could feel the bottom he took off his fins and walked the boat up the rest of the way.

Nate grabbed Hutch's tank and placed it in the boat. The plateau was about two feet above the water's surface and Hutch climbed up until he was on top. Nate adjusted the mounted floodlight to illuminate the plateau.

"It's closer quarters up here than I thought," Hutch said. "It's only about eight feet wide. The ceiling above me is nine or ten feet but we'll be hitting our heads back where the dirt pile seems to come out of the wall."

"Room enough for two up there?" Nate said.

"Should be," Hutch said. "Throw me that other floodlight."

Nate did and Hutch approached the dirt pile. On the right of the pile, about knee high, he saw rock showing amidst the dirt. He placed his foot on the rock, pushing on it, but the rock went nowhere. He bent down and followed the surface into the dirt on all sides until he was convinced that it was a large boulder. He stood back up and shined the floodlight at the top of the pile where it was flush with the ceiling.

"We've got a cave-in, Nate," said Hutch. "It's the only explanation that makes any sense. There's a boulder on the right side of the pile and I'm sure there's more."

"What's your plan?"

"Let's anchor the dinghy out away from the plateau. Then, we'll come up here with the shovels and see what we can dig out."

Twenty minutes later, the dinghy was anchored ten yards away from the plateau and Hutch and Nate had uncovered three boulders. Together they had rolled them to the edge of the plateau and pushed them into the water. Shovelful after shovelful were emptied into the water. Finally, Hutch dug his shovel in and felt it hit something that was not rock. He motioned for Nate to come over and Nate dug out the area around Hutch's shovel with his hands until the object was clear. Hutch's spade had hit a piece of wood.

"What in the hell is that doing back here?" Nate said.

Hutch pulled his shovel from the wood and together they unearthed what appeared to be a beam. They put down their shovels and pulled the beam out. It was surprisingly light, and no sooner had they raised it off the ground when a three-foot section broke off the end. They set the rotted log down and Hutch examined it.

"Looks like something that could have held some weight," Hutch said.

"Yeah, but what's it doing here?"

Hutch shrugged. "Let's keep going."

They cleared the dirt all the way up to where the ceiling was only six feet and found two more beams. Hutch got flush with the wall of dirt and jabbed his shovel vertically up into the ceiling. It sunk in deep, and a load of dirt poured into the opening when he pulled it out. After a few more heaves, Hutch's shovel broke through the top.

"This is where she caved in," said Hutch. "We'll have to be careful as we dig this part out."

They worked cautiously until Nate's shovel hit rock under where the ceiling had collapsed.

"I think we've got another boulder," Nate said.

Hutch came over and they worked to uncover it. Nate put his shovel down and got around to the side in order to push. He felt the dirt up against his back and bent down trying to get leverage. Hutch suddenly stopped shoveling and dropped to his knees.

"What's wrong?" Nate said.

Hutch was furiously carving out the dirt with his hands.

"I'll be damned," Hutch said.

Nate moved around to Hutch, and his eyes widened as he saw what was extending out from under the boulder.

31

They were staring at the rib cage and skull of a human skeleton.

"Do you think it's Daniels?" Nate said.

"Doesn't do us any good to think it's not," said Hutch. "Let's get this boulder off of him."

They dug out behind the boulder and then rolled it away. On their knees, Hutch and Nate dug around until they had exposed the entire pattern of bones. The pelvis and left arm had been pinned under the boulder and the rest of the body smothered under dirt and bits of rock when the ceiling had given way.

"Poor bastard," Hutch said. "Let's move him to the side and dig a little further."

They dug in another foot or two, and then Nate took the light and shined it up through the opening in the ceiling. It looked like a narrow pass that a rock climber would inch up with his back on one side and his feet on the other. Hutch continued to push in further.

"How far back do you think this mound of dirt goes, Hutch?"

"I'm trying to find out," Hutch said. "Keep your eyes on that ceiling. I'll dig from here on out. I don't feel like getting caved in on and suffocated to death."

Hutch was now taking his shovel and seeing how far he could horizontally push it into the dirt.

"It seems to be loosening up," he said.

He cleared another few feet and pushed his shovel horizontally again. Instead of hitting rock, his shovel broke through.

"Sonofabitch. This baby opens up on the other side of the dirt."

Hutch cleared two feet down from the ceiling. He took the flood light and shined it through the opening. His light settled on the back of a wall in the distance. He swung the light back and forth, tracing the small space.

"There's a room in there," Hutch said. "I'll be right back."

"What are you going to do?" Nate said.

Hutch was already crawling through the hole and then disappeared on the other side.

Nate could see the light move around, and then it stopped.

"Give me that shovel and stand back," Hutch said.

Nate obeyed.

Hutch pulled the shovel through the opening he had just climbed through. Using the shovel as a baseball bat, he repeatedly swung at the dirt pile, stopping when there was almost four feet of clearance between the top of the dirt and the ceiling of the small tunnel.

"Come on in," Hutch said.

Nate crawled over the dirt and stood next to Hutch in a dome shaped room. It smelled like urine from the standing water that had pooled in the center. Hutch trained the light near the floor on the right side of the space. The beam showed a wooden chest the size of two shoe boxes.

"Figured you should have the honor of opening it," Hutch said.

They walked over, and Hutch held the light while Nate examined the chest. The carpentry was simple: cast iron strips lined the bottom and top edges, and central strips bound the box lengthwise, breadthwise, and heightwise, making a cross in the middle of each side. Engraved at the center of each cross were the letters JLR.

"The lock has been broken off," Nate said.

He lifted the top. The inside was lined in tattered red velvet, and a folded piece of paper lay in the middle of a piece of wood countersunk approximately an inch from the rim of the chest.

"That's it?" Nate said.

"Carefully hand me the paper, and then try to lift the wooden plate. It's probably a false top to keep whatever's underneath from shifting around too much."

Nate picked up the paper. It was a letter sized sheet folded into thirds. Hutch held the paper and Nate carefully pulled up on the wooden plate. After some massaging, the plate loosened and came up.

"H-O-L-Y shit," Nate said.

The rest of the chest was filled with gold coins.

Hutch's eyes widened. "Let's get this back to the boat."

The sound of rock sliding into the water turned the men's attention in the direction of the plateau.

Hutch handed the light and paper to Nate. In seconds he was over the dirt mound and onto the plateau. He peered into the cave. Water was lapping against the dinghy. His eyes scanned from side to side. Like the rest of the cave, the sides were slimy near the water, but a few feet higher and upward they were bone dry. Seeing past the dinghy was impossible due to the floodlight shining directly at him. He stood motionless and listened. A small piece of stone fell into the water. Hutch watched it sink. He walked to the edge of the plateau and swept his right foot along the edge. More stone fell in. Satisfied that there was no one there, he rejoined Nate in the room at the back of the cave.

* * *

Hutch opened the throttle up and the dinghy gathered momentum toward *Queen*. The paper had been placed back in the chest and Nate held it securely between his legs.

"With a few assumptions, I've got a working theory," Hutch said.

"Let's hear it," said Nate.

"Assuming Daniels is the skeleton we found, I think it's safe to say that the boat I found sunk in the cave was his rowboat," Hutch said.

"Could be," Nate said.

"He must have found the cave when rowing around the island. The log says he routinely took the boat out for exercise. However, the cave was also under the keeper's house, meaning that his sewer line more than likely ran down the inside of the cave and dumped into the water. If there was a problem, he would have had to take his boat into the cave to fix the line," Hutch said. "So, he travels all the way to the back of the cave and places the chest in that room. With wooden beams, he tries to strengthen the ceiling in the tunnel leading from the plateau. Maybe some of the dirt and rock were already starting to cave in. Presumably, on the night of his last log entry or the day after, he goes back to his room in the cave and the ceiling caves in, killing him. Boulders roll off the edge of the plateau and sink his rowboat."

"I've got some questions," said Nate.

"Shoot," Hutch said.

"First, why wasn't this discovered before?"

"I think the answer to that is the lake level. The narrow tunnel before the plateau had at most two feet of clearance, judging from the water line."

Nate interrupted. "At some points today the dinghy had only inches above it. It's a wonder you didn't hit your head on the ceiling when you were swimming back there the first time."

"I couldn't see a damn thing," Hutch said. "When the lake level was up, the back of the cave was sealed off. Someone would have needed scuba gear to dive through the tunnel, and cave diving is dangerous and requires special training. It would have looked like the cave ended at the start of the tunnel."

"Question two," said Nate. "Why would Daniels take it back there in the first place?"

"Maybe he got paranoid with a chest full of gold coins. People do strange things when they get money that they didn't work for. Probably wanted to have it in a place only he knew about. It makes sense that he only said that he had found some coins in the log, without saying where they were kept. That way, he laid claim to them as his property in the most official document available to him."

"Could be," Nate said. "So, how did a lighthouse keeper in 1859 come across a chest full of gold coins from 1643?"

"We're going to try and find out," said Hutch. "I want to know whose coins they were before Daniels found them and how they got to Sanisstey Island."

"Since the coins were all sealed in that chest and you found none on the bottom of the cave, how did one end up on my beach?"

Hutch looked toward the Hampstead shoreline in the distance. "Beats me. For now." He grinned.

High above in the Sanisstey Lighthouse, two men in diving gear watched through binoculars as the dinghy made its way out to where the boat named _Queen_ was anchored. The men lowered their binoculars and headed for their rendezvous. It had been two hours.

32

Brooke Martin lay on the beach reading a paperback about a bipolar serial-killing nun named Katie. On the front cover, the author had been billed as "The next great suspense artist." What a load. The book was predictable—and senseless. On page six, Katie bathed with an overweight priest; on page eight, as he toweled off, she disemboweled him for asking, "What exactly do you know about me, Sister Katie?" Regretting not picking up another O'Hara novel, Brooke was ready to wave the white flag and eat the $7.50 she'd paid for the book, but in the last thirty pages she had latched on to a grocery clerk named Remy. But it wasn't looking good. At present, Katie was hiding behind a bathroom door with a stiletto ready to murder the unsuspecting Remy who had given her a funny look at the store. Damn. Maybe Remy would make it another five pages.

Nope.

"Isn't that outfit illegal, ma'am?" a voice said behind her.

"Not as far as I know," Brooke laughed.

She was wearing a yellow bikini and lying on her stomach with the bikini top unclasped and off her back. She put the book down and re-clasped the top. When she turned around, Tim Gibson was looking down at her.

"That's a relief. I'd hate to have to report this to the authorities," he said.

Gibson was shirtless, wearing a pair of shorts and running shoes. His chest glistened with sweat. He took off his sunglasses momentarily to wipe them on his shorts and then put them back on.

"Getting some exercise?" Brooke said enjoying the view. Must be to have a physique like that.

"Gotta do it," he said. "Whether I like it or not, I'm on the other side of forty and missing a day at this age is really like missing two weeks."

"Sort of like drinking on this side of forty equals missing one week," she said.

Gibson grinned. "I wouldn't know anything about that."

She laughed. "So, what would you know about?"

"Are you trying to continue our conversation from the other night?" Gibson said.

"Are you?" she said back.

"As a matter of fact, it's kind of why I stopped by."

"Really."

"Did Nate talk to you about tonight?" Gibson said.

Her expression immediately turned to annoyance.

"Wrong question?" Gibson said.

"It's nothing," she said.

"Are you sure? It looks like something."

Should she say anything? Tim's manner had a calming effect. "To answer your question, no, Nate has not mentioned anything about tonight. What was he supposed to talk to me about?"

"I don't mean to pry, but is everything okay with you two?" Gibson paused as he lay down on the sand next to her, "I could have taken this completely wrong, but he seemed tense when I came over yesterday."

"You came over yesterday?"

163

He raised his eyebrows, held them there for a second, then let them fall back.

"I swung by to extend a dinner invitation for tonight," Gibson said, "and to let you know how much we enjoyed your company at the bar. The belt you wore is still on my mind."

"It was new," she said.

"It was perfect."

"What did Nate tell you when you invited us over?" Brooke said.

"What any smart man would," Gibson said. "He said he'd have to check with the lady of the house."

"When will it be too late to accept?" Brooke said.

"So there's a possibility we might still be able to get together?"

"I like that," Brooke said.

"Pardon?" Gibson said.

"You have a nice balance of realism and positive thinking," she said.

"Keeps the stress level down."

"If it's up to me, we'll be there tonight, but I need to speak with Nate."

"If you're worried about being a third wheel, we enjoy your company." He leaned closer to her. "We put on a good show."

Her heart rate picked up. "I know it would be a nice evening."

He ran his finger lightly up her arm. "No pressure. There will be other nights if this one doesn't work out."

"You and Jane wouldn't be upset if we had to decline, would you?" she asked.

He stared into her eyes. "Heavens no."

Reading his expression was like rowing a canoe across a glassy pond with the sun just coming up. "Thanks for being understanding," she said looking at her watch; it was almost four-thirty.

"Sounds like you've made up your mind," he said.

"As much as I hate to do this, we have to decline. I don't think it's right to keep you and Jane waiting any longer."

"Can't talk you into it?" he said, brushing a bit of sand from her shoulder.

She knew she should feel uncomfortable, but she didn't. "You're not making this easy."

"I won't apologize for wanting your company," he grinned and stood up, moving far enough away from Brooke to wipe sand off his body. "Besides, there's still a chance I will see you on my walk tonight."

"When do you walk?"

"I leave the house just before sunset," he said stretching his legs. "Goes along with my philosophy."

"And what's that?"

"I try to arrange my life so I always have something to look forward to."

She watched as he bent over and tightened his laces.

"Better finish my workout," he said. "I'll see you later?"

"Maybe," she said.

He turned and began to run down the beach. She viewed, admiring his smooth strides, and thought that she wouldn't mind seeing him tonight.

33

"Did you get ahold of your wife?" said Hutch, walking toward the Fry Daddy in the corner of his kitchen.

"No, I had to leave a message," said Nate as he entered the room after coming back from attempting to call Brooke from Lucille's.

"Will the old lady be pissed?"

"I don't think so. After apologizing, I said I'd be staying late."

"What have you got there?" Hutch said.

Nate brought a package over and set it on the counter next to the stove. "Lucille sent over some fresh vegetables to have with the fish."

"That'll work," said Hutch.

The oil in the Fry Daddy had reached 375 degrees. Hutch turned to the counter and coated six fillets with flour. Next to the plate of fillets was a bowl containing batter ingredients. He picked up a rotary blender and beat the mixture until it was smooth. One by one, he dipped the fillets into the batter and then placed them in the Fry Daddy. They began to turn gold.

"Anything I can do to help?" Nate said.

"Open up the package with the greens," Hutch said.

Nate took the Ziploc bag out of the paper sack Lucille had given him. In the bag were green, red, and yellow peppers, onion, zucchini, squash, and eggplant.

Hutch snuck a peek at the vegetables before pulling a frying pan off the wall from a nail it was hanging on. "That old gem even cut 'em up," he smiled. After turning on a burner, he poured oil into the pan. Then, from a cabinet above the stove, he removed a small coffee can with tiny holes punched in the plastic lid.

"What's in that?" Nate said.

"Old family concoction to liven up the greens," said Hutch, motioning for the bag.

Nate handed it over, and Hutch emptied the vegetables into the pan.

"Bring in a six pack of beer from the garage," Hutch said while turning the can upside down and shaking it over the vegetables. After a mixture of spices had fallen into the pan, he tipped the can up, stirred the vegetables, then turned the can upside down and began shaking again.

Nate left the kitchen, walked through the living room, and opened the door to the garage. The refrigerator was on the wall closest to the door next to a horizontal freezer. There was only a narrow path to the fridge: the garage was packed with furniture covered in sheets. Some sheets along the far wall had slipped down, exposing a large wooden dresser and mirror along with a rack of garment bags. At the end of the rack were Hutch's Coast Guard dress uniforms in clear garment bags. In the opposite corner from the doorway where Nate stood was a conglomeration of curtain rods, some bent in half, that looked like they had been thrown there in a rage. The garage door unit mounted to the ceiling was unplugged and there were no light bulbs in the two sockets. Nate walked to the fridge and took out a six-pack.

When he returned to the kitchen, Hutch had three plates full of food sitting on the kitchen table.

"Who is the third plate for?" Nate said.

"Why, for me of course," Lucille Hawthorne said entering the kitchen. "Didn't think I'd miss his night to cook, did you?"

"You better say somethin', Nate, or she'll keep shellin' ya," Hutch said, winking at Lucille.

"You eat over here once a week?" Nate said.

"Usually," she said sitting down and cracking open a beer. "It's my beer night. I'll only have two though, max."

"Shall we?" Hutch folded his hands, looking at Lucille.

"Good idea, Abner," she said and they all bowed their heads while Hutch led them in grace.

Nate took a bite. "Tasty, Hutch," he said.

"Better than your usual," said Lucille. She turned to Nate, "and his usual is damn good."

Hutch toasted with his beer and then drank.

A loud thump came from the garage.

"What was that?" Nate said.

"Bats," said Hutch. "A royal pain in my ass. You closed the garage door, right?"

"Yes," said Nate.

"Good. Don't need any gettin' in the house," he said.

Nate and Lucille nodded in agreement and continued eating.

"They say you can tell a lot about a man from his garage," said Hutch. "You've seen mine, Nate. What's it say about me?"

The furniture. The garment bags. The broken curtain rods. "That you keep things that mean something to you," Nate said.

"Very intuitive, young man," Lucille said.

"Or it means that I hang on to things and can't let them go," said Hutch. He sat back. "Maybe it's time to move on," he said looking at Lucille, "and I should clean that stuff out."

Lucille reached out and Hutch took her hand. He gave it a tender squeeze. Their hands released and Hutch began to eat again. She turned to Nate. "So, I've made up my mind, Nate."

Hutch shot Nate a look that said: whatever she says next, *agree with it*, because there's no talking her out of it.

"We're all having dinner at my house tomorrow night, and your wife better be there," she said. "It's time I met her."

"I can't pass that up," said Nate.

They devoured the fish, vegetables, and beer. Lucille put on coffee. Then, Hutch led the way to the library where the chest was on the floor next to the desk.

"Dash o' rum?" Hutch said to Nate.

"Sure," Nate said.

Hutch poured two glasses over half full and handed one to Nate. "Cheers."

"Going to regale us with some Shakespeare?" Lucille said.

"Not tonight," Hutch said.

"You read Shakespeare?" Nate said.

"Every wonderful word, right Abner?" Lucille cut in.

"I'm trying to brush up," said Hutch looking at Lucille and then Nate. "My daughter is a Shakespeare fanatic."

"Finished with Macbeth yet?" Lucille asked.

"Last week," Hutch said as if it was old news. "That queen was one wacked out bitch."

"Yeah. We women can get fiery when you men try and overrun us," Lucille smirked, her eyes narrowing. "Now you're on to Hamlet, right?" she said, recalling the list they had made to prepare him.

"Half way through. He's even more messed up than Lady Macbeth," Hutch said and started shaking his head back and forth. "People and their relationships."

Lucille said, "When are you coming over to ca—"

"That reminds me," Hutch said. "I need to call her."

Lucille smiled into her coffee cup.

Hutch reached down and opened the chest. He took out the paper and unfolded it on top of the desk, then put a weight on each corner.

Before dinner, Hutch had radioed Tyee and spelled out a few words for him. Tyee had determined that the letter was written in French. He and Mickey Leif would be over after they closed up their stores.

"Why is Mickey coming over?" Nate said.

"Because he's a friend and I need him to help us with something tonight."

"How did you get to be friends?"

"I've got this one," Lucille said. "Mickey graduated with Tyee from Hampstead High School. He loved to fish and worked for Gary," she took a drink of coffee, "my husband," she said giving Nate's arm a pat, "from the time he graduated until the time he opened the bait shop. Gary supported Mickey and convinced everyone to buy bait from him instead of from another local bait shop owner who kept raising his prices and was badmouthing Mickey. The other shop eventually went under. When Abner first came to Hampstead, he realized that Tyee and Mickey were honest brokers and they earned his respect." She turned to Hutch. "That about sum it up?"

Hutch tipped back his glass of rum, then exhaled. "Along with this fine lady and Tyee, Mickey and his wife helped me out when my wife, well—"

Nate searched for the right words. "Sounds like a good guy."

"Yep," said Hutch.

"How are they getting here?" Nate said.

"On *Magnum*, Tyee's boat. Piece of trash if you ask me but he swears by her." Hutch sat cross legged next to the chest. "Let's see how much loot we've got before Tyee and Mickey get here."

Nate and Lucille joined Hutch on the floor and they emptied the coins onto a blanket Hutch had laid down.

They divided the pile of coins into thirds. At first, Hutch would examine every few with his magnifier, looking for a mint mark in the same place he had found the 'A' on Nate's coin. It was there on every one, and he stopped looking after a while. The final count was 2,684. They refilled the chest and closed the top.

"How much is this worth, Abner?" Lucille said. "Is it crass of me to want to know right off?"

Hutch was rummaging through a drawer in his desk for a calculator. That found, he took out his pocket knife and sharpened a carpenter's pencil from a coffee can full of them on his desk. "Gimme a minute," he said. He opened a cabinet and pulled out a yellow legal pad from a stack of at least fifty.

"This is no time for poetry," Lucille said.

"This is not poetry, woman," Hutch said. He walked over to the fireplace and pulled a book off the shelf over the mantle.

"Poetry?" Nate said.

"He writes beautiful poetry," said Lucille. "*When* he takes his time." She pointed at the stack of legal pads and then at the coffee can. "Those are his tools, only stuff he'll use to write poetry. Coin business must be pretty serious for you to be bringing out the goodies," she said.

"That it is," said Hutch. He sat down in one of his leather chairs by the fireplace and leafed his way through the book until he found the desired page. Putting the pad of paper on the opposite page, he started scribbling down numbers. Lucille left the room to refill her coffee cup. When she returned, she sat down in the other leather chair and watched Hutch.

Nate swallowed a mouthful of rum and sat down behind the desk to study the old document they had found. The format appeared to be a letter, but all they had been able to decipher was a date at the top of the sheet, 20 *septembre 1679*, and the signature at the bottom, *Jean La Rousseau*. Nate had correlated the JLR engraved on the chest to Jean La Rousseau. The rest of the script was faded and in some places illegible.

Hutch punched away at the calculator, wrote more numbers on the paper, and then closed the book. "Ready for the tale of the tape?"

34

"Let's have it," Lucille said.

Nate nodded and took another drink of rum.

"When you first brought me your coin, I said that an authentic louis d'or in very good condition was worth about two hundred and fifty dollars and in extra fine condition around one thousand. Let's put the number of coins in that chest at a nice round twenty-seven hundred. I'm no expert but most of them seem to be in better condition than 'very good'. Again, assuming those are authentic and we can find a mint mark on the rest of them, here are the low-end and high-end estimates. I'm guessing the real value falls somewhere in the middle," Hutch said motioning for them to gather around.

Nate and Lucille moved behind Hutch's chair and gazed at the paper. The fire snarled and snapped, the ebb and flow of the flames putting Hutch's face and the paper in the light and then in the shadows.

Hutch had written two equations at the bottom of the paper:

2,700 in VG ($250) = $675,000.00

2,700 in XF ($1,000) = $2,700,000.00

Nate looked at the numbers again. Before speaking, he did some quick math in his head by taking the worse case scenario of $675,000.00 and dividing it by his teaching salary of $40,000.00. After a few seconds of concentrating, he realized the chest no more than ten feet away from him was worth at least seventeen years' pay.

"That's not bad for a few days of work," Lucille said.

"I'll say," Hutch snorted. "Nate, those numbers meet with your approval?" *Seventeen years of salary.* "Yes, they, do."

The door to the deck opened.

"Evenin'," Tyee said.

Tyee was followed into the room by a short round man with a thick beard and a Bass Pro Shops hat on.

Nate rose and shook hands with Tyee and was then introduced to Mickey Leif. Lucille gave Tyee and Mickey a hug as they entered.

"How'd *Magnum* run on the way over?" Hutch said.

"Same as always," Tyee said.

Hutch showed Tyee and Mickey the coins and then closed the chest while Tyee sat down at the desk with one of Hutch's magnifying glasses.

"You believe this shit, Mickey?" Hutch said.

"You were due sooner or later," Mickey said.

Tyee inspected the letter, adjusting the light Hutch had placed on the desk for him and shifting the paper and glass for the best view. "This may take some time," said Tyee. "I doubt if I'll be able to get all of it."

"You know where the other glass is and my microscope. While you're doing that, we're going to go take care of this," said Hutch picking up the chest. He poured a glass of dark rum and set it on the desk for Tyee. "Be back when we're finished."

"Abner, where are you taking the chest?" Lucille said.

"You know where I'm taking it," Hutch said.

"Why don't you just leave it at my place?" she said.

"Because if anything happens, I don't want you messed with," Hutch said. "Can you keep Tyee company until we get back?"

"I can," she said. "Your kitchen is a mess again. Mind if I tidy it up?"

"Do as you please," Hutch said.

"I usually do," she chuckled and headed for the kitchen.

Hutch led Nate and Mickey down the steps from the deck and opened the storage room.

"What are we doing, Hutch?" Nate said.

"Making sure this doesn't disappear on us," he said putting the chest up on the workbench. "While I get this ready, you and Mickey load the RHIB with a set of dive gear for you and me and two underwater lights."

"We're diving?" Nate said. Mickey was already starting to take the first load down to the RHIB.

"Trust me, Nate," said Hutch. "Off you go."

Nate made three trips with Mickey from the shed to the RHIB loading a tank, regulator, mask, weight belt, dive knife, fins, and a dive light for Hutch and him. Tyee's boat was tied up behind *Queen*. It was dusk, but Nate could still see that Tyee's boat had an all black hull with red letters spelling MAGNUM on the stern.

"Hutch, do we need wetsuits?" Nate said as he returned to the shed.

Hutch had his back to him and kept doing whatever he was doing at the workbench. "No," he said, "but take these out to the boat."

Nate followed the imaginary line created by Hutch's pointing finger to a pair of buoys with chain at the end of each. Mickey took one and he took the other. When they returned, Hutch was wrapping a sheet of 1-inch thick rubber around the chest horizontally. Once it was all the way around, he overlapped by a few inches and made a mark with a white pencil. He removed the sheet and cut it with a knife on a cutting board, which was built into the far end of the workbench. He took the measured sheet and wrapped it around the chest and then took two elastic cords and wrapped them around the rubber, sealing it to the chest.

"Pass me the one over there," said Hutch to Nate, pointing at a rubber sheet that was laying by the sink and was already cut.

He took the sheet from Nate and wrapped it around the chest vertically, and then took two more elastic cords and wrapped them around the chest. Satisfied, Hutch moved the chest onto the cutting board. He reached up to the far right-hand side of the shelves rising up from the workbench and pulled a small handle which unhinged a section of the shelves. The section swung open showing a deep storage bin in the wall.

From the bin, Hutch pulled out what looked like a square plastic suitcase. Nate could see two more in the bin. When the container was clear of the workbench, Hutch closed the shelf door, the handle clicking when it latched back into place.

"What is that?" Nate said.

"It's a modified drybox," said Hutch. "Your typical one at a dive shop isn't very big, so I had Tyee pull some strings to get me three that could carry a lot more."

Hutch opened the box.

"They don't have any padding inside. The only features that are the same as a regular drybox are the outer shell and the rubber seal that keeps the water out."

Hutch placed the chest into the box and then took the scraps left from tailoring the rubber sheet and stuffed them all around, making sure the chest wouldn't move. Then he closed the box. From the top drawer of the workbench he took out two keys and gave one to Nate. Using the other key, he locked the box and then put the key back in the workbench drawer.

Nate picked up the box and held it away from the workbench as Mickey cleaned up the rubber scraps. Hutch turned off the lights and after the men were all out, he locked the shed. The temperature had dropped to around sixty as they walked down the dock. Mickey stepped down into the RHIB and Nate passed him the box.

"Watch out. It's heavier than you think," Nate said.

"About forty pounds," Hutch said as he helped guide the box down to Mickey. Then, he boarded and they secured it next to the dive equipment. Nate cast off the lines and hopped in. Hutch started the engine and pushed the throttle forward, propelling the RHIB away from the dock.

The sun was below the horizon, and the water and sky were the same shade of gray.

"Why don't we have the running lights on?" Nate said, as the only evidence that the RHIB was on the water was the white wake behind it.

"We don't need anyone knowing where we're going."

"Where *are* we going?"

"Diamond Crag," Hutch said.

35

N ate remembered passing by Diamond Crag en route to the Sanisstey Islands. It was just a hunk of rock rising out of the lake.

"Aren't we being a little too cautious?" Nate said. "Why not just keep it at your house, or in your shed?"

Hutch looked at Mickey and then back to Nate. "Anyone can break in and steal stuff from a house or a garage if they want to bad enough. Where we're headed, no one can steal it."

Hutch pushed a button on the GPS unit next to the wheel. The LCD color display illuminated the bearing and range to the waypoint he had programmed in. He verified his course on the binnacle, adjusted, and then pushed the button again to extinguish the light.

"What are the buoys for?" Nate said.

"The buoys should keep the box manageable for us as we move along the bottom. We'll each take a side," Hutch said and pointed at Diamond Crag. "There's a limestone wall that runs down from the surface all the way to the bottom. At the base, there's a crack wide enough for a diver to fit through. We'll go straight in for awhile and then it's a steep angle up to the top. We'll surface inside the rock. There's a room twice the size of the one where we found the chest on Sanisstey."

"Have you been in there where I'm heading, Mickey?" Nate said.

"Once or twice," Mickey said.

Diamond Crag grew larger as the RHIB approached. Hutch checked the GPS monitor once more, made a slight course change, and then the monitor began to beep. Hutch turned it off and stopped the motor.

"Go up forward and drop the hook, Mickey," Hutch said.

Mickey went to the bow and pulled the anchor out from a locker. He tied the end off to a cleat and dropped it over the side.

"She's set," Mickey said.

Waves pushed against the hull hard enough to force Nate to grab hold of the center console as he stood up. He estimated that they were about a hundred yards from Diamond Crag. Swiveling aft, he saw Hutch's dark figure silhouetted against the granite sky.

"How deep are we?" Nate asked as he moved to join Hutch in the stern.

"Forty feet," said Mickey.

Hutch handed Nate a weight belt. "Mickey'll watch the boat while we take care of the chest. Let's gear up."

Both men put on their equipment while Mickey attached the buoys to the dry box.

"All set, Mick?" Hutch said.

"Ready," Mickey said.

"I'll get in the water and then you and Nate hand me the box and buoys," Hutch said, and then turned to face Nate. "I'll sink to the bottom with them and turn on my light. Dive down to me, and then we'll head for the crack. When we get there, I'll back in with my buoy first and then you'll follow me. Don't let go because it's a maze once we're inside."

Hutch clipped an underwater light to his weight belt and breathed into his regulator. Satisfied with his equipment check, he pulled his mask down and jumped in.

Mickey and Nate picked up the buoys and box and lifted it over the side. Hutch took hold and when they let go, left the surface.

"How long should this take, Mickey?" said Nate as he motioned to Diamond Crag and put on his mask and checked his regulator.

"Depends," Mickey said, and handed Nate the other underwater light.

Nate signaled *okay* and then dove for Hutch's light. When he arrived, the box was floating just a few feet off the bottom. Hutch waved Nate over to a rock resting on the sea floor and motioned for Nate to dig underneath the rock. Nate did and saw that the bottom of the rock had been screwed into an auger similar to the one he used to anchor his boat to. He waited for the sand to clear and he could see Hutch again. Hutch pointed to his light and then to his mask, telling Nate to follow the light. Hutch aimed the beam at the sand, illuminating three similarly sized rocks in a row on the bottom ahead of them—a trail. They suspended the chest between them by grabbing the buoy chain in one hand and aiming their lights on the trail of rocks with their other.

Mickey watched from above as the two lights moved away from the boat toward Diamond Crag.

Jackson Floyd ducked as he entered Leonard Shaw's study on board *Triumph*. The yacht was out for an evening test drive to ensure everything was working properly for Shaw's overnight party tomorrow. Local businessmen and a few fellow beach property owners were invited as a gesture of friendship, which Shaw didn't need but could use to pave the way for future projects— political hassles like the dredging of Shelby's Marina a few years back. However, this was not what Shaw had summoned Floyd about. Floyd closed the door behind him.

"Leif, Beecher, Martin, and the woman were at Hutch's house when I left."

"You confirmed what was in the chest?"

"I could see it from where I was on his deck. They were counting the coins—a lot of them. There was also a piece of paper they took out before they dumped the coins."

"Any idea what it was?" Shaw said.

"No. Beecher and Leif showed up and I had to vacate. I had two close calls on Big Sanisstey earlier and didn't want to push it."

"How hard will it be to get our hands on the gold?"

"It's doable, but I think we should wait," Floyd said.

"Why?"

"They don't seem to be in a rush to tell anybody. Watching them another day won't hurt."

Shaw reclined and crossed his hands on his chest. "Where's your partner in crime?"

"Dropped him off before I headed out to the bight. Said to call if we needed him."

"And do we?" Shaw said.

"I think it would be smart to keep him along. For one thing it will keep his mouth shut."

Shaw didn't like it. His one moment of weakness last summer had created a touchy situation that had to be navigated with care. Additionally, Bagley was now under the gun and who knew what might unravel if he went down.

The phone call from Floyd earlier had changed everything. Bagley had just finished explaining that there never was nor ever would be treasure discovered on the Great Lakes and to shift his focus to helping him get his ass out of the sling it was in. The phone had rung precisely after Bagley had shouted, "For Christsakes, Leonard, help me unfuck this mess!" After listening to Floyd, Shaw had smiled and told Bagley to sit down.

The discovery of gold on the Great Lakes went beyond equaling early retirement; it was pure intrigue. But it had to be orchestrated without mistakes. Quietly disposing of a platinum blonde that had threatened to expose Shaw's one and only affair last summer had proven easier than Shaw had expected. Only Bagley, Floyd, and the man Floyd was working with knew about it. However, *easier* didn't mean less expensive. The man Floyd was working with explained to Shaw that it would take cash to keep him quiet. Shaw was tired of paying.

Taking credit for the discovery and cashing in on the treasure was a bigger problem. The only realistic way to do it was to secure the chest and then dispose of the men and woman in an "accident" or series of "accidents". The proposition had tremendous risks. Floyd was right about waiting, but, at most, they had a day until the lid came off.

Shaw stared at Floyd. "All right, let's wait," he said, "but we'll have to make our move in no more than twenty-four hours."

"Understood," said Floyd.

"I want this handled with precision—clean," Shaw said. "Keep the pressure on our man."

"And when we no longer need him?" Floyd said.

Shaw kept a straight face. "You said it."

36

Brooke Martin sat in a deck chair admiring the glow that hung around after the sun had disappeared below the horizon. A glass of red wine sat on the wooden table and Miles Davis was playing at a volume that wouldn't disturb the neighbors. No lights were on inside the house or on the deck.

It was cool but not cold, and she was still comfortable in her shorts and blouse. A cotton sweater hung on one of the empty chairs in case the temperature dropped too much. She took a sip of wine and closed her eyes, listening to the waves break on the shore. "Autumn Leaves" began to play and she leaned her head back. She would listen to the waves and the song, and then head in.

A breeze brought the smell of a bonfire starting down the beach, and the mix of alto saxophone, trumpet, piano, bass, and drums moved within her. Whenever she listened to Davis, she felt transported to a different time and different place—a nightclub in the forties. *She wears a conservative black dress, hair done up in a bun, and sits at the end of a long bar smoking a cigarette that comes from a silver case. She sips amber liquor from a highball glass with scarlet lips. She's alone at the start, but then the door to the nightclub opens and she locks eyes with a stranger dressed in a suit and a Fedora. The man moves with ease across the room to her. Leaning on the bar, he asks if the seat next to her is taken. She says no.*

"Interrupting anything?"

Brooke smiled as she opened her eyes. Coming across the sand was Tim Gibson. "Drifting away to some Miles Davis," she said.

"Good choice of music," Gibson said, stepping up onto the deck. "Makes me think of the terraces where I've longed to dance."

He was wearing the same scent he had had on when he stood next to her, washing dishes. "So, you were right."

"About what?"

"About seeing me again," she said.

"Couldn't stay away from you and the beach," he said, sitting down. "Do I need to ask if Nate is around? It seems every time I ask he's out."

"You're right again," Brooke said. "Pull up a chair."

He was dressed in dark khaki slacks, sandals, and a powder blue v-neck sweater with no shirt on underneath. The wind brushed his hair back from his forehead.

"My favorite time of night," he said.

"It's so calm," she said.

"Can't argue with that," he said. He ran his hand along the bowl of her wine glass. "And what are we indulging in tonight?"

"A little red wine," Brooke said. "Care for a glass?"

"Please."

She left and returned with the bottle and a full glass.

Looking out at the water, Gibson said, "Van Gogh couldn't paint this, not even if he was drunk."

"Should we make a toast?" she said handing him the glass.

"Toasting has become a cliché, flowery words seeping out that are never remembered. However, there is one part of the tradition that I still follow religiously," he said, bringing the glass in front of him.

"What's that?"

"Someone told me that if you don't lock eyes with the person you clink glasses with, then for the next year you'll be cursed with a bad sex life," he said. "I'm not willing to risk something *that* important."

"No words, then." Brooke raised her glass.

Eyes welded together, they gently touched glasses. The sound still hung in the air as they each took a taste.

"Where did you learn to be so joie de vivre?" she said.

"Gentlemen learn to be more," he said. They toasted again.

"Is that one of your own, or from a movie?" Brooke asked.

"From me," he said. "Here's one that isn't. You represent glamour above the decks, comfort below."

"Thank you," she blushed. "Where was that from?"

"A book by David Niven, Bring on the Empty Horses."

She smiled. "Now how could a book with *that* title have a saying like that in it?"

Gibson set his wine glass down. "A conversation for another night," he said. "Care to help me with my Miles Davis fantasy?"

"As long as I don't have to tell you mine."

He thought for a moment. "Agreed. For now." He slid back his chair. "This deck could be considered a terrace of sorts," he said. "Care to join me?"

She moved her chair back and went to the player. Hearing each breath she took, she backed the CD to "Autumn Leaves". The glow on the digital display was the only light on the deck.

She joined hands with Gibson and they began to dance. He moved with a confident, yet graceful sway. She followed, her free hand feeling the small of his back. The evening felt timeless, calm, and secluded in the darkness. The deck became a place where only whispers should be used to communicate.

His hand held hers with a gentleness that felt natural. She was beginning to feel warm all over. He looked down into her eyes and then pulled her closer, resting his cheek against the side of her head. They kept moving.

Her chest rose with a deep breath. He moved his hand across the top of her shorts and then down her waist. They stopped dancing and he began to move the hair away from her face.

His lips were inches away from hers. She turned away.

"You move well," he said. "So far my fantasy has been everything I ever wanted."

They began dancing again. This time he let her take more of the lead. "I thought up a phrase the other day," he said. "Care to hear it?"

The talking relaxed her. "Sure," she said.

He stepped back and looked into her eyes. "Promise not to make fun?" he grinned.

"Promise," she said.

He stepped forward and started in. "It goes something like this: I risked it all and lost, but I'd risk it again."

"Must have been about something important," Brooke said. She was moving with more ease again.

"Let's just say I was inspired," he said.

The trumpet started in again, and Gibson took the lead as the alto sax took the pair in a circle. He held her close enough that their bodies rubbed against each other.

"So, you have me curious," he said and lowered his head to where she wouldn't have to answer in a tone above a whisper.

She obliged with a soft response. "About what?"

"What your fantasy is."

"I thought I didn't have to tell," she said.

"I'm sure it's better than mine."

She began to describe the nightclub in the forties.

"Do you look like yourself, or do you resemble, say, Deborah Kerr in An Affair to Remember?" Gibson said.

"I've never seen it."

"It's a must see," he said. "Back to your story. After the gentleman sits down next to you, what happens?"

"We have a drink together and talk like old friends."

"Old friends? I thought this was a fantasy."

"Well, not old friends. I—I can't think of how to put it."

"But there is mutual attraction, right?"

"Yes. He is handsome, and—"

"And?"

"And I don't worry about things moving too fast."

He pulled her closer and then rested his cheek against the side of her head once again. His cologne smelled stronger. "That's better," he said. "You were starting to worry me with that old friends line."

She let out a laugh.

"What happens next?" She went to answer, but he cut her off, "Wait. If I were him, I'd ask for a dance so that I could hold you close."

"Dancing is *always* nice."

A breeze blew across her face. She closed her eyes and took a deep breath.

He brought their joined hands under her chin and gently lifted up until their eyes met. "Does the dance lead to anything right away, or does that come later?"

"I haven't thought that far ahead yet."

"Thinking always ruins it. What do you *want* to happen?"

She stopped dancing and moved away. "I've never been one to not think things through."

"Something wrong?" he said.

She retreated another step. "I need to clear my head. I—I should head inside."

Gibson frowned. "Are you sure?"

"Yeah, I'm sure," she said, turning toward the house.

He shrugged, and left.

Brooke entered the house. Using her phone's caller I.D. function, she scrolled through the numbers until she found the one she was looking for. She wrote it down, then dialed it, and soon heard the voice of Lucille Hawthorne on the other end.

37

ate and Hutch reached the bottom of the limestone wall. Hutch aimed his light to a spot ten yards to the right and Nate saw a crack that was around five feet wide and ran about six feet up from the bottom until it narrowed to a close like the shape of a tent opening. A school of fish swam by to inspect the box and then left. Hutch led the way in and Nate followed. The inside was larger than he had expected, and the main tunnel they traveled had a good six feet of clearance on all sides. As they kicked further in, Nate saw that the passageway was full of branches that led off into darkness. He could see how getting lost would be easy, and he gripped the chain tighter, focusing on Hutch. The tunnel rose upward and Nate's legs began to tire. Then, the passage narrowed. They slowed and Nate tugged on the chain below him to get the buoy to pass through.

The top opened up and Nate saw that Hutch was no longer swimming upward but treading water. He kicked hard and soon broke the surface next to Hutch.

Hutch pulled the regulator out of his mouth. "Follow me over to the side," his voice echoed.

They swam over until they were both hanging onto the side of the cave. Together they lifted the box out of the water and slid it onto a level surface.

"Hold your light on me," Hutch said.

Nate aimed the beam at him and watched as Hutch got out of the water and stripped off his gear. Then, he walked over to a metal box that had a crank on the side of it, like an antique telephone box. Hutch cranked furiously for a minute and then flipped a switch on the top of the box.

The entire cave illuminated. There were lights hung on the ceiling above the water where they had surfaced, on the wall above the crank box, and on the opposite wall. Nate got out of the water and as he took off his gear, Hutch cranked for another minute.

The cave was close to circular. The platform was widest where they stood, about 20 feet, and rose about a foot above the water. The wall above the crank box looked like a miniature version of Hutch's storage shed. Two complete sets of scuba gear and accessories hung on hooks and racks that had been anchored to the rock wall.

The cave looked to have a spare room past the dive gear, and as if Hutch had read Nate's mind he picked up the box, now detached from the buoy chains, and said, "Follow me."

Hutch handed the box to Nate and then cranked a handheld flashlight for thirty seconds and then turned it on. They entered the small room and Nate froze as the light stopped on a cross rising up from the rock.

"Meet my wife," Hutch said.

"Your wife?" Nate said.

"She left it up to me where to bury her. We had the funeral at my house and when I asked my daughter where she wanted her mother buried, she didn't want to talk about it. I had Sherry buried in the back yard, but I never liked her there. When I found this place I decided to move her out here."

"You mean, you took her body—"

"Oh, hell no," Hutch said. "She was cremated. I just took the urn out here."

"In one of the dryboxes?" Nate said.

"Yep."

"Was it in the box that we brought the chest in?"

"Could have been, I guess."

Nate swallowed.

"Don't worry, she won't bother us," Hutch laughed. "She's just going to watch over the chest."

Hutch set the drybox down in front of the cross, and they returned to the main room.

"How'd you find this place?" Nate said, joining Hutch on a natural rock bench that extended out from the wall.

"Did you see the wood and other junk at the bottom of the limestone wall?"

"Yeah, I wondered what that was," Nate said.

"Bunch a shit down there from a couple o' wrecks. Nothin' worth writin' home about. I was pokin' around one day and saw that crack. Figured I'd see where it led to," Hutch said.

"Mickey told me he'd been here," Nate said.

"He, Tyee, and Lucille all have," said Hutch. "They came to the burial ceremony I had after I found the place. Out here, I can be completely alone with my wife. You know by now that I'm not the most sensitive person in the world."

"I didn't pick up on that," Nate joked. "Lucille dives?"

Hutch broke a smile. "Swims like a fish," he said and then stood up. He walked over to the wall with the scuba gear and hung the buoys and chain on two hooks. "Let's get back and see what Tyee's been able to find out."

* * *

Tyee was at the desk writing on a piece of paper when they returned to the house.

"Mrs. Hawthorne headed out awhile ago," said Tyee. "Said to give her a buzz on VHF later."

Hutch nodded as he walked to the desk and picked up the decanter of dark rum. He poured fresh glasses while Mickey disappeared down the hallway. There was the sound of a door being opened, shuffling footsteps, then the door being closed. Mickey reappeared holding a rocking chair.

Tyee put down his pencil. "That's all I can get from this," he said rubbing his eyes and then took a drink of rum.

"What do you make of it?" said Hutch. All attention turned to Tyee.

"The letter is written by Jean La Rousseau. He doesn't say where he's from or who he is. I'd say he's a French noble. He writes that he was picked up at St. Ignace on the morning that he started writing the letter by a ship that had stopped en route to Niagara. The name of the ship was written down, but no matter what I did, I couldn't make out the name. It didn't help that it was on a fold in the paper either. Anyways, the ship sets sail from St. Ignace with Rousseau aboard. Then, the letter gets pissy. He says that he was guaranteed passage to Niagara, but after one of the crew members went into the ship's hold and looked at what was in Rousseau's chests, Rousseau was brought topside and questioned."

Hutch broke in, "Did you say *chests*, Tyee?"

"I'm getting there. The captain—his first name started with an L but the rest was illegible—questions Rousseau and makes for an un-named island on the horizon. The ship anchors and Rousseau is marooned with only one of his chests. It appears he gets some revenge, though. Right after he is marooned, a fall gale hits. As the ship gets farther away from the island, Rousseau says the seas become enormous and at one point he sees the ship's masts tip over and touch the water. The weather temporarily subsides about an hour later, and the ship is gone. The gale picks back up again and storms for four days straight. He says he has found shelter but doesn't know what will become of him. He ends the letter saying that he hopes he will be rescued and his eleven stolen chests returned to him."

"Twelve chests total," Hutch announced.

Tyee stood up and walked over to Hutch, handing him his notes. He downed the glass of rum and looked at his watch. It was almost eleven o'clock. "You ready to head out, Mickey? We'll let these gents toy with the letter."

Mickey threw back the last of his own rum and got up. "Sounds interesting, Hutch. Let us know if you put anything together."

Hutch handed the paper to Nate and walked with Tyee and Mickey toward the dock. Nate said goodbye and received two waves in return. Their voices faded as they disappeared down the stairs to the dock.

Nate said it out loud. "Twelve chests." He picked up the calculator and shuffled through papers until he found the sheet with Hutch's calculations for one chest.

He calculated for twelve:

2,700 in VG ($250) = $675,000.00 x 12 = $8,100,000.00

2,700 in XF ($1,000) = $2,700,000.00 x 12 = $32,400,000.00

Hutch returned and peeked over Nate's shoulder.

"That's a lot of dough that was never carried on the Great Lakes," he snorted. "Equal partners if we find the rest?" Hutch said extending his hand.

Nate stood up. "Equal partners," he replied and the men shook hands.

"A fifty-fifty split of either of those two numbers would set me, and you and your honey up for life."

"I can't believe this," Nate said, peering out the large windows at the black water in the distance.

"Believe it," Hutch said.

"My father had a knack for storytelling. He used to sit with me on my bed at night when I was a boy, telling me of the gold hiding beneath the surface of the Great Lakes. I would have my flashlight on and his face would glow as he spun yarns of divers looking for treasure and the perils of the deep," Nate said. "I wish he were here to see this."

"Like life, the sea gives and takes away, Nate. Always has, always will. We don't have a sunken ship or the other eleven chests, but we do seem to have proof that gold was carried," said Hutch.

"It's enough for me. Anything beyond this is gravy. I'm not holding my breath for the other eleven, but Brooke is going to flip when she finds out what we may walk away with from just one."

"Then, we've got our conversation starter for dinner at Lucille's place tomorrow night."

"I'd love to stay and talk about everything, the gold and the letter, but I better go."

"I'll let you know if I find anything out. If the eleven remaining chests seem like a dead end, we'll go down to the Hampstead bank tomorrow and see what the procedure is for the loot."

Hutch walked Nate to the front porch and duct taped a flashlight onto Nate's handlebars.

"Take it nice and slow," Hutch said.

"I will," said Nate, turning to go. He stopped the bike and looked back, "We might have the answer to one of our questions though."

"And which one would that be?"

"If the ship did wreck and spilled her guts all over the bottom, it could explain how the coin washed up on my beach."

"Just maybe," Hutch said.

Nate put his right foot back on the pedal while keeping his left foot on the ground. He thought about all the gold that could be out there for a moment, and then started to pedal again.

Hutch watched as the bike vanished into the woods. Excitement rose from his stomach all the way up to his eyes. There was only one ship that he knew of that was lost during that period. If he was right, it would solve one of the oldest shipwreck mysteries in the world.

If they could find it, they'd be a part of history, which was important to some people—verified their existence or profession—but for Abner Hutch, finding it meant taking something back from the sea.

But, before he hit the books, he had a phone call to make.

38

As Nate pedaled around the final turn before reaching the clearing, he could see the lights from Lucille's porch. He braked and the bike came to a stop just short of the wooden post. He turned off the flashlight and began walking the bike toward the porch. He was surprised to see two figures sitting in the wicker chairs: Lucille—and Brooke.

Brooke leapt off the porch, and he dropped the bike as she rushed into his arms.

"I love you, Nate," she said and held him like she hadn't seen him in years.

"How did—"

She kissed his mouth.

Their lips parted and she hugged him again. "I missed you," she whispered into his ear.

"I missed you too," he said, and they held hands approaching the porch.

"This is better than anything I see on T.V. these days," Lucille said. "Now get up here and have some coffee."

"How did you end up out here?" Nate said.

"I called Lucille," Brooke said. "She told me about the chest and the coins. Incredible!"

"Now I can see why you're so torn coming out here day after day, Nate," Lucille said while they sat down, "having to leave someone this pleasant." She poured each of them a cup of coffee.

Brooke smiled. "Lucille was just telling me about how she had invited us to dinner tomorrow night."

"Glad I didn't have to wait until then to meet you," Lucille said. "I've been askin' about you for a few days now."

"Oh, have you?" Brooke said looking at Nate with a smile.

Nate lifted his coffee cup to cover his face, then peeked around the side.

A voice from the end of the porch turned their attention. "You've got a full house tonight," Hutch said.

They all rose like the President had entered the room.

"You back here again?" Lucille said.

Hutch stepped onto the porch, carrying a backpack. "And who might this be?" he said reaching out his hand to Brooke.

"Brooke Martin," she said shaking his hand.

"Not a bad man you've got here," Hutch said pointing at Nate.

Lucille pointed at Hutch's backpack. "Gift for me in your bag?"

Hutch laughed. "Only if you like books about French currency, shipwrecks, and history."

"I'll pass," Lucille said. "Cup of coffee, Abner?"

"Might want to make another pot. Lots of readin' to do tonight."

Brooke began to rub Nate's leg. "Well, we'll get out of your hair," Nate said.

"Don't let me run ya off," Hutch said.

"No, we need to be getting home," said Brooke. She put her arm around Nate. "I have what I came here for."

"A late dinner tomorrow night, kids?" Lucille said.

"Wouldn't miss it," Nate said, then he turned to Hutch. "Call me tomorrow if you find something?"

"I'll call you anyway," Hutch said.

Lucille couldn't hide her smile.

Nate and Brooke walked to the Jeep and drove off into the woods. When the house was out of sight, Brooke said, "Stop the Jeep."

Nate did. "Is everything okay?

Brooke kissed him hard and began to lift his shirt up. "Not yet," she said.

Hutch sat on the davenport in front of the phone once more. Lucille took her station in the rocker. There was no music in the background this time, just a ceiling fan. He took out the piece of paper and dialed the number.

"Hello?" Melanie answered.

"It's me," Hutch said.

There was no answer back, but Hutch could hear her breathing into the phone. "Melanie, I have some things I want to say and all I'm askin' is that you hear me out. If you still don't want to communicate, it will be hard, but I'll respect your decision."

Again, nothing back, but the breathing was still there.

"I've made my share of mistakes, and unfortunately, many of them have been with you. Starting when you were young, I wasn't there for you as much as I should have been. I had made a commitment to my country, and looking back—"

Lucille nodded as if saying: *you're doing fine.*

"—I know it must have seemed like I was putting that in front of my family. Your mother, God rest her soul, ran the show for both of us and I talked myself into believing that you were getting everything you needed from her. That was wrong. I don't regret my service, but I do regret not explaining to you that you and your mother were both more important to me than my service."

"Oh, Dad," Melanie broke in, sniffling.

"I want to see you. I *need* to see you. I want to pick up those grandkids and never let them go. I want to get to know your husband Jim better. I—" he clinched his fist trying to hold his emotions off for one more second "—love you. Please forgive me."

He heard more sniffling on the other end, and his eyes welled up. Then he heard, "I love you, Dad. I have needed to hear those words for so long."

"I needed to say them," Hutch said, regaining his composure.

"We want to see you."

"I would like that," said Hutch. "You know that California is not my speed, but if you've got an opening in your schedule I'll be there pronto. And your family is always welcome to come here—on my dime."

"I'll take a look and get back with you in the next couple of days, okay?"

"That'll work," Hutch said. After a long pause, he added, "I won't take up any more of your time tonight. Give those grandkids a bear hug for me and I'll look for your call."

The call ended and Hutch fell into Lucille's open arms. She said, "See. You should never give up."

39

"Hello?" Nate said.

"Good morning," said Hutch, a bounce to his voice that Nate had never heard before. "Interested in searching for a shipwreck today?"

"So, you found something last night," said Nate looking at his watch; it was nine o'clock. "Late start this morning?"

"Not really. I was up until after three, sort of slept for an hour, and then had coffee with Lucille. After that, I had to gas up *Queen* and rig the towfish winch. However, it sounds like you just woke up."

"Don't know why I even asked." Nate shook his head.

"Ah, don't worry, it's fun to get called out and then bombshell someone back," Hutch laughed.

"You're going to have to teach me how to do that," Nate said.

"Takes years of experience," Hutch said. "But we'll see what we can do."

"Fair enough," he said. Nate thought about transportation. Since he was leaving the Jeep—Brooke was going to relax from their night of athletics in bed and later hit the play that the Hampstead Players were putting on at the high school—he would have to bike the entire way. Then a thought came to mind. "I probably won't be out there until ten. I'm bringing *Speculation* over."

"That'll work. Mickey's driving to Lucille's so there'll be plenty of room at the dock. Tyee has to work, so it'll be you, me, and Mickey out on *Queen* today. Give me a shout on the radio when you round the bight and I'll come down and help you tie up."

"What were you able to find out?" Nate said.

"I'll wait until everyone's here to explain. You're a teacher; I'm sure you don't like having to repeat things more than once."

"Very true," said Nate. "On my way."

He hung up the phone and packed his gear. Grabbing his boat keys, he kissed Brooke on the cheek.

"I'm heading out," he said.

She turned over. "Did he find anything?"

"He's waiting to tell me, must not be too earth-shattering."

"Okay," Brooke said, "just give me a call when you're ready for me to come out for dinner, babe."

"Will do. Have fun at the play," Nate said.

"The Hampstead Players are superb," she said. "They deserve their own playhouse."

"Oh, I'm sure someone is schmoozing one of the beach mansion owners for the funding," Nate said.

Hutch sat behind the desk in his library drinking straight from a thermos of coffee. Nate and Mickey were each sipping on their own cups and sitting in the leather chairs.

"I'm going to break this into two parts," said Hutch. "First, I'll tell you what I found out about our French friend Jean La Rousseau, and then I'll talk about the ship that supposedly marooned him."

Nate and Mickey set their cups down and listened.

"First, some background. We have to go back to Louis the Fourteenth's seventy-two-year reign. Louis's father was Louis the Thirteenth and his mother was Queen Anne. Anne had miscarried four times and after twenty-three years of marriage people doubted that she would ever produce an heir. It probably didn't help that her husband liked young men, either. One night, because of weather and the King's quarters not being ready, Louis was forced to stay with the Queen and they conceived. The birth was considered a miracle or an act of God. Sort of like you finding that coin, Nate."

The men laughed, and Nate raised his cup of coffee in a toast. Hutch continued.

"Even King Louis and Queen Anne agreed that the baby's birth was a miracle and named their son, Louis-Dieudonne, meaning Louis, the gift of God. However, since he was born so late in the marriage, he was only five years old when his father died and he inherited the throne. Hence, the picture on the 1643 coin is him as a child. When a king inherited the throne at such a young age, a Regency would take over until the king was old enough to rule. So, from age five until his early twenties, the country was run by the regent, sometimes his mother but mostly a Cardinal named Mazarin. As a young child, Louis saw that he could rely on almost no one, because he believed—and rightly so—that people were only out to weaken his power or take it away. When he finally became king, he removed all the aristocrats from his council and came down hard on the nobles. This may or may not have had an effect on what the person who was in charge of Louis' finances, Surintendant Nicolas Fouquet, did. In fact, it's generally accepted that Fouquet was bent and would have stolen from Louis anyways. Fouquet's power was based on the classic strategy of making his job out to be so complex and confusing that only he could understand it. Besides, the king had more important things to do than swamp himself in the inter-workings of his empire's wealth. For a while, Louis let

Fouquet believe that he was happy with his work. However, he secretly had people investigating where all of his money was going. Meanwhile, Fouquet was using the advantages of his position and taking money from the Treasury. Fouquet was wetting the beaks of all the nobles shunned by Louis. Of course, he was also having a state-of-the-art chateau built on his estate of Vaux, which still stands today. It all came to an end when King Louis imprisoned Fouquet for life in September of 1661 and did away with the political position."

"Did he ever get his money back?" Nate asked.

"Right after he put Fouquet away, Louis came out swinging at the nobles. There was a large operation to get back as much of his money as possible, but it would take years to discover who everyone was that had benefited from Fouquet. Some probably never got caught."

Hutch reached down to the floor and picked up one of the two books that Tyee had given him.

"And that is where I stopped reading the other night. So, when we saw Jean La Rousseau's name on the bottom of the letter, it didn't click," said Hutch while opening the book to a page he had earmarked. "Last night, I found out that Jean La Rousseau was one of the few nobles who left France to go explore the New World—and a member of Fouquet's party. It says La Rousseau left his estate in 1677. The date is important because that was the year nobles who wanted influence in the government were selling—or at least moving out of— their glamorous chateaux to occupy small residences in Versailles called garrets," Hutch said.

"Do you think La Rousseau was on the take from Fouquet?" Nate said.

"Hard to imagine someone in his own party who wasn't," said Hutch. "We have no proof, but why he would up and leave with such a big portion of his fortune doesn't smell right—especially because he did it during the year when the nobles were moving to Versailles."

"He probably went unnoticed during Louis' initial attempt to recoup," Mickey said. "After all, he left sixteen years after Fouquet was imprisoned—maybe his name was on the long list to check out and his number had been called."

"Where do you think he ended up?" Nate said.

"Who knows," said Hutch. "Maybe someone will find his bones buried in a cave one day."

"I guess we'll never know how Daniels found his chest on Big Sanisstey, either," Nate said.

"Safe assumption," Hutch said.

"What about the ship that marooned La Rousseau?" Mickey asked.

40

"Finding out about some noble and his fortune stolen from the government is all fine and dandy, but what really has my juices flowin' is the ship I believe he was on," Hutch said and then gulped from his thermos. "And King Louis leads us right to the name."

"King Louis the Fourteenth was involved in multiple wars in Europe, most notably with Spain. A bit ironic, since his mother, Queen Anne, was King Philip the Fourth of Spain's sister. Queen Anne had sent and received correspondence that had her nailed to the wall as a traitor. The birth of Louis ended up saving her from prosecution, since the mother of the next king couldn't be tried for treason. Strange way of life back then," Hutch shook his head.

"That aside, Louis was not only interested in fighting his neighbors, but also in exploring the New World. His most notable explorer was Rene-Robert Cavelier, Sieur de la Salle. Now, La Salle was not a pleasant man to work for and he struggled to keep a crew. There are said to be over sixty desertions, which is a fact we need to keep close at hand as I continue. To adequately explore and expand the fur trade, La Salle needed a sailing vessel. So, he borrowed money at a high interest rate and had the Great Lakes' first sailing vessel, *Griffon*, constructed in 1679. It was named to honor a French Governor whose coat of arms had a griffin. A griffin has the body of a lion and the head and wings of an eagle," said Hutch leaning back and scratching his cropped hair.

"You think the ship La Rousseau was on was the *Griffon?*" Nate said.

"Before I go any further, let me say this. I read numerous accounts last night of people who have claimed to have found the *Griffon*. In fact, there is a vessel on the bottom of Lake Michigan right now that seems to fit the description, but no one's diving on her because of various lawsuits. It seems like our account from Jean La Rousseau would disprove that ship as a candidate, but who knows. Hell, the literature I've read can't even agree on how long the ship was, how many cannons she carried, who was on her when she supposedly went down, and who was the last person to see her. So, what I'm going to present to you is my best guess from what I've been able to piece together. After all, the only people who know what really happened aren't around anymore are they?" Hutch took a deep breath, held it for a moment before continuing.

"A griffin was placed on the bow and the stern, and the ship was probably made of white pine and iron. She was a sixty to seventy-foot-long Barque armed with five to seven cannons. Her hull was rather square—had a high stern—and could have had two or three masts. Minus what La Rousseau's letter said, the only chronicled events come from the diary of Friar Louis Hennepin. Hennepin claims that when the ship was completed, it sailed Lake Huron, made a stop at Ft. Michilmackinac, and then continued on to its destination, Green Bay. At Green Bay, they loaded the ship with beaver pelts. La Salle was in debt from building the *Griffon* and the cost of his voyage, so he had his pilot, 'Luke the Dane,' and five other crewmembers set sail for Niagara with the pelts to pay off his loans. Hennepin wrote that Luke ignored what the natives said about an upcoming storm, and the *Griffon* left Green Bay in September of 1679 and was never seen again."

"Now, enter all the scholarly theories of what could have happened to her. The overriding generalization has been that the first vessel to sail on our beloved Great Lakes, the *Griffon*, is also our first shipwreck. Now, the possibilities. Let's start with La Salle. He believed that either *Griffon* went down in a storm or that Luke ordered the crew to help him steal the pelts, sell them, and then sunk the *Griffon* on purpose to hide any evidence. Where that would have happened, is anyone's guess. If it happened in Lake Michigan, then the wreck I talked about earlier that may really be the *Griffon* is just waiting to be confirmed because of the lawsuits. If it went down somewhere else, then she's still out there waiting to be found. Now, Luke was close to seven feet tall and a brutal man, who had no respect for superiors. I led similar scoundrels in the Coast Guard."

"I've taught a few like him," Nate said.

"Hutch, isn't your nephew coming out for his annual visit soon?" Mickey said.

"Yeah, the little shit is so full of himself that sometimes I could break him in half," said Hutch. "But he's family, so I'll keep tryin' to bring him around."

Nate said. "Sorry to get us off track. You were talking about La Salle's pilot Luke."

"I think back to La Rousseau's letter. Remember when he named the captain, but all Tyee could make out was the 'L'? It *could* be Luke; he would have been in charge so La Rousseau would have considered him the captain," Hutch said and took another pull on his coffee.

"But, before we get on that, let me finish the possibilities of the *Griffon* being in Lake Michigan. One year after the disappearance, La Salle starts to get reports as to what happened to his ship and crew. Some Potawatomi Indians tell him that they saw the *Griffon* moored in the northern part of Lake Michigan a couple of days after she had left Green Bay. Then, a few years after that, a man tells La Salle about five white men paddling down the Mississippi in canoes carrying furs. They were captured and all but one was killed. The one who got away could have been Luke the Dane." Hutch stood up and stretched. "And those are the theories that support Lake Michigan as the final resting place of the *Griffon*. The Lake Huron theories are less concrete."

41

"Three possible theories argue for the wreck to be in Lake Huron," said Hutch. "One: A wreck near Russell Island fits the size and shape of *Griffon*. In 1955, some experts saw it and found hand-made bolts that were old enough to be the *Griffon*. The other two possibilities are on Manitoulin Island. There was a wreck on a rocky beach but it was striped by settlers and not much was left for identification. Experts were brought in again and they decided that the wood and caulking left matched the period the *Griffon* was built. Naturally, the wreck sunk back into the water," Hutch grinned.

"Lots of mysteries around Manitoulin," Mickey added.

"Right where I'm headed, Mick. The last clue to where *Griffon* might be is from the late eighteen hundreds. A lightkeeper and his assistant found a cave with the skeletons of six men. I guess local residents kept the skulls as souvenirs, but rumor has it that one skull was a lot larger than the others. Some guy said it was so large, he could easily fit the jawbone over his own. The larger skull could have been Luke the Dane's. Naturally—" Hutch's smile widened again "—the skulls have disappeared."

Nate and Mickey sat in silence, trying to piece together the pieces of information that Hutch had provided. A few times, Nate went to speak, but then returned to his thoughts, shaking his head and rubbing his temples.

Hutch broke the silence. "Now, let's look at our old friend, Jean La Rousseau. I think wherever the *Griffon* may have ended up Luke and the other five crew members were never coming back for La Salle. One account I read says Luke and the crew of the *Griffon* were owed an entire year of pay, which seems to fit La Salle's character. As a side note, his treatment of subordinates eventually did catch up with him and he was shot in the back of his head by his own crew. It happened in Texas of all places. It makes perfect sense that Luke would pull in at St. Ignace on his way to Niagara, sell the beaver pelts, re-supply, take on this man La Rousseau—who I think had had enough of the New World and was headed back to France—finds out he's a noble with chests loaded with gold and dumps him off on an island in Lake Huron. Then, Luke's overconfidence gets the better of him and instead of waiting out the storm, heads full into it. This theory is supported by Hennepin's report of Luke throwing caution to the wind when leaving Green Bay. Hennepin also says that on the way from Niagara to Green Bay, *Griffon* almost sunk off of Long Point, but Luke was able to steer her through fog without any navigational aids. That'd be like trying to drive blind today," said Hutch. "You guys followin' me so far?"

Nate and Mickey nodded that they were.

"Well, gentleman, unless there was another sailing vessel that left St. Ignace in September 1679, or Jean La Rousseau is a liar, or he was seeing things after he got marooned, I believe *Griffon* went down somewhere between Hampstead and Big Sanisstey. What do you think?"

Nate spoke up. "I wonder why no one in St. Ignace ever recorded seeing the *Griffon*."

"I thought about the same thing last night, but it is what it is. No one did. Maybe they got bought off by Luke. Also, La Rousseau said they picked him up in the morning. Maybe there weren't many people around when he came in, or he anchored down the coast—rowed in, traded the pelts, picked up La Rousseau and got out," Hutch said.

"What happens if we find the rest of La Rousseau's chests?" Mickey said.

Hutch scratched his beard. "Well, I did a little looking into that too. The concept of paying money *for* money is as strange as it sounds. If we were French citizens and found treasure, we'd have to declare it and would only be reimbursed for our expenses, while the whole lot would go to the French government. If we didn't declare it, we could go to prison for theft and fraud. However, we're not French citizens and are in a unique position. The gold we have found—and maybe will find—belongs to the descendants of Jean La Rousseau. But taking into account that it was illegally acquired from the French government over three-hundred and fifty years ago, that it was found on U.S. soil, that La Rousseau had left his country and possibly tried to establish himself in the New World, it's anybody's guess who it belongs to or when they would be able to cash in on it."

"Should we report any of this before we start to look for the ship?" Nate said.

"I'm against that for two reasons. One: just look at how slow the lawsuit over the wreck in Lake Michigan is going—and that's just to establish who gets to *try* and identify the wreck. Two: nobody's gonna tell me when or where I can take my boat and dive."

"Let's say you do find the ship and the chests," Mickey said. "Are you going to get a cut?"

Hutch stood up. "Ultimately, I can't see how anyone could keep us out of some of the kitty. We'll have as much right to it as anyone else, and as for the one chest we already have from the cave—we found it."

He walked over and opened the door to a rectangular cabinet in the wall. The inside looked like a mailroom with twenty evenly cut out square slots. Hutch moved along the slots, looking at the labels he had on each one. When he found the one he wanted, he pulled out a rolled up nautical chart. He closed the cabinet drawer and unrolled the chart on the desk, using the heavy-duty rum glasses from the previous night to hold the corners down. He took out a pencil from the coffee can and a sliding ruler from the drawer and waved everyone over.

Nate noticed that it was a large-scale chart that showed the Hampstead coastline, including the bight and Hampstead Point near the bottom. A quarter of the way up from the lower edge was Diamond Crag and near the top were the Sanisstey Islands.

"What are you doing?" Nate said.

Mickey motioned quiet, let him finish.

When he was done, Hutch had drawn a large box, which equated to a small area of water—no more than a few square miles.

He put his pencil back in the coffee can and used the ruler to outline the box. "That's our search area for today," he said.

42

I t was five o'clock and Nate and Mickey sat on the deck in *Queen*'s stern finishing a quick snack of fish sandwiches Hutch had put together for them. Mickey walked over and took a can of coke out of the cooler. Hutch was in the wheelhouse steering the boat and watching the side scan sonar display on the laptop. The four-foot towfish was deployed and being pulled one hundred and fifty feet behind the boat at a depth of twenty feet.

Nate entered the wheelhouse and looked at the laptop's screen. "Anything?" he asked.

Hutch shook his head 'no'. "You both finished with the sandwiches?"

"Yeah. How much longer do you think we'll be out here?"

They had eaten lunch after looking at the chart in Hutch's library. Then they'd loaded the rest of the gear and started at the NW corner of the box Hutch had laid out. Since then it had been the monotonous routine of traveling up the box, turning around at the far edge, and traveling down the box— steadily covering the area from north to south.

"You know how to plot a fix?" Hutch said.

"I do," Nate said.

"Where'd you learn that?"

"Taught myself a few summers ago."

"You're provin' useful," said Hutch. "Mark our spot so we'll know where to start tomorrow."

Nate looked at the GPS coordinates and then plotted their position on the chart.

"Got it?" Hutch said. "Take the wheel."

Hutch slipped out of the way and walked to the chart. He rolled it up and put a rubber band around it, and then slid it underneath his chart table. Positioning himself in front of the GPS console, he brought up the waypoint function. Nate had remembered the latitude and longitude of the point where they had stopped and started to call out the coordinates to Hutch when Hutch raised his hand to silence him.

Hutch pulled a piece of paper out of his pocket and then started punching in coordinates. When he was finished, the machine gave a bearing and range to the waypoint.

"Drive to that," Hutch said. "I want to see something before we head in."

They approached the waypoint and Hutch watched for an image to appear on the laptop's screen. Nate was still at the helm. They were at the drop-off Hutch had told him about earlier, where the depth changed from thirty feet to three-hundred feet and then back up to fifty.

Hutch had showed Nate the piece of paper that had decided the course. It was a sheet from the plotter showing the faint outline of what could be a ship's bow close to the right edge of the image. The printout was from the hull-mounted wide-scan beam that Hutch had turned on when they were coming back from their first trip out to Sanisstey Island. Nate recalled Hutch writing down the latitude and longitude of the spot—it seemed like that day was months ago.

The boat passed over the waypoint and Hutch froze the screen with the push of a button. A much clearer picture confirmed what Hutch had seen in the first.

"Whatever it is, it doesn't look too big," Hutch said to Nate. He turned toward the stern. "Winch in the fish, Mickey. We're gettin' wet."

Nate went forward to drop the anchor. Hutch took the wheel and turned *Queen* around, going over the waypoint in the opposite direction. Twenty seconds past the waypoint, Hutch pounded on the wheelhouse's front windows for Nate to drop the hook.

The sound of the engine lowered and then stopped. After setting the anchor, Nate walked back and hopped down into the stern.

"Who's divin'?" Mickey said.

Hutch came out of the wheelhouse with a load of gear and a Styrofoam cup. "Nate and I will head down and see if this is anything. If it is, then I'll send up this cup. If you see it, Mick, come down and join us."

Nate looked over the side. Two seagulls floated on the blue-green water, which was not as clear as it had seemed when they were in the box using the towfish. He swiveled his head to the right. Fifty yards past the bow, the water turned to navy. His attention returned to the seagulls, which after a minute shook their wings and lifted into the sky. A shadow covering the water crept toward the boat and engulfed it as the sun disappeared behind a wall of clouds. All the water turned to gray.

Hutch emerged from the cabin in his wetsuit and Mickey lifted a tank from a metal rack that Hutch had installed against *Queen*'s port gunwale.

"Ever dived a wreck, Nate?" Hutch asked.

"No."

"Then follow me and do exactly as I do," Hutch said.

They sat on the starboard gunwale and strapped their fins on over their booties and then secured their dive knives. Mickey brought over three dive lights. One was the size of a household flashlight with a drawstring on the end to attach around the wrist. He handed it to Nate. The second light was exactly like the one Hutch had used in the cave, which looked like a radar gun. Hutch took it in his left hand and then opened his right hand as Mickey lifted the third, which was the size of a watermelon cut in half. The light face was flat and the rounded half-sphere was made of yellow plastic. A semi-circular metal handle came out from the sides of the light and joined in a rubber handgrip. There was a molded eye on either side with around three feet of wire clipped between the eyes. Hutch grabbed the rubber handle.

"We'll follow the anchor line down, Nate. When we reach the bottom, I'll secure this light to the anchor line and turn her on. This will be our safety spot in case of any hiccups. We'll also come here before we ascend. I know it's still daylight out and we'll only be down around thirty feet," said Hutch anticipating Nate's question, "but with cloud cover like today, it can get dark down there in a hurry. Just remember, always swim to the light and follow the anchor line up to safety."

"Where's the wreck?" Nate said.

Hutch stood up and looked at the direction the anchor line was tending and then used the Sanisstey Islands as a visual marker, which were a few points off the bow to port. "We don't know it's a wreck yet, but the object of interest is almost directly in front of the bow, maybe twenty, thirty yards away," said Hutch. "Meet me up forward." He put the regulator in his mouth and holding it and his mask in place, flipped back into the water.

Nate followed Hutch. His drop had taken him no more than ten feet under. The clouds were still blocking out the sun and it was darker than he thought it would be. He switched on his underwater light and followed _Queen_'s hull toward the anchor line. The wooden hull was spotless. He saw a light up ahead and was soon at the line with Hutch. They began their descent and reached the bottom in less than thirty seconds. Hutch secured the safety light to the anchor line and turned it on. A beacon of light rose toward the surface. Hutch studied his compass and then directed Nate to follow him.

Nate concentrated his light forward and lined up behind. Hutch kicked a few yards in front, aiming his light in a tight arc from side to side. They traced the bottom for twenty yards. Then, Hutch stopped and Nate drew even with him. They were looking at a wreck, but not the one they expected.

43

In front of them lay the forward part of a modern sailboat. Hutch thought about letting go of the Styrofoam cup so Mickey could come down, but instead stuffed it inside his wetsuit. The bow was ten yards away and pointed at them as if on a collision course. There was no trace of the mast in the immediate vicinity. Hutch signaled to Nate that they would circle the boat first. They swam to the right and as soon as they came parallel with the bow, saw that the entire stern of the boat was missing. A few kicks further and Hutch drew Nate's attention away from the boat and to the sea floor. No more than ten yards past the boat, the bottom disappeared.

They stopped short of the edge and Nate looked right and then left, seeing the cliff extend indefinitely in either direction. Hutch had shown him on the laptop screen that this larger cliff's edge was around two hundred yards in length and the crater was more of a trapezoid shape like a flattened coffee filter. From edge to edge the crater spanned approximately one hundred yards.

Nate swung his light around and aimed it into the deep. It was nothing but a penlight of yellow that barely penetrated the black chasm. He turned and followed Hutch to where the stern of the sailboat should have been. The bottom was deeper than where the bow lay and as he followed it back, he saw that the cliff edge was caved in toward the crater. It was as if someone had taken the stern in one hand and the bow in the other and snapped the sailboat in two. Hutch pointed at a dark shape protruding from the sand and gave Nate his light. Nate held both beams steady on the object and Hutch dug until he had uncovered enough to pull out a piece of wood that was an arm's length long and several inches thick. It definitely didn't belong to the sailboat and seemed to puzzle Hutch. He set it down and they swam toward what remained of the sailboat.

There was no real danger of getting caught or snagged on the inside of the wreck because there wasn't much there. However, Hutch continued to take every precaution. They stopped at the opening and Hutch shined his light into a hatch that led to the boat's v-berth, which was the only compartment left. From what they could see, the inside had been done in all wood and brass fittings. Hutch aimed his light away and got Nate's attention. He signaled that it was okay to look around but that penetrating the hull into the v-berth was off-limits, and to stay within sight. Nate signaled back that he understood and they broke eye contact.

Hutch disappeared from view, and Nate shined his light on the inside of the wreck again. He assumed that this was where the galley had been, but there were no traces of plates, cups, or silverware on what remained of the deck or on the sand in front of him. He checked his pressure gauge and saw that they had a half hour left before they would need to start heading back. A few fish were swimming in and out of the top hatch, and Nate could now see Hutch's bubbles up forward. He swam over the deck and estimated that the boat had been broken in two just forward of where the mast was. But where were the mast and the stern? Had it broken in two on the surface, and the stern and mast were closer to where *Queen* was? No, it would have shown up on the sidescan. The rest of the sailboat must have slipped over the cliff edge and was most likely in over three hundred feet of water. It would explain why the bottom was carved out aft of the wreck and why the cliff edge was indented. But where did the piece of wood they found come from?

Nate swam to the port side of the boat and continued forward. The boat's lines were beautiful on what was left of the white hull. A two-inch-thick navy stripe ran back from the bow and an inch underneath it was a thick golden stripe. He kicked another two strokes and found Hutch directing his light where the bow met the sand. Hutch was moving sand away and as Nate looked closer he could see something attached to the hull. Hutch continued to uncover the black object and then froze. Coming out from the bottom of the object were two wires.

Hutch squeezed Nate's arm. The older man's eyes were on fire and said: Don't touch it, follow me *now.* He pointed in the direction of the safety light, and they kicked toward *Queen.*

At the light, Hutch signaled for Nate to wait there. Then, he pointed at himself and to his watch. He held up one finger and then all five. He pointed back toward the wreck, to himself, and then to the light attached to the anchor. Nate nodded. Hutch pointed at his watch again and held up two fingers and then made a zero. He pointed at himself and gave the sign for trouble. He pointed to Nate and motioned for him to surface and get help. Nate's eyes widened behind his mask, but Hutch gave him the okay sign, turned on his light, and took off toward the wreck.

Hutch swam past the wreck, clearing the side by twenty or so feet. He circled around back and picked up the piece of wood he had examined earlier. Then he moved back toward the edge and chose a random area to dig with his hands. He would occasionally look up at the sailboat, as if playing peekaboo with the devil, and then look back down at the place he was digging. He found nothing. He moved closer to the edge and was now looking up at the sailboat from a thirty-degree angle. If the sailboat slipped back now, it would carry him with it over the edge and into the deep. He started digging again.

This time he felt wood and continued to clear. The piece was much larger and Hutch couldn't pull it out. He looked at his watch. He had five minutes left before he had to head back to the light. He swam to the edge of the cliff that had been caved in and shined his beam straight down. As he examined the cliff face it got darker around him. He glanced up and guessed that the sun must have gone behind another cloud. Hutch held the light out in front of him and disappeared over the cliff.

He followed the cliff face down and observed that the wall had been torn apart. The aft section of the sailboat must have exploded and—at least some of it—slid down the cliff-side. But where did the wood he had found come from?

He had never dived around the drop-off before but knew that on one of the sides of the crater there was a shelf at a depth of around sixty feet. He had thought it was this side, but wasn't sure. Other than the pass with Nate a few days ago, he hadn't been out here since the first summer he'd spent in Hampstead. During that summer, he'd been a passenger on Lucille Hawthorne's son's boat. After a tour of some of the family's favorite fishing spots, he'd taken Hutch to the crater and told him that the fishing there was terrible and the scuba diving dangerous. The only thing worth going down for was a shelf that ran approximately two hundred feet along the cliff-side and extended forty or fifty feet out into the cavern before dropping straight down to three hundred feet. Hutch had never bothered to see it.

His depth gauge read forty feet...fifty feet...fifty-five feet. His feet hit bottom, and he shot the light down at his flippers. He'd reached the shelf; his depth gauge read sixty-two feet. If there was anything left of the sailboat some of it might have landed here instead of going into the deep. He began to kick along the wall, aiming his light out onto the shelf. The beam hit an object sticking up from the sand and leaning against the wall. The light reflected off the object and soon Hutch was touching a portion of the sailboat's mast. The section was about ten feet long. He attempted to pry it loose from the rock and sand, but it was no good. He decided to move out onto the shelf and search.

He kicked fifteen feet out and then swam parallel to the cliff face. His beam was pointed at the sand and after a few kicks he saw something glittering up ahead. A metal fixture from the sailboat?

It was not metal. It was gold—a gold coin to be exact. He read the inscription on both sides and, after placing it in a pocket in his wetsuit, kicked further. He was surprised when he flew past the shelf edge and was surrounded in darkness. If it had been on land, he would have been dropping to his death right now into the chasm below. However, he just floated in space with over two hundred feet of water beneath him and the shelf edge a few kicks away. It sure didn't seem like it was as big as Lucille Hawthorne's son had described it. He thought about it a minute, and started to trace the edge of the shelf. There was an eerily similar pattern starting to form, and as he swam backwards out into the open water while shining his light on the edge, it became apparent that there must have been a secondary explosion when the stern of the sailboat landed on the shelf.

Satisfied, he began to head toward the place where he had found the coin, but two lights descending down the cliff face grabbed his attention. He looked at his watch. It had been twenty-two minutes.

He swam toward the lights and was soon in the company of Nate and Mickey. He signaled that he was okay and saw that they had brought him a new air tank. He still had fifteen minutes left on his tank but switched over to the fresh one. He motioned for Mickey and Nate to gather around. He pulled the coin out and opened his hand, watching the men's expression go from concern to jubilation. He got their attention again and signaled his search plan. The men got into formation abreast, with Nate hugging the wall, Mickey in the middle, and Hutch the furthest out onto the shelf. They aimed their lights at the floor and kicked together. After no more than ten seconds of kicking, Nate turned into the cliff face and vanished. Hutch went after him and then almost dropped the regulator out of his mouth. Nate had discovered a cave under the cliff face, and, rising up from the cave floor was the hull of a wooden ship lying on its side. The cave was enormous, and the keel, which was closest to the shelf floor, was still under the cliff face. Rocks ripped off from the explosion littered the shelf. Nate's light was dancing all around and then it became focused on one point. Hutch arrived to see what he was pointing at.

At first, he didn't see it. Nate swiveled him into position and then it was unmistakable. The carved figure on the bow had a lion's body with the head and wings of an eagle: it was the *Griffon*.

Mickey arrived, and seeing the carved figure, high-fived Nate. Hutch calmed them down and signaled for no one to penetrate the wreck. He proposed they all swim the length of the wreck to see how much was down there. Nate and Mickey signaled back to him that they understood. Mickey swam above, between the starboard side of the ship and the top of the cave, while Nate and Hutch followed either side of the keel.

Most of the hull was intact, preserved by the chilly fresh water of Lake Huron. During the secondary explosion, some of the cliff that had been camouflaging the wreck must have slid off the shelf into the deep; the rest was strewn on the shelf like a shattered glass ball.

As they approached what Hutch considered the middle of the ship, they saw the hull had come apart and provided an opening large enough for someone to enter. Hutch stopped to look at the wood. There were axe marks at various points, showing that the wood had been hand-crafted. He continued along and saw one more point where he might be able to enter the wreck, but it was tighter than the first. The keel began to curve deeper into the cave as Hutch reached the stern. He waited for Nate and Mickey so all three could search for the second griffin seal that was believed to be mounted there. They found nothing. The stern was more heavily damaged and it was difficult to make anything out from the scraps. Either the seal was amongst the rubble, had been broken off, or had never been a fixture on the stern.

They regrouped, and Mickey signaled that there was also no sign of the masts. He focused his beam into the cave showing a maze of wood, rock, sand, and debris. If that was where the masts and the rest of the wreck were, there was no way that someone was going to try and swim in there. Hutch motioned the other two to follow him, and he led them back to the smaller of the two openings in the hull.

There, he stationed Nate. Hutch switched lights with him, giving Nate the more powerful light for steady illumination and taking Nate's smaller light. Mickey then followed Hutch to the larger opening where Hutch signaled for him to do the same thing as Nate. Mickey signaled back and went inside the opening and backed up to give Hutch room.

Hutch entered the wreck. Aided by Mickey's light, he could see about fifteen feet. There were collapsed bulkheads and broken decks, but he was able to move along the keel. Then he found an opening further into the middle and took a left. The beam from Mickey's light was still visible, but Hutch could no longer see him. He navigated around a collapsed deck and found another opening to the right. Now he could see the beam from Nate's light. He was in a space big enough to take a break and he settled onto the bottom. He aimed his light at the sand and moved it around the space. In a corner he saw something light colored and moved toward it. He reached down and picked it up. It was a skull. Beside it was a large bone which looked like a femur. He decided to move on.

He entered a narrow passageway between decks where Nate's beam was stronger. He maneuvered away from the light and found himself in a space that was twice as large as the room with the bones. He put his beam to the floor and his eyes almost burst out of his mask.

Nate felt relieved as he saw Hutch's light get closer and closer to him. Hutch exited the narrow opening and they swam back to get Mickey. When they reached the large opening, Mickey saw their lights and was half-way out of the wreck when the regulator popped out of his mouth. He seemed to shout in pain and was dragged back in.

45

Hutch lurched inside and seized Mickey's arm. Together, he and Nate pulled Mickey almost all the way out before they saw what had him. A barracuda-like fish at least six feet long had a hold on Mickey's calf and was shaking its head back and forth. Blood oozed from Mickey's leg. Hutch pulled out his knife and got behind the fish. Clamping the body in-between his thighs, he stabbed it and sawed its head off. Then, another one shot out at Nate from inside the wreck and went for his elbow with its needlelike teeth. Nate dodged and caught the fish by its large tail. The fish jerked and Nate held on with both hands. Hutch plunged his knife into the side and dragged it along the body as far as he could. The fish's motion slowed and he withdrew his knife and motioned for Nate to let it go. The fish swam away trailing a stream of blood in its wake.

The three men were outside the wreck and Mickey gave a sign that he was okay and that he could still kick with his other leg. Hutch took Mickey's weight belt off and left it on the bottom. Then, he positioned Mickey between Nate and himself and Mickey grabbed hold of their weightbelts. Nate and Hutch held their lights in front of them and pulled Mickey to the surface.

* * *

"What in the hell were those things?" Nate said as they climbed aboard.

"Two very large and very pissed off Muskies," Hutch said.

"Muskies?" Nate said.

"Muskellonges," said Hutch. "A rare game fish. I've heard that they can get to be six feet and around ninety pounds. I'd say both of those were that, and then some."

"I've never seen them get that big before," Mickey said.

Hutch started to treat Mickey's wound with the first aid kit he had on board.

"We found ourselves a ship, gents," Mickey said.

"Not just *a* ship, *the* ship," Nate said. "We found the *Griffon*."

"Wanna know what else we found?" Hutch said.

"What?" Mickey said.

Hutch made fists with both of his hands and raised them in front of his chest. The men's eyes followed. He opened his hands and showed nine fingers. "Nine chests, gentleman. Nine chests," said Hutch and he lowered his hands.

"What shape are they in?" Nate said.

"Seemed intact," Hutch said. "You might be retiring." He lifted Mickey's leg. "I'm just glad you had your knife on your leg, Mick. Or I'm afraid that set of teeth would have done a lot more damage than that," Hutch said, finishing with the dressing. "Might need stitches though."

"Feels better already," said Mickey.

"If she's been on that shelf all this time, why hasn't anyone discovered her yet?" Nate said.

"Could be a variety of things," said Hutch. "Thinking off the top of my head, a cave—a covered cave before the ass end of the sailboat explosion opened her up—tucked underneath the cliff is the perfect place for a wreck to be concealed. If the drop-off is like a blue hole, then the whole thing could have been a cave complex. Who knows when the original part collapsed? Mrs. Hawthorne's son dove on that shelf and never noticed the cave—not that he was looking for it. Plus, I've been down on a wreck before during the day, had a storm blow over that night, and dive the next day and have it look completely different. The cave and *Griffon* have had over three hundred years of storms to work on them. At least some of *Griffon* broke off just aft of what's left of the sailboat."

"The wood that you dug up," Nate said.

"Yes, sir," Hutch said. "I only saw nine of the eleven chests that are supposed to be aboard. I'll bet one of those missing spilled all over the bottom, which could account for why that coin showed up on your beach, Nate. It's like any wreck that someone finds. As soon as it's located everyone can't believe that they didn't search there. I wish I could say what the cliff face looked like before today, but I can't. It could have completely hidden the wreck, or there might have been openings large enough for a diver to enter, but even if there were, cave diving is a dangerous business—especially for amateurs. Lotta wannabes have permanently left the building messing around in places they shouldn't have."

"Like you almost did when you first discovered the room in Diamond Crag?" Mickey joked.

Nate tried to hide his smile.

Hutch laughed. "You just worry about your leggy, shitstick. When it's my time to go, it's my time to go."

"Leg's fine, but I'm not sure about your logic," Mickey said.

"Look at the odds," Hutch said. "Even using the best technology for finding wrecks doesn't mean that we're going to find all six-thousand that are out there in the Great Lakes' ninety-five thousand square miles of water. All that matters is that we found ours."

"What do you think about the sailboat?" asked Mickey.

Hutch stared out over the water. "I don't know. Can't say that I've ever seen one that was rigged to blow on purpose."

"What kind was it?" Nate asked. "I didn't see any markings."

"A big Hunter," Hutch said. "Luxury sailboat. Makes even less sense. Who in their right mind would want to scuttle a Hunter?"

Nate thought. Was Jeff Sawyer's boat a *Hunter*? He couldn't remember.

"What about the gold?" said Mickey.

"We'll discuss that on the way in," said Hutch. "It's seven now. We'll be back before eight." He looked at Nate. "Dinner with everyone might have to wait until tomorrow night."

46

There was over an hour of daylight left when *Queen* reached Hutch's dock. Mickey was sitting in the fighting chair with a bag of ice wrapped around his leg. When Hutch was satisfied with *Queen*'s mooring, he shut off the engine and then helped Mickey up onto the dock.

"Help Mickey up the stairs while I dash up and get a fresh bag of ice," Hutch said to Nate.

Mickey put his arm around Nate's neck and they were soon at the bottom of the steps. They started to climb with Mickey in the lead. When they reached the half-way point, Nate was surprised to see Hutch coming down the stairs without a bag of ice.

"Out of my way," he said and slid past them.

"What's up, Hutch?" said Mickey.

Hutch ignored him as he reached the bottom of the stairs and marched over to the shed.

Mickey and Nate turned around, and as they went back down the stairs heard the shed door open and then close. When they arrived at the bottom, Hutch was locking the door back up and had a shotgun lying on the dock next to him.

"What is it, Hutch?" Mickey said.

Hutch stood up with the gun. "We've had visitors. The inside of my place is all ripped apart."

"Looking for the gold," Nate said.

"Appears so," said Hutch.

"What are we going to do?" Mickey asked.

"We need to get you to a doctor first," Hutch said.

"The hell with that."

"Mick, I—"

"Won't listen to it," said Mickey.

"Sometimes I think you're more stubborn than I am," Hutch said. "I radioed Lucille while I was up there and she's fine—dinner has been postponed." He looked at Nate. "She hasn't been able to reach your wife, but will keep trying."

Nate nodded.

"I also contacted Tyee. We know the treasure is safe out at Diamond Crag, but I don't know what these yahoos are going to do next. I want to be prepared." Hutch scratched his beard for a moment. "Mick, you stay here while Nate and I go to Tyee's and hook up the winch. I told him that I want to dive first thing tomorrow morning and haul up the chests. He's meeting Nate and me at his dock and then coming back with us to stay over tonight. I think it'll be quiet while we're gone. Whoever is messing with us, has already been here and not found what they wanted."

"No problem," Mickey said.

"Nate, go up and get Mickey a chair and a bag of ice," Hutch said.

"Got it," Nate said, and he clipped up the stairs.

Hutch hopped down into the RHIB. From a compartment next to the helm, he pulled out a portable VHF radio and a black leather case.

He climbed back onto the dock and turned to Mickey. "Mick, I need you to stay on the dock and wait for us. We'll radio you when we're close to getting back. In the bag is a pair of night vision goggles so you can keep an eye on Diamond Crag. Like I said, I don't expect anything more tonight."

"Who do ya think is fuckin' with ya?" Mickey said.

"Not sure yet," Hutch said.

Nate came down the stairs with a bag of ice, a chair, and a bar stool.

"What's the bar stool for?" said Hutch.

They sat Mickey down in the chair and Nate placed the bar stool in front of the chair. "Elevation. It'll keep the swelling down," Nate said.

"Good point," said Hutch. "You think pretty well on your feet."

Nate propped up Mickey's leg, made sure the wounded part was raised higher than Mickey's heart, and then wrapped the bag of ice around it.

Hutch handed Mickey the radio, black case, and shotgun. He turned to Nate, "Let's go."

Lines were cast off and Hutch backed *Queen* away from the dock, navigating it around *Speculation*. Nate performed a radio check with Mickey, then looked at Hutch. "Do you think we should radio the police?"

"Wouldn't do much good right now," said Hutch. "They'd take forever getting out here and we'd lose time that could be spent going to get the winch. And when they did get here, they'd look inside my house and then tell me what I already know—that someone broke into my damn house."

Queen heaved forward and Hutch's house became smaller and smaller. They passed the bight and headed for Tyee's at full throttle.

47

The Four-Runner pulled into the driveway of Tim and Jane Gibson's and rolled toward the house. A few yards short of the front porch, the driver stopped the vehicle and then turned off the engine. She looked at the address she had written down on a notepad, then looked at the house. The numbers on the paper matched the numbers on the house. There was no outside light on, but at least one room was lit on the inside. She got out and walked to the front door.

After two knocks, the outside light turned on and the door opened.

"Can I help you?" Jane Gibson asked, looking into the face of a young woman she had never seen before.

"May I speak with Professor Gibson please?"

"I'm afraid he's not here," said Jane. "You look familiar. Do I know you from the Hampstead Country Club?" she lied.

"No. I'm not from around here," the girl said.

"Oh," said Jane. "My husband is taking care of some business down in Ann Arbor and won't be back until at least tomorrow. Is everything okay? Is there something I can help you with?"

The girl stared at Jane. "May I come inside for a minute, Mrs. Gibson? I've had a long drive."

"Please, call me Jane," she said, holding the door open for her.

Jane ushered her into the living room and offered her a seat. "Can I get you anything to drink?"

The girl shook her head no. "He always said this place was a shack in class."

Jane gave her a half-smile and winked. "Well, Tim's modest."

The girl raised an eyebrow.

"You said you had a long drive. Where are you from?"

"Pennsylvania."

"I don't understand," Jane said.

Then, the girl told her...and Jane Gibson screamed.

The Hampstead Players performance of *42nd Street* had been exceptional—and had run over. Brooke Martin entered her house and hurried down the hallway toward her bedroom to change clothes for dinner. With the exception of picking up a bottle of wine and attending the performance, she had stayed inside and had not seen or heard from Tim Gibson all day, which had been a relief. As she entered the bedroom and kicked off her shoes, the phone rang, startling her. She did not check to see who it was, assuming it was Nate at Mrs. Hawthorne's.

"Hello?"

"It... it's Tim," Jane Gibson said.

"Jane?"

There was no response.

"What's wrong?" Brooke asked, her stomach rising to her mouth as she asked the question.

Brooke waited for her to continue, but all she heard was sobbing. "Jane, what *about* Tim? What's going on?"

A voice came on the phone that Brooke did not recognize. "Hi, Mrs. Martin. Jane is not doing well right now and said that you are a friend of the family who lives nearby."

"I live a few houses down the beach. Who is this and what has happened?" Brooke demanded.

The voice continued to be calm. "I think she needs to have a friend here with her right now, Mrs. Martin. Could you come over?"

"Of course I can, but could you please tell me what's going on?"

"Please come over."

"I'm on my way," Brooke said and hung up the phone. She was in such a hurry that she did not see the digital '2' blinking on the answering machine in the kitchen as she left the house.

The door opened and Brooke was greeted by a young woman. She led Brooke into the living room, and no one was there.

"Where's Jane?" Brooke asked.

"She's in her bedroom upstairs," the girl replied.

"Where is her husband?" Brooke said.

"Ann Arbor."

Brooke started toward the stairs and the girl grabbed her arm. "I want to fill you in before we go up there."

"Please do," Brooke snapped.

"I attend the University of Michigan and took a class from Professor Gibson last semester. I'm pregnant with his child."

48

*Q*ueen cruised by Diamond Crag on its way back to Hutch's. The stars were out and the last remnants of sunlight had vanished around a half-hour ago. The stainless-steel arms of the large winch rose from both gunwales and joined into a hooked 'V' a few feet aft of the transom. Wire cable ran from the metal spool, screwed into the deck where the fighting chair had been, up into the pulley located where the steel arms met, and finally down from the pulley to end in a clasp attached to a rectangular stainless-steel cage.

Tyee was in the stern using a red lensed flashlight to guide himself as he made a few adjustments to the gas-powered motor that operated the winch. Nate was with Hutch on the fair-weather level.

"We'll be back to my dock in about ten minutes," said Hutch, passing the VHF handset to Nate. "Give Mickey a call and see if everything's okay."

Nate tried to reach Mickey on Channel 6 first—the channel they had agreed upon before leaving. No answer. Next were Channels 12 and 16. They were the most commonly used VHF channels, and Hutch had the handheld Mickey was using set to scan traffic on them. No answer.

Hutch grabbed the handset and tried. Static.

Tyee finished with the motor and shut off his red light. Nate moved over to make room as Tyee climbed up the ladder and joined them.

"No radio contact with Mickey," Hutch said to Tyee.

"What do you think?" Tyee asked.

Hutch threw Tyee a set of keys from his pocket. "Go below and load two guns from my safe."

Tyee climbed down the ladder and was soon out of view below.

"We may have some trouble waiting for us back home," Hutch said.

When they were in visual range of the dock, Hutch pulled a spotlight out from a compartment underneath the helm and handed it to Nate. Hutch's entire property was dark. Nate turned on the spotlight. Other than the RHIB and Nate's boat, the dock was bare. Mickey was nowhere to be seen—the chair, stool, radio, shotgun, and night vision goggles were gone.

"Where in the hell did he go?" said Hutch. "Turn off that light."

Tyee appeared in the stern wearing a pair of night vision goggles with a shotgun slung over his shoulder. He began to scan Hutch's property.

Hutch turned off the running lights and the dark shape of *Queen* crept to the dock.

They tied up and met in the stern. Hutch had the other gun that Tyee had brought up. It was a revolver and was wedged between Hutch's belt and shorts.

"Okay, let's not get jumpy. He might be okay, and the last thing we need is us shooting each other. Tyee, you stay down here and Nate and I will check the house."

The men split up and Hutch led the way up the stairs. He paused at the top and crouched with his eyes at deck level. Nothing moved in the house.

"We'll enter through the library door. Stay right next to me."

"Hutch, I don't even have a weapon to defend myself."

"When we get indoors, I'll fix you up."

238

They sprinted across the deck and were inside the library in seconds. The room was dark with the exception of the stars and moon shining through the large windows. Hutch went to the desk and from the bottom drawer pulled out a k-bar that he'd been given from an inter-service function with the Marines years ago. He threw it to Nate, and Nate looped the sheath through his belt and then took out the knife. Hutch walked over to the VHF set and keyed the mic. Dead. He toggled the switch and got no response.

"Someone's been in here since we left," Hutch whispered reaching behind the box, feeling for the cord. "The set was on when I first came up here and saw the place trashed. You didn't turn it off when you came up to get ice, did you?"

Nate shook his head no.

Hutch felt the end of a frayed wire. "Sonofabitch," he said.

"What?" Nate said.

"Someone's cut the cord." He looked into Nate's eyes. "Be ready. You may have to use that," Hutch said pointing at the knife.

Nate's palm was moist and he gripped the knife harder.

Hutch began to move toward the kitchen. Then the smell hit him. He rose and bolted for the front door.

Nate ran after him and they were soon side-by-side on the porch. Hutch turned on the lights and the entire dirt clearing angling down to the woods lit up.

"Help me up onto the roof," Hutch said.

Nate paused, smelling smoke.

"Now, goddamnit!" Hutch ordered.

Nate flexed his legs and locked his hands. Hutch stepped into them and was soon standing on Nate's shoulders. Grabbing the top of the roof, he pulled himself up. Hutch treaded upright to where the roof angled up and then leaned over, putting both hands on the shingles. He climbed to the peak and held on to the chimney to steady himself. His eyes saw the orange glow rising from woods in the distance. He slid back down the roof and swung onto the porch.

"I'll be right back," he said to Nate.

"Where are you going, Hutch?" Nate said.

"Lucille's house is on fire," said Hutch running toward his garage. "Gotta make sure she's okay."

There was a level of concern in Hutch's words beyond merely hoping someone wasn't injured—it was the fear of *losing* someone. The front door opened and Nate pulled his knife back, ready to swing.

Tyee appeared, and Nate lowered his knife. Hutch was opening the garage door and they ran to him.

"Hutch, I found blood on the edge of the dock where you moor the RHIB," said Tyee. "I boarded and found a few drops on the deck. Then I felt the engine. She's been used recently."

"Jesus, Mickey," Hutch said to himself, "tell me you aren't that stupid."

"Do you think he went to Diamond Crag?" said Nate.

"Lookin' that way," said Hutch, who was clearing a path to an object in the corner covered by a sheet. "Someone's gotta run the RHIB out there and get wet."

Nate spoke up. "I can check on Lucille. I'm sure she's fine. You know Diamond Crag the best, Hutch." He would now find out how much Hutch trusted him.

Hutch turned around and studied Nate. "Okay," he said. "Use this." He pulled the sheet off, and a dirt bike stood resting on a kickstand. Hutch wheeled the bike out of the garage and pointed off to the left. "See that opening?"

Nate nodded as he saw where the trees thinned on the outer edge of the dirt plot.

"That's the back way to Lucille's. You'll be there in a few minutes on this puppy. Keep your head low to the bike. There are hanging branches that'll have you seein' stars if you don't."

It made sense to him now. The bike path always seemed to be winding to the right when he was coming out to Hutch's. This emergency path must be a straight shot.

Hutch started the bike and turned on the round headlight. Nate hopped on and held on for dear life as he shot into the woods.

"We've gotta call the fire department," Hutch said. "Fuck, I guess it's time I got a phone out here."

"I've got my cell phone," Tyee said.

"Call it away. She may have called already, but we can't take that chance."

"You headin' out to the Crag?" Tyee said.

"On my way," said Hutch. "If what I think has happened *has* happened, Mickey may no longer be our friend. Don't trust him if you see him, and stay on the dock until I get back."

Joshua David Bagley was almost finished screwing the daylights out of a Hampstead High School senior who had been hired by the Shaws to clean their house for the summer, when his stateroom phone aboard *Triumph* rang, and kept ringing. He ignored it as he pumped away at the tiny blonde. Two shot glasses and half a bottle of tequila sat on the nightstand, and a trail of clothes led from the private balcony into the room and up to the foot of the bed. The phone stopped ringing as he finished with the girl. Out of shape and exhausted, he flopped on his back next to her. She slid her knees back down and lay on her stomach.

"Want another shot?" she asked.

"Baby, I feel like I've just been shot," Bagley said.

There was a knock at the door.

"Go away, I'm busy," Bagley said.

The knock got louder.

"Who the fuck wants me now?" he said and then patted the girl's ass as he got up.

Bagley threw on a robe and the girl went into the bathroom.

"This better be goddamn import—"

"Important?" said Leonard Shaw, wearing a black tuxedo and standing in the doorway. "It is. Get dressed and meet me in the study in five minutes."

The toilet flushed in the bathroom.

"Company?" Shaw said.

Bagley tried to come up with an answer but thought too long. Shaw was already walking away.

The lights flicked on in Shaw's study and Bagley followed him in. Shaw closed the door.

"How old was that girl?" Shaw said.

"What difference does it make?" Bagley said. "She was good and experienced. They seem to start earlier and earlier every year. You got anything to drink in here?"

Shaw poured Bagley a snifter of brandy and they sat down at Shaw's desk.

"So what's going on?" Bagley said and took a sip.

"Good news and bad news," Shaw said.

"The bad."

"Someone found the sailboat," Shaw said.

"What sailboat?" said Bagley raising his glass again, but stopping and almost dropping it on the desk. "You mean *the* sailboat?"

"Yes."

"I don't understand. Floyd told you he took care of it last summer. Said something about scuttling it in some cavern that was over three-hundred feet deep where no one would find it."

"That's what I thought. You know what he did?"

Bagley shook his head no.

"He rigged it with explosives. How could he be that stupid? I told him to sink it, not sink it and blow it up."

"Well, how much did they find?"

"Just a portion of it."

"Any identifying marks?"

"Thank Christ, no. The bow was the only thing left."

"And the girl?"

"Floyd says she was in the stern with the majority of the explosives. And no body or body parts have washed up this year, so I think we're still safe."

"Why didn't he make sure everything was gone last year?"

"How the hell should I know, Joshua? Anyways, he didn't have time to explain it all to me. He's got more important things to take care of right now."

"What could be more important than taking care of that?" Bagley said, standing up. "Does the other party involved know about it?"

"I told him and he's helping Floyd out right now."

Bagley was pacing. "I'm lost, Leonard. You should take care of the sailboat and then concentrate on whatever else you've got going on. Maybe you should cancel the overnighter until you've got this tightened up."

The intercom on Shaw's desk beeped and he looked at the number. It was the bridge and he pressed a button to answer. "Yes?"

"Sir, all the guests are on board and we're ready to get underway," a voice said.

"Thank you, Captain. Cast off," Shaw said and hung up. He gestured for Bagley to sit. "Relax, Joshua. I'm not going to disappoint our guests. Believe it or not, we're going to be able to enjoy ourselves tonight, fix the sailboat issue, and celebrate the good news that you haven't asked me about yet."

Bagley sat and took a stiff belt from his brandy. "All ears, Leonard."

49

Nate zoomed through the woods, the smell of smoke getting stronger. The path was worn down enough for him to keep his speed up, and after a short dip he could see the house from the top of the rise. The upper floor and roof were engulfed in flames but the fire had not reached the first floor yet. How much time did he have until it started collapsing? The path began to drop again and Nate held on as the bike flew down a steep hill. An attic fire? Had to be. He prayed that when he reached the house, Lucille would be out in the clearing and would tell him that the fire trucks were on their way.

The woods opened up and the path leveled off as Nate drove into the backyard. The screen door was open on the deck and he started moving toward the house when he heard a branch crack behind him.

He turned around to see a dark figure swinging a baseball bat at his head. Nate ducked and the bat whiffed through the air. Still crouched, he lunged at the man's legs and tackled him.

The man dropped the bat and they rolled on the ground, ending with the man on top of Nate. He grabbed Nate's neck and began to squeeze. Nate struggled and tried to pull the man over to one side, then the other, but the man's knees were anchored to the ground on either side of Nate's chest. He began to feel lightheaded; in a few more seconds he would pass out. Reaching down, he pulled the k-bar from its sheath and with a swipe, gashed the man's left shoulder. Warm blood poured from the wound onto Nate and the man released his grip. Nate coughed as he refilled his lungs and then swung the knife again, but the man had moved off him and was crawling for the bat.

Nate hit him from the side and the man fell to his back. The man reached for the bat, which was less than an arm's length away. Nate drove the knife into the man's forearm just as the man had closed his fingers around the bat's handle. The knife went through his arm and into the ground. The man yelled, releasing his grip. Nate took hold of the bat midway down the barrel and with a quick jab, brought the end down on the man's face. The sound of wood breaking bone preceded blood oozing out of the man's nose, and his body went limp.

Nate sheathed his knife and then placed his hand on the man's neck. Who was he? After registering a pulse, he rose and ran for the deck with the bat still in his other hand.

Another man rose in the woods. He watched as Nate entered the burning house, then he sprinted across the backyard. Stooping down over the body, he snapped the man's neck and pulled the corpse into the woods with him.

The smoke was billowing down from the stairwell and Nate shouted for Lucille. He passed through the living room and entered the kitchen. She was lying on the tile floor unconscious. Nate picked her up over his shoulder and carried her back through the living room and out the front door. As they cleared the porch, the entire second story collapsed.

The sound of fire engines and police cars could be heard now. Nate looked at the back yard. The body was gone.

✳ ✳ ✳

246

Hutch stopped the engine and threw the RHIB's anchor over. He scanned the horizon for any boats nearby and saw none. He threw on a tank, mask, and fins and with his dive light on, dropped over the side. He located the line of rocks and followed them up to the limestone wall and swam into the crack. Everything in the underwater tunnel looked normal—until he started to make his final ascent into the room. The lights were on above him.

He turned off his dive light and instead of surfacing in the middle of the pool, he swam over to the far corner which was hidden behind a short wall of rock. It wasn't enough to hide his whole body, but it was enough for him to get his head out of the water and look around without being noticed. He reached the corner and was a foot below the surface when the lights in the cave went out.

Surrounded in darkness, Hutch raised his head out of the water and listened. Perhaps there was a diver about to enter the water and Hutch would have to be ready. He unsheathed his dive knife.

Nothing moved or sounded in the cave, and he waited. He submerged for a moment and shined his dive light beneath him. No one was coming up from the bottom. He raised his head out of the water again. Still no sound. He decided to make a move and shined his light quickly at the ceiling and then shut it off. He listened. Nothing. Someone had been in the cave, that was for certain, but could it be that the overhead lights had simply lost their charge? Time to find out.

Hutch swam over and exited the water as quickly as possible, ready for someone to jump him. The cave remained quiet, except now he could hear a dripping noise. He started cranking the power box for the lights and they began to flicker since the toggle switch had never been turned off by whoever had been in the cave. He cranked a few more times and then gasped in horror. Hanging on one of the hooks in the wall was the body of Mickey Leif.

50

Hutch fell back against the cave wall, vomited, and then approached the body. Mickey hung motionless as blood ran from the two chest wounds where he had been shot, forming a pool underneath him. His eyes stared straight ahead and his neck was cold and clammy. Hutch knew there wouldn't be a pulse, but he went through the motions of checking, just in case. There was none.

Hutch left the body and went over to where he had placed the chest. It was gone and someone had dug up the urn and smashed it on the rocks.

"Sorry, my love," Hutch said to the ashes and pieces of urn. "I thought you'd be safe out here. I promise to come back and get you." He couldn't fall apart; he had to focus on what needed to be done now.

He raced back to the main room of the cave, turned off the lights, and swam for the RHIB.

Hutch was met at the dock by Tyee and Nate. Nate explained that Lucille had regained consciousness and was on her way to the Hampstead Hospital. The fire was out and an investigation had started. The firefighters and cops had asked Nate if everything was okay out at Hutch's and he had lied and said it was fine. Then, he told the story of his encounter and Hutch spoke up.

"Mickey is dead."

"Dead?" Tyee said.

"He led whoever it is that's after the treasure out there, and once they had the chest, I guess they figured they didn't need him anymore."

"The chest is gone?" Nate said.

"Gone like your students at the end of a school year," said Hutch, "leaving us with a problem."

"What?" said Nate.

"It's a good bet that before Mickey kicked the bucket they got the location of the wreck out of him," said Hutch walking toward the shed. "That's why we're diving tonight and getting it up before those bastards get their hands on it."

"You don't think they'd go after it tonight, do you?" Nate said.

"Well, I didn't think my house would get the shit stripped out of it, Mickey would betray us, or that they would set Lucille's house on fire. Do you really wanna wait?"

Before Nate could answer, Tyee said, "Shouldn't we tell the cops about Mickey?"

"What good would it do right now? He's not going anywhere," said Hutch. "Let's get *Queen* loaded up."

The powerboat came alongside *Triumph*'s port quarter and maintained station directly beneath a boat davit. A crew member was stationed at the davit control console and pushed a button to lower a heavy-duty cable from the davit. The end of the cable arrived at the powerboat and the man who was not driving clamped the end to a steel ring mounted in the center of the boat over the helm console, then gave a thumbs up to the davit operator. The operator pushed another button and the davit took the weight of the powerboat and the two men in it.

The winch stopped, and three crew members helped steady the boat against the rail as the two men disembarked and took their cargo into *Triumph*'s interior.

The guest list for the overnight cruise included Hampstead's mayor, police chief, country club owner, district judge, two beach mansion neighbors, and even marina owner Kevin Shelby. Their significant others were aboard and of course Shaw's wife and Bagley, which put the number of guests at seventeen. It was nearing eleven o'clock and the lights were turned down in the main entertainment room. The talk of politics along with having his ass kissed by every local was boring Leonard Shaw to death. At least the jazz musician he had flown in was gorgeous. The music, booze, and Bagley's courtroom war stories—'They didn't know they were dealing with the *master*'...'I *destroyed* him'—were flowing. It was doubtful that Bagley and Kevin Shelby would make it to midnight at the pace they were going, but it didn't matter.

Deep, or not so deep, into a conversation with Hampstead Mayor James "Jimmy" Wagner about what it would mean for Hampstead to construct a brand-new Community Performing Arts Center for the Hampstead Players— which of course Jimmy wanted Shaw to pay for—was cut short when a crew member approached the men. *Unfortunately*, Shaw had to excuse himself for a minute. He thought about motioning for Bagley to come with him, but took one look at Bagley's eyes and determined that it would be pointless.

Shaw entered his study and two men were seated on the couch inside. On the table in front of them was a chest.

"Excellent, gentleman," Shaw said approaching the couch.

One of the men was Floyd and the other was a man he had not seen since last summer. Just seeing him brought back visions of an event that Leonard Shaw had hoped to never think about again. The two of them on the sailboat, wining and dining Shaw's mistress and then taking turns with her below. The man had introduced her and had even *shared* her with Shaw, but it had spun out of control fast. Floyd scuttling the boat was supposed to be the final act of an affair gone terribly wrong, with the end result being that the girl and boat would never be found. The man's trump card of videotape and pictures of the three of them together had kept the man alive and his pockets full during the past year, but that was coming to an end. The man had no idea that he wasn't being cut in on the treasure—or that Floyd would be killing him later tonight.

Floyd remained seated but the man next to him stood up and extended his hand. Shaw shook it heartily as if they were best friends.

"It's good to see you again, Tim."

"Pleasure is all mine, Leonard," said Tim Gibson.

"How are things proceeding, Floyd?" Shaw asked.

"We had a setback with the house fire and I had to finish off the new guy before his body was found."

"Who was he?" Shaw asked.

"The helmsman who took Tim and me out to the island the other day. No one will miss him."

Shaw started to shake his head.

"Don't worry, I took care of it. His body won't be found," said Floyd. "The house is clean too. I made it look like an attic fire. Tim took care of Leif and I helped him bring up the chest," Floyd said.

"What happened to Lucille Hawthorne?" Shaw said.

"She's probably in the hospital by now," Floyd said.

"We missed our chance to get rid of her quietly," said Shaw, "but she still needs to go."

"They'll keep her there for at least twenty-four hours. I'll drop by the hospital tomorrow and take care of it carefully," said Floyd.

"So that leaves Martin, Beecher, and Hutch?" Shaw asked.

"Correct," said Floyd. "And there's been a new development—an opportunity."

"What's that?" asked Shaw.

"It looks like we've forced their hand. They're gearing Hutch's boat up to dive on the wreck tonight and recover the rest of these," Floyd said, patting the chest.

"Will they all be on the boat?" Shaw's eyes glinted.

51

The future mother of Tim Gibson's illegitimate child had left the house and Brooke sat across from Jane in the Gibson's living room. Jane was now on her third drink in the past hour.

"May I tell you something, Brooke?" Jane said.

"Of course," Brooke said.

"I'm scared of confronting Tim."

"None of this must seem easy," Brooke said.

"No. You don't understand. I'm afraid of what will happen to me."

"Oh, I don't think you have to worry about Tim becoming violent with you. It sounds like he has really messed up, but he doesn't seem to have that kind of streak in him."

"That's not what I mean, Brooke." Jane took a long drink. "We're in debt. Major debt."

"But I thought," Brooke said looking around their house, "that you were set financially."

"Appearances," Jane said. "Ann Arbor is a last-ditch effort for us. Tim has some friends in the program; they juried our way in. Based on our salaries last year, we'll have to work until Tim is in his late seventies just to break even.

However, Tim has been able to make some payments this year with money coming from somewhere that he won't tell me about." Jane began to sob. "Tim is a serious gambler, Brooke. It didn't start out that way, but it's gotten worse as time has gone on. And not just gambling at the casinos or on horse racing or other sporting events. After one good property investment a few years ago in Florida, we tried to break into buying and selling real estate, but we got in way over our head. We'd buy, buy, buy and then couldn't sell. Then, Tim began gambling to try and recoup our losses, but our debt doubled. We *own* virtually nothing right now."

"I don't know what to say," Brooke said. "Do you have anything in reserve? A nest egg?"

Jane said, "My father left us a good amount of money, and Tim blew it all." Her voice broke again. "And now this, Tim getting involved with a student. She claims she's pregnant with Tim's child! I can't handle this!"

Brooke looked at the carpet, thinking how she had almost given into Tim's charms, and then lifted her head. "I'm so sorry, Jane."

Nate listened to the roar of *Queen*'s engine winding down as he waited at the bow with the forward anchor and Tyee waited in the stern with the aft anchor. The engine went to idle as they reached the target position.

"Drop your hook, Nate," Hutch ordered.

Nate released the brake on the windlass, and the anchor began to drop. They were in thirty feet of water, and Hutch wanted to go with a 6:1 ratio on both anchors.

As Nate's rode continued to pay out, Hutch backed up past the target point and had Tyee drop his anchor. Then, it became a matter of paying out the stern rode while taking up the bow rode, until 180 feet were deployed forward and aft. This procedure eventually centered *Queen* above the target: a position ten yards parallel to the drop off and directly over where *Griffon* rested on the shelf.

Hutch's mastery with the throttle along with his patience paid off. *Queen* was anchored like an Olympic gymnast sticking a landing.

"I think that'll do it," said Hutch, and he shut off the engine.

Nate, Tyee, and Hutch changed into wetsuits. After helping each other strap on tanks, Hutch loaded and hid a shotgun in the aft locker. The only boat they had seen on their way to the wreck was Leonard Shaw's *Triumph*, which was now out of sight. The men finished putting on their gear and stood in the stern.

"Tyee'll go down first and make sure the aft anchor is settled in and secure the safety light to it. Then, he'll check the forward one. After that, he'll surface and he and I will take the cage down together and place it next to the large opening in the middle of *Griffon*'s hull where I entered earlier today. Remember to be careful because that's where I had to slit those two giant Muskies. I'll place lights at that opening and the smaller opening. When the winch stops paying out, it'll mean that we've got it where we want it and that's your cue to get wet, Nate. Follow the cable down and meet us," said Hutch.

Nate watched as Hutch went over to a box that had been placed next to the rack of tanks during the onload. Hutch bent over and opened it, showing the men what was inside.

"From my inspection earlier today, I don't think the chests will stay together. So, Nate and I will be putting each one into these heavy-duty wire-mesh bags. That way if the chests do come apart we won't lose any coins. We'll bring the bags out to the cage; I figure we can fit three or four bags per load. Once she's loaded up, Tyee, you'll swim up and start the winch."

Tyee looked confused.

"What's wrong?" Hutch said.

"Why doesn't Nate just stay up here and operate the winch?" Tyee said. "You and I can handle loading the bags in the wreck."

Hutch smiled. "Because you're too goddamn big to move inside the wreck without risking bumping into something and causing the thing to collapse. It'll be a tight fit for Nate and me as it is."

"Probably a crummy time to blame my parents for their genetics," Tyee said.

"Amen," said Hutch. "Nate'll follow the cage up and make sure she doesn't get fouled on the aft anchor line or clip the edge of the drop off. While he's doing that, I'll get the next load ready and then come up to join Nate and help bring the cage back down after you've offloaded it, Tyee. Any questions?"

Tyee walked over to the starboard gunwale and sat with his back to the water. He put his mask on and Hutch handed him the large underwater light. Tyee turned it on and flipped back into the water.

Nate and Hutch stood at the rail, watching as Tyee swam over to the stern anchor line and shortly after, started his descent.

Then, Tyee's light went out.

52

Hutch and Nate looked into the water, waiting for the light to reappear.

"The bulbs might have gone bad," Nate said.

"Not likely," said Hutch.

They scanned the water, waiting to see Tyee's back-up light come on. When it didn't, Hutch took his knife out, flipped on his dive light, and dove in.

The large Indian shuddered as the knife sliced up his side and then punctured his right lung. He was still fighting, and Floyd thought that if he hadn't had the element of surprise they would have been evenly matched. Floyd pushed the knife in deeper and the man's strength lessened. He pulled the knife out and got around behind his victim. Snatching the Indian's hair with his left hand, Floyd sliced the man's throat with the right. The body twitched, and then sank motionless onto the shelf, blood gushing out of the neck and chest.

* * *

Fiddling with his own gear, Nate followed Hutch's light as it searched back and forth, preparing to go in after him. He did not hear the sound of a diver easing up onto the swim step. By the time he felt the boat move, it was too late.

Nate turned around and saw a diver pointing a spear gun at his chest. The diver removed his mask with the other hand. It was Tim Gibson.

"Take off your mask and fins, Nate. I don't want you going too far if you decide to jump overboard," said Gibson.

"What in the hell is going on, Tim?" he asked.

Gibson pointed the spear gun at Nate's feet and then his head. "Fins and mask, please?"

Nate took them off and set them on the deck.

"First, I'm rigging a horrible accident at sea. Then, I'm going to do the same thing that you're here for, Nate: bring up a bunch of gold," Gibson said shaking the water from his mask. "I'm sorry about your Indian friend, but he got in the way down there, much the same as your friend Hutch is right about now."

Nate's eyes slanted at the water and then back to Gibson. "What about Mickey Leif?" Nate said.

"Met him only once—when I killed him. Mr. Leif didn't see me come out from under the dock. By the time he did, I had him underwater, wore him down. Then, I was able to coax the necessary information out of him by threatening his family. Spilled his beans and earned two rounds to his chest."

Nate shook his head. "So he wasn't in on this?"

"No way," Gibson said. "Just another obstacle like you."

The speargun had lowered while Gibson was talking. As he began to raise it, Nate leapt over the side. Gibson shot but it went high. He loaded another spear and put his mask back on. Without fins, Nate couldn't get far. Gibson sat on the gunwale and then rolled into the water.

* * *

Hutch's light found Tyee, and then found the largest diver he'd ever seen coming straight at him. Hutch bit down on his mouthpiece and kicked hard to meet him.

At the last possible moment, Hutch went low. Using the serrated edge of his knife, he tore across the man's leg, right behind the knee. He was in the process of turning around to make another pass when he felt two huge hands wrap around his neck. Hutch gagged and the regulator fell out of his mouth. The diver's strength was overpowering, forcing Hutch to drop his knife and then use both hands to try and pry free. He got one hand off and shook his windpipe loose. He kicked at the man, buying enough time to locate his regulator and take a breath. The man grabbed Hutch's right arm at the wrist and just below the shoulder. Lifting his good leg, the man applied pressure with his knee on the middle of Hutch's arm. Hutch saw his arm straighten, shake, and then felt his elbow pop as his arm broke inward. Hutch writhed in pain, his arm feeling as if it had been placed in an oven. The man backed off and reached down for his knife, which gave Hutch a split second to decide what to do. He couldn't fight the man toe to toe with one arm. He still had two good legs.

Hutch bolted for the wreck. After a dozen powerful kicks, he looked back. The diver was following, but had to stop every few kicks due to his leg. Hutch dove to the lifeless body of Tyee and grabbed Tyee's knife. Then, he kicked for all he was worth toward the wreck. Inside the *Griffon*, maybe he could even the odds.

Floyd tried to catch the man, but couldn't. One of the tendons on the back of his left knee was severed—his whole leg throbbed. He watched as the man entered the wreck. Then, he saw a light enter the water on the surface. He watched it for a moment and then continued swimming toward the wreck.

Nate found his regulator and put it in his mouth. He was only a few feet beneath the surface when two hands grabbed him from behind and pulled him underneath *Queen*. Nate lashed out with his arms but could see nothing. His body slammed up against the hull. Then, he felt a terrible pain in his thigh. The water began to feel warm around him, and he reached down and felt his leg. In the meaty part of his quadricep rose the end of a metal spear. The opposite end had come out the other side of his leg and was embedded into the hull of *Queen*. He no longer felt Gibson and could make out a light moving away from him.

Hutch hid in the wreck and watched as the diver entered through the larger of the two openings, waving a light back and forth. Hutch waited, his knife in his good hand. When the diver was in deep enough, Hutch swam up from behind and cut the man's air hose. The man grabbed at his regulator. Hutch dropped the knife and moved above. Finding an opening, he reached in and ripped off the man's mask. The diver turned around slashing with his knife, but Hutch had already kicked past him and was headed for the other opening. The man thrashed out of control, dusting up sand everywhere and then one of his arms hit wood and a wall collapsed on him. His inaudible scream sent a column of bubbles up.

Hutch reached the opening and waited outside the wreck. The diver never re-appeared. Then a light struck Hutch from behind.

* * *

Each movement of his leg sent needles of pain through Nate's body. He put both hands under his thigh and pulled on the spear, but it would not dislodge from *Queen*'s hull. He repositioned and tried again with the same result. Nervousness and pain were making him breathe faster. He let go of the spear and instead grasped his thigh with both hands. Yelling bubbles of air in agony, he pulled his leg off of the spear.

Free from the hull, he kicked up and willed himself over *Queen*'s starboard gunwale, landing on the deck. Blood splashed onto the stern's deck boards. He donned his mask and fins, and dove overboard.

Under the surface he shined his light up at *Queen* and saw that the entire hull had been wired with the same type of explosives he had seen on the sailboat. Next to the last set, he saw a timer that was at thirty seconds and counting down. Nate turned and kicked with his good leg toward the two lights he saw below—at close quarters.

Hutch tried to keep the diver off him with his good arm, but Gibson twisted around and took advantage of his weakness, plunging his knife into the shoulder of Hutch's wounded arm. Hutch shook in pain and reached over with his left hand and tried to remove it, but instead got his arm pinned back. Gibson pulled the knife out and with a clear shot at Hutch's midsection, drove the knife forward. Hutch's eyes opened wide, helpless against the inevitable.

With the knife inches from Hutch's chest, Gibson's head jerked back and the blow missed. Nate Martin held Gibson's tank strap and pulled him away from Hutch. Gibson tried to spin around, but Nate held the strap in an iron fist. They were twenty feet directly below *Queen*'s hull.

Nate slashed Gibson's air hose with his knife and Gibson spit out his regulator after sucking in water. Nate held him down for a few seconds, then released, and dove, trying to get as deep as possible while Gibson raced toward the surface.

Gibson's outstretched arm was inches from fresh air, his lungs aching, his eyes pleading, when *Queen*'s hull exploded.

The shock sent Nate torpedoing through the water and he would only remember a hand grabbing him, someone pulling him aboard a boat, and then waking up in the hospital.

EPILOGUE

I t was a rainy October day as Nate Martin and Abner Hutch exited the Hampstead Bank parking lot in Nate's Jeep. Fifteen minutes later they arrived at Lucille Hawthorne's house, finished a month ago in exactly the same place her old one had stood.

The rain drenched the red, yellow, and purple leaves as they took seats on Lucille's porch. Nate gave Brooke a kiss on the cheek, and then he rubbed her belly.

Hutch spoke to Brooke. "Has he finished the nursery yet?"

Nate tried to hide behind Brooke.

Hutch grunted. "I'll take that as a no. Better get on that, Nate. You've got five months left."

"Plenty of time," Nate said.

"I'll keep on him," said Brooke.

Lucille emerged from the house and poured them each a cup of cider. "And how did we do, gentleman?" she said.

In June, the story of their historic find ran on the front page of all the major newspapers. By the following week it was a paragraph on the back page, and two weeks later it fizzled out of the editorials. Below the final editorial in the local paper was the announcement that Leonard Shaw had listed his beach estate with Hampstead Reality, and noted that his yacht was for sale.

Nate pulled a folded bank statement from his pocket and placed it in front of Brooke and Lucille, saying, "this is what we each get."

Brooke's eyes widened.

The Government of France had determined the total value of the ten chests of gold—the stolen chest had been anonymously dropped off on Hutch's front porch the day after they had brought the other nine up—to be worth 22.2 million dollars. Nate and Hutch got half. They decided to split the money with Tyee's next of kin, his sister Levana, and Mickey's son Marty—who was now running both the hardware store and bait shop. It was the right thing to do.

Lucille glanced at the numbers and then locked eyes with Hutch. "Well, at least now I get a proper wedding," she said.

"Who says we're tyin' the knot?" Hutch winked at Nate and Brooke.

"You did, one month ago on this porch," she said. "Thank you very much."

He leaned toward her. "So I did."

AUTHOR'S NOTE

Thank you for reading my book. As an independent author, my success greatly depends on my readers. I know it can be a pain, but I would appreciate it if you could take a moment and leave a quick review (Amazon, BookBub, and/or Goodreads).

If you would like more information on upcoming books, please sign-up for my email list through my website (landonbeachbooks.com) or follow me on Facebook, Twitter, or Instagram.

If you enjoyed the book, please tell others about it!

My sincerest thanks to all who helped bring *The Wreck* to life—you know who you are.

As far as *The Wreck*...

It's mostly fiction, my friends. However, the *Griffon* was a real ship and is a very real ship*wreck*—perhaps, the first on our beloved Great Lakes—located somewhere unknown, far beneath the waves. It is simply not possible to list all the references I have read over the years to gain knowledge and ideas for this book, but there are a few that stand out: *The 100 Best Great Lakes Shipwrecks, Volume I*, by Cris Kohl; *Ships of the Great Lakes*, by James P. Barry; *Shipwrecks of the Great Lakes*, by Paul Hancock; *Guiding Lights, Tragic Shadows: Tales of Great Lakes Lighthouses*, by Edward Butts; *Lighthouses of the Great Lakes*, by Todd R. Berger; *Ghosts of the Great Lakes*, by Megan Long; and *Louis XIV: A Royal Life*, by Olivier Bernier. I hope *Griffon* is found one day, but until then I will continue to grin at the thought of Nate and Hutch finding her first.

Happy Beach Reading!

L.B.

If you enjoyed *The Wreck*, expand your adventure with *The Sail*, the second book in The Great Lakes series. Here is an excerpt to start the journey.

THE SAIL

Landon Beach

PROLOGUE

NOVEMBER 10, 1975 - 7:00 P.M.

The seaplane was off course. Twenty minutes ago the navigation systems had failed, and now Captain J. W. Wilson was piloting a descent through a storm. He should radio for help, but no one was supposed to know that they were up here tonight. Nothing was visible: his backup option was pissing away with the barrage of raindrops obscuring the windows and trailing off into the wind. If he could only see a strip of water where they could land, anchor the seaplane, and ride out the storm on the beach.

A bolt of lightning lit up the sky outside the co-pilot's window. Thunder boomed as loud as if it were fed into the earphones the men were wearing. The plane banked to the left as Wilson jerked the controls—eyes wide open—and then eased them back to level the plane.

"Sweet Jesus that was close, pally," said the co-pilot Jimmy Morris.

"Almost too close," Wilson said taking a sip from a flask. The liquid burned on the way down. A little Jacky Dee to calm the nerves.

He screwed the top back on and then placed the flask inside his flight jacket. Well, flight jacket was generous. It was a dirty parka with *J. W.* stitched on the breast and *Captain* stitched underneath. They had been advised to fly without any identification in case they were searched. But Captain J. W. Wilson didn't give a shit. No jacket, no flight. No wallet, no flight. No flask, no flight. Why not? He was down to a pint a day.

"We should start seeing water soon," Morris said, peering out the window. "There's no way we could still be over land."

And how would you know that, Jimmy boy? We haven't known where we were for the past twenty minutes. Wilson jerked his thumb toward the aft of the plane. "Bring the bags forward and have them ready in case we've gotta ditch. I'm not showing up with nothing."

Morris looked back at the black bags heaped on each other behind the back bench, then his eyes met Wilson's. "Ditch? Man, you think it'll come to that?"

Wilson brought the bill of his tattered Boston Red Sox baseball cap—he'd never seen a Red Sox game—down close to his eyebrows and then focused on the descent again. "Just get them."

Morris unbuckled his safety harness and moved out of the cockpit. Lightning flashed again and the plane dipped to the right this time, enough for Morris to lose his balance and hit his head on the cargo door. "For Chrissakes, keep her level, pally. I just about left the building."

Wilson ignored him and continued to ease the controls forward. The rain stopped. There seemed to be an opening in the clouds below and he flew toward it. As they descended, it began to snow.

Morris got his footing and then knelt on the back bench. He grabbed the two bags and placed them on the seat next to him. Sweat beaded on his forehead, slid down his nose, and dripped onto the bench as he turned around and sat down. He started to unzip one of the bags.

"Keep it closed," Wilson ordered from the cockpit.

"Aw, c'mon, man. Don't you want to know what we've been carrying for the past six months? Especially now, since we might pay the piper."

"You know the contract," Wilson said. "Besides," he paused, "you don't want to end up like Wilford, do you?"

They both thought back to June.

Five Months Earlier

The plane glided to a stop on the moonlit surface of the water. Wilson shut down the engine and Morris moved aft to open the cargo door. Water lapped against the seaplane's pontoons, and a stiff summer breeze blew into the plane. Wilson joined him and together they positioned the two bags on the back bench. Once this was done, Morris jumped down onto one of the pontoons. Wilson passed him a pair of binoculars.

Morris scanned the horizon. "We radio them, right?"

"We maintain radio silence, Jimmy."

Morris dropped the binoculars around his neck. "Oh, right," he said.

Wilson could see that Morris was nervous. Couldn't blame him, though. Wilson had been scared out of his crow his first time. "Don't be asking any questions when they show up. Just pass the bags to the boat crew *very* carefully," said Wilson. "Then we get right back in the plane and head home."

"Do we ever find out what's in the bags?" The binoculars were up again as Morris scanned for the boat.

"Don't you listen?" Wilson said. "It's all part of the deal. The bags take off from Vancouver by truck, travel through Winnipeg, and end up at our seaplane dock in Lake of the Woods where we load the bags and lake hop until we touch down here in Lake Superior. We deliver the bags, don't say no fuckin' word to nobody, and then head back and wait until we're needed again."

"Okay, okay, pally. Lighten up," Morris said. "Where do the bags go after we transfer them?"

"No clue," said Wilson, "and I don't wanna know."

"What happened to your last co-pilot?"

The motor of a powerboat in the distance could be heard. Wilson looked at his watch: 1:25 a.m. "It's them. Get ready."

Morris scanned left and saw nothing. Holding on to the wing with one hand, he leaned out over the water. Farther to the right he thought he could see the outline of a boat approaching them with no running lights on. "I think I've got 'em."

"Remember, not a word," said Wilson.

"Aye, aye, sir," Morris saluted with a shaky grin.

Wilson didn't hear him as he ducked back in the plane. He moved to the cockpit and retrieved a revolver from under his seat. If they thought of pulling anything tonight, he'd be ready. No way would he be taken as easily as Wilford had been. Dumb. So dumb. Why did Wilford have to look in the bags? Why did he have to ask the men on the boat about the contents? Stupid. Captain J. W. Wilson had been sober for three years, but when they took Wilford away that night, he'd broken at the first waypoint home. The metallic scraping sound of the lid being unscrewed. The aroma from the first whiff as he put his nose over the bottle. The watering of his mouth. The sweat on his neck. The feel of the smooth bottle in his weathered hands. The slow deep breaths and the thump of his heart as he raised the bottle to his mouth. And, finally, the first warm spirits hitting the back of his throat as he sucked on the bottle and gulped. Liberation. Heaven. The dulling of pain.

The memory of Wilford's screams lanced through his mind, and he had to shake his head to snap out of it. He slid the gun in between his belt and trousers and then untucked his shirt to cover it.

The boat approached, and two men in dark t-shirts and blue jeans—one he'd dubbed "Tall" and the other "Gun"—walked to the stern of the cabin cruiser. Tall picked up a line as the third man—the helmsman—backed down the boat and then cut the engine. Tall threw the line to Morris. His hands were sweaty, and he almost dropped it but got a grip and secured it to the pontoon.

Tall and Gun pulled on the line until the starboard gunwale was a foot or two away from the pontoon and then tied the line off to a pair of cleats.

Wilson tapped Morris's shoulder, and Morris looked back and then took the bag Wilson was holding out. He transferred it to Gun, and Gun passed it to the helmsman who stowed it below.

When Morris passed the second bag over the gunwale, Tall spoke to him.

"Come aboard. We've got something to show you," Tall said.

Morris snapped his head around to Wilson and looked at him as if asking: *what do I do?*

Wilson just nodded.

The helmsman took the second bag below as Tall and Gun helped Morris board. Wilson began to slide his hand under his shirt but stopped when the helmsman reappeared. Tall uncleated the line and threw it to Wilson.

"We'll be back in ten minutes," said the helmsman.

Wilson gave a thumbs up sign and began coiling the line. Fifty-fifty chance he'd never see Morris again.

The helmsman turned on the engine and drove the boat away. Three minutes later, he shut off the engine and Tall went below and returned with a weight belt, mask, and dive light. "Strip down to your skivvies, Jimmy," Tall ordered.

"What the—"

Gun cut Morris off. "Are you supposed to be talking?"

Morris shook his head and began removing his clothes.

Tall motioned to the water off the stern. "We need a little help tonight. There's some...some *thing* down there that we need to make sure is staying put." Tall bent down over the transom and dipped his hand in Lake Superior. "Water's not too bad tonight, but I advise that you make it quick."

Morris was in his underwear now, ghost white legs and sunken chest with small patches of hair exposed to the night air. He shivered as Tall passed him the equipment.

"It's about fifteen feet straight down, toothpick. We'll wait for you up here," Tall said.

Morris sat on the deck and swung his feet over the stern. The water rose up past his ankles. His rear began to feel cold as the water on the deck soaked his underwear. He turned on his light and jumped in.

The shock of the cold water made him shake, and he almost dropped the light. The weight belt did its job: he continued to sink. Once he made it to the bottom he would look for this thing and then get the hell out of there. Yes, he was freezing, but this should be easy.

It came out of the dark as his feet hit the lake floor and he swung his light around. A human body with no arms, one eyeball missing, and small bites taken out of its face and legs. The legs. The legs were anchored to the lake bottom by heavy duty rope and two cinder blocks. Morris went to scream, but then he saw a silver chain around the neck. He reached for it. At the end of the loop was a flattened rectangle of silver. Holding the rectangle in his hand, he aimed the light down and read the inscription: "Fast" Eddie Wilford. Now he screamed, sending a stream of bubbles up.

The sound of the motor starting above made Morris drop the chain, release the weight belt, and he kicked upward.

His head broke the surface of the water, and he looked up into the eyes of Tall, peering down at him over the transom. "Don't ever look in the bags or talk about your job," Tall said. Morris nodded. Then, Tall turned around, and the boat sped away.

Fifteen minutes later, the seaplane was taxiing toward Morris.

Wilson steered the plane through the snowy gap in the clouds, and he could finally see below. "Water, Jimmy."

Morris rejoined him in the cockpit and strapped back in. The plane continued to angle down, and the storm began to let up. Morris looked at the water. "I told you we had to be over water, J. W. Now, we just gotta find a place to let her down near shore."

7:10 p.m.

Enormous waves crashed over the "Pride of the American Flag" *Edmund Fitzgerald*'s deck. Loaded with 26,116 long tons of taconite pellets from Burlington Northern Railroad Dock at Superior, Wisconsin, the 729-foot ore carrier pitched and heaved in the churning water, trying to find a magic line through the eighteen-foot seas. Water crested over the port side, spread across the deck and over the hatch covers, and then slid over the starboard side back into the lake. At the dock in Wisconsin, deckhands had secured the 21 hatch covers—each hatch needing 68 clamps manually fastened. Thankfully they hadn't broken this routine or they might have sunk hours ago.

Captain Earnest McSorley stood in the pilothouse clinging to a radar console that was bolted to the deck—and inoperable. The bow rose as the *Fitz* climbed a wave. McSorley lunged for the radio console and held tight as the ship dipped and screamed into the trough. Fresh vomit from the quartermaster slid on the deck toward McSorley's feet and then slid back as the bow began to rise again. The veteran captain grabbed the radio's microphone. In 44 years he had never been in conditions like this, and for the first time he felt fear—not for himself, but for the twenty-eight other men onboard that were his responsibility.

His ship had been traveling with the *Arthur M. Anderson*, a freighter also carrying taconite pellets, since yesterday. The *Anderson* was presently aiding the *Fitz* in navigation; McSorley had radioed *Anderson*'s captain, Jessie B. Cooper, two hours earlier to explain that *Fitz* had a bad list, had lost both radars, and was taking heavy seas over the deck. Additionally, the *Fitzgerald* carried no fathometer or depth gauge. To measure the depth of the water, the *Fitz* still used a hand lead. A crew member would stand at the bow and drop a line with a weight attached to the end overboard. When the weight hit the bottom, the crew member would report the depth. Sending a man out to do that now would be sending the man to his grave.

"*Fitzgerald* to *Anderson*, over," McSorley said into the microphone.

Another wave: McSorley lost his grip on the radio console and the sixty-two-year-old fell to the deck and slid away, arms grasping for anything to hold on to.

"This is *Anderson*, over," a weathered voice answered over the speaker.

McSorley's right hand found a fire extinguisher bolted to a bulkhead, and he held on as the next wave began to lift the *Fitzgerald*. When the ship began to level out, McSorley pulled his way back to the radio console.

He keyed the microphone. "Read you loud and clear, Cap. How is our heading and position?"

"Caribou Island and Six Fathom Shoal are well behind us. There's a line of ships nine miles ahead that will pass you to the west," the first mate on the *Anderson* answered. "How is *Fitzgerald* handling?"

McSorley looked out the pilothouse windows at the snow falling down and limiting visibility to no further than just beyond the bow: they were blind. He looked up at the anemometer. *65 knot winds.* He was about to speak into the microphone when waves crashed over the pilothouse sending a wall of water over the deck. The seas had increased to twenty-five feet. One cargo hold hatch had failed...maybe more. *We may not make it. My crew is sick, beaten up, and this witch of a November gale is wearing down the old girl.* He keyed the mic. "We are holding our own."

"Look at that sonofabitch twist and turn," Morris said. He was looking out the seaplane's window at a huge cargo ship being tossed by the gigantic slate colored seas below.

J. W. Wilson swiveled his head and took a quick peek out Morris's window. "I'm glad we're up here, Jimmy," said Wilson. He tried the radio switch. Dead.

"Please don't try and land us down there," said Morris. "Those waves would bend this plane into a pretzel."

"I don't plan on it," said Wilson. Then, he motioned down to the ship. "She must be headed for the safety of a harbor or bay. We might be close to land." Wilson steered the plane to the right.

"Hey! I can't see her anymore," Morris said.

"I'm going to try and parallel her course," said Wilson, "it's our best chance of surviving this thing with our radio and nav equipment fried." Wilson began to steady up on a course. Then, he looked out his window. "Okay, Jimmy. You can sneak a peek of her—oh my God!"

Morris almost joined Wilson in the captain's seat as both men looked below.

The giant ship had nearly folded into a 'V'. A few mangled lifeboats floated away in the huge seas as the water lifted the ship—flattening it out for a moment—and then snapped it in two.

"She's goin' down!" Morris shouted in terror.

First the fore, then the aft section slid below into the deep. For a few seconds nothing remained on the surface. Then, the Great Lake seemed to burp, and a few pieces of flotsam came up, including what looked like an inflatable life raft.

"Gone," Wilson said.

Morris sat back in his seat and, for some reason, began to cry. Wilson circled the spot where the ship had been. He saw no one in the water. "Gone."

Wilson pulled out his flask and took a healthy pull. Morris was sniffling and looking out the window at the snow. The winds had shifted. There was nothing they could do about the ship. How many had gone down with her? Wilson screwed the cap back on the flask, leveled the plane out, and steadied onto the course that the ship had been steering.

* * *

Wilson's hands began to feel cold. He looked down at the heater. The familiar hum from the vents had disappeared. All he heard now was the steady sound of the propellers, engine, and Morris's snoring. Shit. What else is going to break? The cold moved to his neck. He shivered and slapped both of his cheeks. How much time had passed? A half-hour? An hour? Fifteen minutes? The blank stare syndrome reserved for monotonous spaces of time had taken hold of him. Wilson could see himself loafing around the mall, high, listening to Milt Jackson or in his senior year algebra class hearing the bell ring, the teacher starting to talk about something he had no interest in, staring at the wall—zoning now—noises dissipating, a white blur, other thoughts that refused to become clear, and...the bell announcing the end of class. Another forty-five minutes lost to the ages. Same deal for driving on a long boring interstate: jolting upright in one's seat—*where in the fuck am I?*

Wilson pulled on a pair of gloves and woke Morris.

"Heater's gone, Jimmy boy," said Wilson, "better put on your jacket."

Morris squinted and then rubbed his eyes. "Where are we?"

The snow was gone and the plane seemed to be descending.

"See that?" Wilson pointed out the window.

On the horizon was land.

Morris sat up. "Yee haw, bubba! We're gonna make it out of this mess after all."

"Just in time," Wilson said. "If the heater's gone, I don't wanna find out what's next."

"I'm gonna get me a paper tomorrow and see about that ship we saw go down. We'll be celebrities being the only ones who know how she sank."

Wilson pulled on Morris's collar and brought the co-pilot's face to within six inches of his own. He stared into Morris's eyes. "We're not talking to anyone," he ordered. "Have you forgotten what we're carrying back there?"

Morris broke eye contact and looked toward the back bench. Then, at Wilson.

"Uh huh," Wilson said. "We've gotta figure a way to get that delivered before we say a word about the ship." He released Morris's collar. "Understood?"

Morris sat back. "Yeah."

Wilson began to focus on flying again. Suddenly, the plane dropped. "What the—"

"Look!" Morris said.

The right propeller began to slow down...then, it stopped. For a moment, both men just stared at the motionless blades. They both shot their eyes to the left propeller and watched it slow down, sputter, and then stop...

Scrambling in the cockpit: Morris in the backseat reaching for the bags, Captain J. W. Wilson fighting with the controls.

The plane diving toward the water.

Screaming...

...Impact.

Explosion in the fuselage—one man burning. More screaming. One man trying to exit the plane, but pinned.

Water flooding the cockpit and fuselage.

Fire on the water.

The wreckage sank below the surface, putting out the fire, leaving only the moon's reflection on the black water.

Landon Beach

PART I

Preparations

Landon Beach

LAKE HURON

OFFSHORE HAMPSTEAD, MICHIGAN, JUNE 1995

The bow flattened the waves and the wake gurgled as the thirty-six-foot sailboat came about.

"Trist, get ready to tighten her up," Robin Norris shouted over the wind to his son as the boom swung overhead and snapped to a halt.

Tristian Norris pulled on the mainsheet, and the sail became pregnant with air. *Levity* heeled to starboard, and the smooth wooden hull began to slice through Lake Huron.

Robin looked up at the tattletales on the mainsail; both were streaming taut, parallel to the boom. "Cleat her," he said and sat down behind the wheel. Trist did and sat back down on the starboard cockpit bench.

"She looks seaworthy to me," Trist said.

It was the final trial run—an overnighter—before they left for their summer sail, *the* summer sail that Robin had promised Trist since they had purchased the boat three years ago. The previous day had been filled with practicing procedures they would carry out in emergency situations: man overboard, collision, fire, abandon ship, loss of equipment, foul weather, and any medical situations that arose. When they had bought the rotting, abused, and broken boat from marina owner Ralph Shelby for practically nothing—Shelby said it would never float again and just wanted to get it off his hands—Robin had set the bar at not only getting the yacht to sail again but to circumnavigate Lake Superior the summer before Tristian's senior year in high school.

Last night, they had anchored, tested the new grill Robin had mounted on the aft rail, and slept under the stars. There were always *problems* with a boat, but it appeared that there was nothing to stop them now from attempting the voyage.

"A few days to load supplies, get this beast on a trailer, and take her up," Robin said. "Tomorrow's your last day at the hardware store, right?"

"What's mom going to do with us gone all summer?"

Robin watched as Trist's black hair blew across his forehead. His hair was smooth and longer like his mother's and behind Trist's Ray-Ban sunglasses were the same brown eyes as hers too. Trist's skin was a blend of Robin's Caucasian and Levana's Chippewa heritage—closer to Levana's in the summer, Robin's in the winter. Why was he noticing these things at this moment? He knew. Since the diagnosis, he had been in a hyper-sensitive state of observation. Familiar things: the amount of air in the tires on the car, exactly how much toilet paper was left on the roll in each bathroom, how many beers were on the top shelf of the refrigerator, the bottom shelf. Weird things: a detailed inspection of how much dirt was on his socks before putting them in the hamper, how much dust was on top of the fridge, how many napkins were in the holder on the kitchen counter. Even sentimental items: what earrings Levana had on (he'd never taken time to notice before), the family photographs in the hallway, and now his son's skin color, which he'd known from the moment Trist had come out of the womb and Robin had picked the doctor up, thrown him over his shoulder, and—he still didn't know why—spanked the doctor's bottom in celebration.

"Dad?" Trist said.

Robin's head jerked. "Yeah, bud?"

"You're zoning out again. I just asked what you thought mom would do while we're gone."

Was he being too selfish? Should they not go? Christ, after the past year, did Trist even want to go anymore? Should Levana come with them? No, she had made that clear. This was his time to make things right with his son.

"Probably relax without us bothering her," Robin said. A safe and weak answer. "What time does Uncle Tyee want you in tomorrow?"

"Same as always, seven." Trist looked at the shoreline in the distance. "Yeah, mom deserves some alone time."

He might have had most of his mother's looks, but his frame was a carbon copy of Robin's, only—and Robin hated to concede the point, though couldn't tell you why he struggled to—Trist was actually two inches taller than his 6'1". *Enjoy the 170 pounds at 17, kid. The question is: could you keep it under the 200-pound line for 20 more years like your old man had?* Robin paused, letting the question ruminate. Another small battle lost in the fight to not ask himself questions that he would not be around to answer. Well, Levana will see if he can do it. Maybe next month's test results will bring the unreliable and unrealistic word of 'hope' out of the graveyard. He was glad that Tristian didn't know about *that* yet.

How many times had he wanted to bring it up as an eye-opener, a bargaining chip? But he had resisted. Pity was not the way to curtail adolescent behavior. And *that* was *not* the way to let a child know that his father was on borrowed time. Parents are the bones that children sharpen their teeth on. And as much as Trist's teenage years had gnawed away at Robin's skeleton, and as many nights as he had wanted them to be over, now, he wished they would go on.

"Dad?" Trist said.

Sweat beaded on Robin's forehead, and he ran a hand over his closely cropped hair. His stomach felt queasy. Water was building behind his eyes, and his sunglasses were on the verge of becoming blurry. He gripped the steering wheel harder. He would not lose it here.

"Dad." Trist said louder.

Robin turned his head toward Trist. "What's up?" He mumbled.

Trist pointed up at the main sail. "We're luffing."

Thank God. Something else to concentrate on. "Good call. We fell off a bit."

"*You* fell off a bit."

Robin ignored the critique. Don't fire back at him when he challenges you, Levana had said. Robin turned the wheel, and as the boat changed course, the sails became full again. "Ready to head in and start our preps?"

"I guess so," Trist said. "Need me up here right now?"

It had been like this since they had left yesterday morning. When he wasn't needed, Trist wanted to be as far away from Robin as possible—down in the cabin getting lost in a movie or book, or napping. At least they didn't have enough money for one of those ridiculous sat phones, or cell phones, or whatever the hell they were. What a waste of time and money that would be. However, he could see the day coming, and Robin Norris detested it.

"Trist—" Now was not the moment to fight him about time spent together. "I—"

Trist exhaled.

Maybe it was. "Well, you know we're going to be spending a lot of time together over the next 3 months."

"Yeah, I know. What's your point?"

"What I mean is that we can't spend the whole time just sailing and when the work is done go off into our respective caves."

"Do we have to talk about this now?"

Yes! He wanted to spend every waking minute he had left with him. "No, but I want you to think about it."

Trist rose and headed for the hatch leading down into the boat's cabin.

"Trist?"

Trist paused at the top step. "Call me when we get close to the marina," he said and then disappeared below.

ABOUT THE AUTHOR

Landon Beach lives in the Sunshine State with his wife, two children, and their golden retriever. He previously served as a Naval Officer and is currently an educator by day and an author by night. Find out more at landonbeachbooks.com.

CPSIA information can be obtained
at www.ICGtesting.com
Printed in the USA
FSHW022206030920
73561FS